PORTRAIT OF A SIOUX

PORTRAIT OF A SIOUX

ROBERT J. STEELMAN

63782

DOUBLEDAY & COMPANY, INC.

GARDEN CITY, NEW YORK

1976

All of the characters in this book are fictitious,
and any resemblance to actual persons, living or
dead, is purely coincidental.

Library of Congress Cataloging in Publication Data

Steelman, Robert.
Portrait of a Sioux.

I. Title.
PZ4.S8145Po [PS3569.T33847] 813'.5'4
ISBN: 0-385-11625-X
Library of Congress Catalog Card Number 76-3124

"During his long fight to salvage something of the Sioux's ancestral lands, Sitting Bull was grateful for help from virtually any quarter—even from a New York society woman. In the spring of 1889, Mrs. Catherine Weldon, a smartly outfitted widow in her middle years, arrived at the reservation on the pretext of painting the chief's portrait. Moving in with him and his two surviving wives, she had ample opportunity to achieve the real purpose of her mission: she persuaded the famous chief to make a tour campaigning against the government's efforts to open Indian reservations to white settlement—a cause that deeply concerned her as an activist in an eastern humanitarian group, the National Indian Defense Association.

"Alarmed, the Sioux's Indian agent, James McLaughlin, scuttled the plan by refusing to give the chief a pass to leave the reservation. To drive the disruptive matron away, McLaughlin circulated rumors that she was in love with Sitting Bull, and had tried to arouse his warlike impulses by reading him biographies of Napoleon and Alexander the Great.

"During her stay in his home, Mrs. Weldon did arouse other impulses in the chief by cooking his meals and doing housework. Sitting Bull, interpreting these activities by Sioux standards, proposed marriage. Shocked and irate, Mrs. Weldon left the reservation soon afterward, leaving the finished portrait behind. When Indian police tried to arrest Sitting Bull a few months later and ended up killing him, one of the policemen slashed the portrait—as if to kill him twice."

The Great Chiefs

Time-Life Books,

New York, N. Y. 1975

CHAPTER ONE

Old Wah Chee, the laundryman, was the best-informed man in Deadwood, Dakota Territory. From the hillside Centennial Wash House, perched on stilts above the main street, he stood at his sad-irons and watched all that went on below. The ninety-pound Chinaman rented out cell-like "rooms" in his ramshackle structure for three dollars a night; though he seldom spoke, English being difficult for him, he made a point of always listening intently to his guests. When he delivered shirts and collars to the townsfolk Wah Chee also listened, though the bland Oriental face gave no hint of interest or comprehension. "A good Chink," Deadwood decided. But the citizens would have been surprised and agitated to know the true extent of the Chinaman's knowledge.

Now, waxen yellow face wreathed in steam from the shirt he was pressing, he stared through the fly-specked window. An August sun of late afternoon lit the scene. There was a raucous background of whistles and saw-whinings from the new planing mill, reports from powder blown off in anvils, cheers from a knot of spectators watching two miners—the Welshmen who called themselves "Cousin Jacks"—pummeling each other. There was an occasional gunshot, a thin pure bugle call from the post that laced the dust like a silver thread.

Julian Garner, counsel for the Indian Commission, strolled the street with a lady on his arm. Wah Chee did not know the lady—yet—but he had seen her arrive on the stage the day before, with several heavy trunks and a strange latticelike structure of scantlings he did not know the purpose of. The laundryman watched as the pair paused delicately before a conclave of miners who blocked their way. Some doffed stained and dirty hats; one even managed a rough bow as Garner and the lady passed through. Julian Garner was an important man in Deadwood. As representative of the Commission, he was managing the agency's effort to buy the Sioux lands in *Pa Sapa*, the Black Hills, to persuade Walking Bull and the rest of the savages to leave their gold-rich mountains, to enter peaceably into the reservation prepared for them on Whitewood Creek.

Wah Chee watched, his hand moving mechanically back and forth as the pair mounted the long slow grade, paused at the foot of his rickety steps. He was folding a shirt—Judge Yount's best China silk shirt, with the ruffles along the front—when he saw shadowy forms through the draped cheesecloth protecting the doorway of the Centennial Wash House from Deadwood's many flies.

"Wah Chee?" Garner called. "Are you there? May we come in?"

Mr. Garner was a polite man. In the frontier atmosphere of Deadwood City the lawyer was an anomaly with his claw-hammer coat and polished Wellington boots. But the lawyer was pleasant enough, bringing seven shirts each week to Wah Chee's laundry. The Chinaman did not dislike Garner; he only reserved judgment. Wah Chee was a member of an oppressed minority, like the Sans Arc band of Sioux who were barring the way into Pa Sapa.

"You sure come in," the Chinaman invited, "and bring lady, too."

She was a lady, no doubt about that. Dainty in balmoral skirt and snowy muslin waist, there was cool and well-bred confidence in her manner. Under the flower-sprigged hat, dark eyes stared appraisingly at Wah Chee; the eyes, deep and penetrating, were surmounted by heavy brows. A wealth of glistening black hair framed the lady's face, with its aquiline nose and thin lips. The excess tresses were neatly swept up with a horn comb to disappear under the fashionable bonnet.

"Mrs. Brand," Lawyer Garner said, "this is Wah Chee, a respected citizen of the town, and an excellent laundryman."

Mrs. Brand inclined her head slightly. Wah Chee noticed under her arm a black volume with stamped gold letters—the white man's Bible book.

"I am pleased," she said, "to make your acquaintance."

She took the chair the laundryman offered, crossing her small feet daintily together. She looked, Wah Chee thought pleasurably, like a delicate porcelain from the Han dynasty.

"Eh?" Wah Chee asked, startled. In his reverie he had not been aware Garner was speaking to him. "What you say?"

The lawyer was patient.

"I said—I understand a Mr. Rollins has lodgings here."

Wah Chee wet his finger, tested the sole of the iron, put it down again on the stove.

"Jack Rollins? Sure, he live here. Owe me eighteen dollah for room. Bad pay!"

Garner coughed. "His debts do not at the moment concern us. Is he in?"

Wah Chee held up a pair of ladies' drawers from one of the numerous "hurdy-gurdies" that flourished in Deadwood to entertain and divert the rowdy miners; hastily he dropped them into the basket again.

"Rollins?" He chuckled. "He in—and out."

"Whatever do you mean?" Mrs. Brand asked.

"Rollins in—he sleeping off a drunk, like always this time of day. He out, too—out of his head with whiskey. Take three men bring him here last night, put him to bed."

Garner was embarrassed, but Mrs. Brand only smiled tolerantly.

"I want to talk to Rollins," she said. "Do you think you could wake him, Mr. Wah Chee? It's very important."

"Mrs. Brand," Julian Garner interrupted, "do you really think you should—"

"Yes," she said quickly. "I should, sir. I must. And at once."

Wah Chee shrugged, drew aside a baize curtain. He shuffled away into the rabbit warren of tipsy passageways, flimsy walls, and rough-hewn posts comprising his lodginghouse. Felt slippers made hardly any noise on the earthen floor. Pausing before a board cell built partly into the hillside, the Chinaman lit a sulphur match and touched it to a candle in a sconce.

"Jack!" he called. "Rollins!"

In the gloomy interior was a sagging cot, smell of unwashed flesh, a small scurrying as if a rat had suddenly left the premises.

"You, Jack Rollins!" Wah Chee demanded. "Where in hell you?" He rummaged in the tangle of bedding. "Goddam, Jack, where you? Jack, you here?"

There was a strangled oath; the bedding suddenly erupted. Snarling, a small shabby dog rushed at the Chinaman. A naked figure sprang from the bed, holding a gun.

"Who the hell is it?" Rollins demanded. Blinking in the light from the candle, he shoved the barrel of the carbine at Wah Chee. "What's your business? Who—"

Patiently Wah Chee tried to disentangle the dog's teeth from the hem of his gown. "Get up!"

"I am up," Rollins sighed. "Oh. It's you!" He swallowed, licked his lips thirstily, laid down the weapon. "Rufus, turn him loose! Well, I tell you—I haven't *got* eighteen dollars! After last night, I haven't even got eighteen cents! But I promise—"

"You don' promise me anything," Wah Chee said. "Rollins' promises worth dirt—no more." He jerked his head toward the sagging door on its leather hinges. "Lady out there want see you."

Rollins put both hands on his head, cradling his skull. "I think my head is about to fall off," he complained. "Put out that damned light! It's bright as a locomotive headlamp!"

Rufus whined in sympathy for his master.

"Only goddam candle," Wah Chee said. "You come?"

Rollins was a tall, almost gangling man, with pale blue eyes, now bloodshot, and a sheaf of wheat-colored hair in need of cutting. His hands were big and raw-knuckled, and the bladelike nose was curiously askew, perhaps once broken. He raised his head like a hunting dog, listening.

"I heard my name spoken," he said.

Wah Chee listened also. Through the thin partitions could be heard a faint rustle of voices. *I'm not sure this is very wise, ma'am. Rollins is a rough and violent man—a drunkard, too.*

"By God, that's right!" Rollins admitted with some pride. "How does it go? 'I'm rough and ready and full of fleas—never been curried below the knees.' Ow—my head!"

Moving cautiously, he slipped into torn jeans and fastened his shirt with the single remaining button. "That sounded like that dressmaker's dummy Garner—Julian Garner. Now what in hell does he want with me?" Rollins bent to pull on his boots. One was split at the toe, the other had a loose and flapping sole. "And who in hell is the lady? Didn't you say there was a lady, you slant-eyed bandit?" Grumbling, yawning, he shambled after the laundryman, trailing the carbine after him. Rufus ambled at his heels. "I don't know any ladies," Rollins mused. "Not—*ladies!*"

In the laundry he stood in the unaccustomed light of day, scratching his armpit. His reddened eyes adjusted, the focus hunted back and forth, sharpening finally on Mrs. Henry Brand.

"Ma'am," Julian Garner said with some distaste, "this is the man Rollins—Jack Rollins."

Rollins tried to stand up straight, wincing a little as he did so. In his disrepair he fidgeted, swallowed, fumbled with the dangling shirttail.

"John Rollins, ma'am. John Fitzhugh Rollins." The single shirt button gave way and he tried to pull the gaping edges of the bosom together. "You don't see me at my best, ma'am, but I can explain. I—"

"That won't be necessary," Garner interrupted. "This lady— Mrs. Henry Brand—has a business proposition to discuss with you." In lawyerly fashion Garner pressed the tips of his fingers together, cleared his throat. "Rollins, you've heard of the Brand Patent Plow and Harrow? Well, I guess everybody has! Mrs. Brand is the wife—I should more properly say the widow—of Mr. Henry Brand. She is also a portrait painter of note, with works hanging in many eastern galleries. In pursuit of her art, she has come all the way from Philadelphia on the cars and by other conveyances. She—"

Mrs. Brand made a small impatient movement. The lawyer broke off in midsentence.

"I'll take care of this, Mr. Garner! Thank you very much." She turned toward Jack Rollins, addressing him in a voice deft and businesslike, yet with a throaty murmuring quality he found pleasant.

"I understand you are a good friend of Mr. Walking Bull, chief of the Sans Arc Sioux."

Compassionately Wah Chee took from a pile a freshly pressed dark coat and handed it to Rollins to cover his nakedness.

"I understand also that you know the Sans Arc people well, speak their language."

"I have done Walking Bull some service," Rollins admitted. "And I speak the lingo."

"I hear from Mr. Garner you recently returned from Mr. Walking Bull's camp in the Black Hills, what the Indians call the *Pa Sapa*, where the chief has gone in protest against being forced to sign the government's offer of a dollar and a quarter an acre for his lands."

Warily, Rollins buttoned the coat. Rufus watched Mrs. Brand also. In Deadwood these days, any friend of Walking Bull was suspect. The Sans Arc chief, resolutely holding out against the government's offer, was barring gold-hungry miners from the rich Black Hills country. There was great pressure on Walking Bull to sign, but he refused. Because of his stubborn example, none of the rest of the Sioux hierarchy would sign. It was a stalemate, a growing peril to the peace of the Territory.

"Well, it isn't very much money," Rollins said. "I don't blame Walking Bull. It would be like selling his mother—the Indians are devoted to their land in a way we don't savvy. On the other hand—"

She gestured again, an impatient movement of the gloved hand.

"I'm not asking you to explain, Mr. Rollins. It's only that I need your help. You see, I have painted many famous men back East—soldiers, industrialists, statesmen—even our beloved President Grant. Now I want to do a series of portraits of great men of the frontier—men like your own Judge Yount here, and others—and my work should certainly include distinguished warriors like Walking Bull and some of the other Sioux; Red Cloud, Sitting Bull, oh, so many!"

Rollins shook his head, pushed back a hanging lock of sunbleached hair. "He's at Rainy Butte, ma'am, and that's at least fifty miles from here. And believe me, Walking Bull ain't—isn't—about to come back to Deadwood for anything. He's afraid of treachery—" He stopped, looked at Julian Garner. "No offense, Mr. Garner, but the Sioux have been treated poorly, they feel. So they're rightly suspicious."

The lawyer inclined his head stiffly.

"But that's exactly what I'm talking about, don't you see?" Mrs. Brand broke in. "I want to go to Walking Bull's camp, see him in the savage element, speak to him—get to know him. Finally, I hope to persuade him to sit for his portrait."

Rollins frowned, stroked his broken nose.

"No, ma'am—that wouldn't do!"

"But why not, pray?"

"It's a long way, through rough country—very rough country. There's heat, cold, storms—rattlesnakes, bears, panther. A passing Crow or Blackfoot might take a notion to lift your hair." *That beautiful black hair, soft and silklike*; Rollins licked his lips, stammered on. "The Territory isn't any place for a lady."

Lawyer Garner agreed. "Mrs. Brand, can't I ask you to forego this undertaking? The letters you brought left no doubt I am obliged to render you every assistance. But in these troubled times—the Indians surly and the miners clamoring for the Army to eject them—I cannot be responsible for your safety!"

Mrs. Brand rose, swept toward Jack Rollins, eying him coolly. "I am a very good judge of men! When my husband became ill with his final sickness, I played no small part in the conduct of his business. In the Brand Iron Works, I grew to know how to deal with men." Bible still clamped beneath her elbow, she opened her reticule and drew out a document. "I have shown this to Mr. Garner, and he agrees it is properly drawn up. You may read it if you wish, Mr. Rollins, but I can explain it more quickly. It is an agreement between you and me—an agreement that you undertake to deliver me and my luggage to the camp of Mr. Walking Bull, in the mountains; Rainy Butte, I think you said. You will outfit a proper expedition, see me safely there, and use your good offices to introduce me properly to the chief. Upon completion of the portrait which I mean to paint of him, you will return me safely to Deadwood City and receive the sum of five hundred dollars for your efforts."

Rollins blinked. He stared into the soft-lashed eyes, so penetrating, so unwomanlike.

"Five hundred dollars, ma'am?"

She looked triumphantly at Garner. "Yes, five hundred dollars! I will, of course, pay in addition all the expenses of the journey. I take it you will have to purchase supplies, provisions—perhaps a wagon."

Rollins was discomfited. Five hundred dollars! Yet he felt his headache returning, his broken nose hurt.

"Come, come, Mr. Rollins!" Her voice was sharp. "I made you a perfectly legitimate business offer, and I am quite serious about it!"

"A wagon couldn't go through some of the places!" he warned.

She turned to the lawyer in exasperation. "Don't they just—well, pack things on mules or horses or something?"

Before Garner spoke, Rollins said, "I guess we could take care of your traps—I mean your baggage, trunks and things. But *you*—I mean how—"

She smiled; he knew he had lost.

"I am an expert horsewoman, Mr. Rollins. In Philadelphia, I ride in Fairmount Park every Sunday. *Every* Sunday, without fail!" She plucked a pen from an inkstand on a shelf where Wah Chee used it to cast up his accounts. "Will you sign?"

Rollins looked helplessly at Julian Garner. The lawyer shrugged, turned away.

"All right. Might as well." The money was the thing; he needed money badly. Gambling debts, a liquor bill at the Paradise Card Room—many things.

She watched him scratch his signature on the document. Though Rollins was indifferent, she asked Garner and Wah Chee to witness, and handed him a copy of the contract.

"There! I feel ever so much better! Now when will we be able to leave for Rainy Butte, or whatever it is called?"

Rollins rubbed his cheek, uncomfortable to feel the coarse blond stubble. How long had it been since he shaved? He must look to her like a scarecrow, a fugitive from a neglected cornfield. Once he had been careful, much more careful, of his appearance. Once he had—

"When, please, Mr. Rollins?"

"Two days, ma'am. Maybe three, till I rustle a proper outfit together. I'll be in touch with you."

"Good! You will find me in my rooms at the Grand Central Hotel. Judge Yount has made me very comfortable there." She nodded briskly, thanked Wah Chee, and gestured to Julian Garner. "Oh, there's something I forgot!" She took the small Bible from under her arm, leafed through it. "Do you know, I can never find a proper prayer when I want one! Well, I'll just make one up!"

Bending her head, she began in a clear sweet voice to pray for success of their venture.

"Oh Lord, look down in thy infinite wisdom and love on us sinners here below. Look with favor on our undertakings, and bestow on them thy blessing. Watch over Mr. Jack Rollins here as he goes about the task of suitably equipping us. Bless Mr. Julian Garner for his efforts in our behalf. And thank Mr. Wah Chee also for his kindness and co-operation."

From the corner of his eye Jack Rollins saw a look of Celestial bafflement on Wah Chee's rotund face. Rufus cocked his head in wonder.

"Preserve also Mr. Walking Bull at his camp on Rainy Butte, and cause him to look on our mission with favor. We ask all this, Lord, in our belief that our undertaking is right and proper, and that it will be crowned with success to your greater glory. Amen."

"Amen," Julian Garner said noncommittally. Wah Chee looked stunned. Jack Rollins felt his skull again with tender fingers. He needed a drink, badly.

"Oh!" Mrs. Brand cried. She fumbled again in the purse. "The money for your supplies!" She handed Rollins a sheaf of bills. "Here is a hundred dollars. If you need more, come to me."

Julian Garner offered his arm, and they left. Rollins wrinkled his nose, sniffing. Against the smell of steam and hot cloth and boiling rice, a faint fragrance laced the air. It was not opium; he had smelled opium often enough, even smoked some. No, it was a flowery smell. Heliotrope—magnolia—what? No, those were southern fragrances, well known to him; Mrs. Brand was from up North, in Philadelphia. But the money was the thing. He took off the borrowed black coat and handed it back to Wah Chee.

"Thanks," he said. Counting carefully, he peeled notes from the sheaf and handed them to the laundryman. "There; paid in full! And don't come bothering me again about that niggardly eighteen dollars!"

Wah Chee objected. "That not your money, Jack. Lady say money to pay for horses, beans, bacon—stuff you need go Rainy Butte!"

Rollins laughed. He was feeling good. "Doesn't matter! She's got plenty! Didn't you hear her say 'If you need more'—"

Wah Chee shook his head, the pigtail bounced. "I don't take lady's money. And I don' know why I let you sleep here either, you no-good bastid!"

"That's right!" Rollins chuckled. "That's perfectly right. I'm a no good bastard! But if it wasn't for sinners like me, who would handsome churchgoing widows pray for? How would they ever do good works, without someone to do them for?"

Carrying the carbine in the crook of his arm, he left the Centennial Wash House and strolled down the street, smiling and affable. He had never cared for the bulk of a handgun tugging at his belt, so he bore the old Spencer about always, ready for what might come. Deadwood was a violent place. Some people were distrustful of a man who consorted with Sioux, especially with rebels like Walking Bull. Jack Rollins understood that. He could appreciate both sides of the argument, and knew that neither side had completely the right of it. In the war he had seen enough limp bodies, clothed in both blue and gray, each believing he was custodian of the Right. So Rollins was wary of causes; he would have none of the current argument, would not take sides in the Pa Sapa controversy.

He said hello to Lawyer Grubb, stopped for a while to talk with old Jake Van Meulen at the harness shop, rumpled little Jamie Burns's tousled blond hair. Jamie was the son of the town's best blacksmith, and had been known to steal one of his mother's dried-apple pies from a windowsill in exchange for King Arthur stories told him by Jack Rollins. In the Crown Mercantile, Rollins bought a handful of Cuban cigars and three bottles of the expensive whiskey he favored but was not often able to afford. Outside, he walked carefully in the crowd, shielding the precious bottles, savoring the flavor of the cigar, a swaggering Rufus at his heels.

On the porch of the Grand Central, Judge Yount watched Rollins pass, and spoke to the man called Peach who stood behind him, leaning against a doorway. Peach nodded. A mournful strain from a mouth harp, a falling cadence of minor notes, reached Rollins' ear. Peach played the mouth harp, and rather well.

Lew Searles had a dray-wagon backed up to a storefront. He and the driver were nursing a hand press down on rollers. Already the printer had hammered together a counter and a few type racks inside the sagging building. On the window was an inexpert sign in fresh paint the color of blood; *Territorial Argus.*

Rollins handed Searles a cigar while the printer wheezed for breath.

"Now where did you get that Havana, Jack?" Searles bent to the light Rollins offered, puffing. "You look somehow like the cat that swallowed the canary. What you up to?"

Rollins let the smoke roll round in his mouth. "A little good luck. By the way, I thought you were moving on to Cheyenne City, after your—accident."

The printer shook his head. He was a terrierlike little man with a veined bulbous nose and a fringe of wiry gray hair, almost obscured by an enormous bandage.

"They can't scare me out of this place!" He waved his arms. "I don't scare easy!"

"They beat the hell out of you," Rollins observed. "Don't you know the powers that be don't want any newspaper here, poking its nose into civic affairs?"

Searles wiped his sweating face with an ink-stained rag, leaving a smear across one eye.

"Fair is fair, ain't it, no matter who a man is dealing with? Understand—I'm no Indian lover, give me that! Hell, I had a cousin —name was Homer—had his hair lifted, up on the Musselshell. Lived to tell about it, but went barefoot on top of his head for the rest of his life. Nice feller, Homer; I liked him a lot. But that ain't to say it's right to flimflam ignorant savages out of their birthright. Them Sioux was here thousand of years before us, living a good and peaceful life when we had rings in our noses and painted ourselves blue!" Searles spat into the dust, and shook his fist. "A lot of things makes me mad, but this bamboozling the Sioux is the worst! A dollar and a quarter an acre—why, that's thievery pure and simple! The Indian Commission ought to buy Julian Garner a black mask to wear when he dickers with the Sans Arcs!"

Rollins looked around uneasily. He did not favor controversy. Too, a crowd of spectators began to gather before the office of the new *Argus*; their faces were bleak and hostile.

"You agin the gov'mint, Searles?" a miner called.

There was muttering from the crowd, and a man in a checkered vest and straw hat stepped forward; Dickybird Conway, a Welshman turned politician in the steamy tension of Deadwood City.

"Troublemaker!" he shouted to Searles. "We just might run you out of town on a rail, printer!"

Rufus growled uneasily. Rollins picked up his sack of bottles.

"Well, this time look out for slow music, Lew."

"What in hell do you mean by that?"

Rollins looked meaningfully at the veranda of the Grand Central Hotel. "Be careful someone isn't composing a funeral march for you."

Searles patted his hip. "I can take care of myself."

Rollins found Nobie Ferris in her quarters at Mlle. Sophie's, above the Paradise Card Room. The coverlet of the brass bed was turned back, the pillows rumpled. Nobie sat on the edge of the bed, legs crossed, combing hair red as a fox's brush.

"Jack!"

She flew to him, turning her face upward for a kiss, throwing her arms about him and pressing her lips tightly against his, body wriggling with delight against him, like a small animal. There was no deviousness in Zenobia Ferris, no deceit; she knew no maxim except to be honest. It was what Rollins liked about her; that, and the small compact body, the daintiness, the cleanliness of her, though considering her business that was probably the wrong word.

Carefully he laid the bottles on the bed. It was getting dark. Nobie lit the lamp and adjusted the wick, looking at him with childlike fondness.

"You been asleep?" he growled, looking at the unmade bed.

She giggled. "Major Toomey just left!" Quickly she smoothed the sheets and brought two tumblers while he pulled out a cork with his teeth.

"Blasted hypocrite!" he muttered, jealous of her favors. "John Toomey goes to the Methodist Church on Sunday, and sings the loudest. He's got a wife and three kids at home!"

"Four," Nobie corrected, scratching Rufus' ears. "Ellen—that's the oldest—then there's Charlie and Harry and—"

"I don't give a damn!" he howled.

Drawing him down on the bed beside her, she breathed warmly into his ear. "Jack, you were gone so long! I was afraid for you, with rampaging Indians and all. What were you doing?"

He had been gone a long time, and savored the elastic warmth of her body against his. "Found a little color at my New Ophir mine, up by Rainy Butte. Thought maybe I could bring out a few ounces before the dam breaks and those damned Cousin Jacks overrun the country. But the vein petered out. That's always the way it is." Taking pleasure in the surprise, however, he rolled on his side, took out the sheaf of bills, and threw them into the air.

"My God, Jack! Where did you get all that money?"

"There are other gold mines in the Territory." He snatched up a handful of the bills, pressed them on her. "Here—take some!"

She drew back. "You know I don't never take no money from you, Jack."

Lighting a fresh cigar, he propped himself on his elbows and dredged the greenbacks into a neat pile.

"Where did you get it, Jack?" Her voice was accusing.

"Rich lady." He shrugged. "Wants me to take her into the hills, take her to see Walking Bull. Wants to paint his picture, she says."

"I saw her!" Nobie said fiercely. "I saw her come in on the stage yesterday! She's staying at the Grand Central." She took his face fondly in her hands, brushed back the errant strand of blond hair. "She's pretty, Jack. Do you—do you like her?"

He laughed, easily. "Now, Zenobia—"

"Don't call me that!"

"But Zenobia was a queen! She was a real Cleopatra! In history books they speak of her 'dark beauty, her energy, her chastity'— well, maybe that's a little too much—but Zenobia was a great female. Once she ruled all the eastern part of the Roman Empire!"

She eyed him suspiciously. "Is that true?"

"Of course it's true!"

Mollified, she lay again beside him, stroking his cheek with her fingers. "Oh, Jack, you talk so pretty! And you know so much! Why won't you teach me to read, like I want you to?"

It was an old issue between them.

"Because," he said, "reading would spoil you, dear girl. You're a child of nature; what's written in books would only confuse you, make you dissatisfied and unhappy. Anyway, books are filled with rubbish; high-sounding phrases and lofty sentiments and claptrap about patriotism and honesty and humility. And it's all a pack of lies, you see! We're born, we live, we die—that's all there is to it. The only thing that counts is the few days we have here on earth —getting through life the best way we can and enjoying it while we go, without any of the sickly pap that's in books. You're already expert at living, Nobie—better than me!"

Unconvinced, she tried to show him a child's reader she took from the litter on the bureau. "Mr. Searles just give me this. Show me the letters, Jack—I already know a lot of the alphabet—and tell me how to put them together to make words."

He snatched the book and tossed it to the floor.

"Let's have a party! Get Jennie and Phoebe and Sibyl and—" He paused, looked at the clock on the bureau. "They're not working, are they? The rush hasn't started yet. We've got to have a few drinks. I'm dry as a bone!"

"But, Jack—"

He slapped her bottom. "Go! Quick! And on the way tell Eddie to send over to the hotel for a sliced beef and cheese and a few bottles of French wine!"

At the thought of a party, she forgot about the reader. "And oysters, Jack; I saw whole barrels come in today on a freight wagon, packed in ice!"

"Oysters," he agreed. "And champagne—two bottles. Make it three." He waved the sheaf of bills. "It's the money that counts in this life, girl! Money makes life bearable! Money and—" He pulled her to him, kissed her. "Now *run!*"

Sometime early in the dawn he woke. His mouth was thick and furry. He licked his lips, feeling the tongue strange and cumbersome. Rufus slept soundly in a chair. Rollins sat up; an empty bottle rolled from the bed onto the floor. Moonlight slanted through the open window. Hands hanging limp between his knees, he stared at the moonlit dishevelment of the room. Bottles, bottles everywhere—empty bottles. Rinds of cheese, oyster shells, half a coconut cake—smell of stale liquor, flat beer, tobacco, sweat, women's powder and paint. A garter hung on a bedpost.

His head hurt, but he was almost sober, he figured. Walking carefully, he went to the window. Deadwood slept, almost slept, in the lime-white glow of a hunter's moon. From far down the street, toward the hotel, he heard an uncertain tinny chording, a piano. But as he listened, the piano stopped. In the hush a cat stepped into a patch of silver dust, holding each paw high. Perhaps it was stalking a rat. There were a lot of rats in Deadwood.

He was about to turn away when he saw a man cross the street. He carried a lantern, the wick turned low. As Rollins watched, the silent figure stopped before the new office of the *Territorial Argus*. Moments later there was a faint tinkling sound, like tiny bells. What was going on?

Leaning on the sill, he listened, but heard no further sound. Well, it wasn't any of his business. Hitching up his pants, he fumbled in his pockets. The money—where was the money Mrs. Brand had given him? Was it possible—had he spent the whole hundred dollars? He looked on the bureau, searched again in his pockets. It must have been one hell of a party!

Whistling to Rufus, he went down the dark stairs into the street. Somewhere he heard music, eerily soft and sweet, in a minor key. He was still pondering the mystery of the money when he passed the offices of the *Argus*, saw the blaze within. For a moment he stared, watching flames bite into the dry boards, swirl around the Washington hand press, burst a bottle of ink and gather new strength as they hungrily drank the fluid.

"Fire!" he called in disbelief.

He turned to run, to seek help. But something hit him with bludgeonlike force behind the ear. Rollins did not immediately lose consciousness. He remembered Rufus barking and snarling. As he slipped down, farther and farther into the well of blackness, he continued to hear the mouth harp. He remembered the tune from Petersburg. On a still night they could hear the Yanks singing it from their works across the way. "Weeping Sad and Lonely," that was the name of it. It went:

> Weeping, sad, and lonely,
> Hopes and fears, how vain!
> When this cruel war is over
> Praying that we meet again.

Jack Rollins would hope to meet again the man who had just hit him behind the ear. His groping hand caught at a post, found no purchase. Slowly, very slowly, he slid down and lay on the boardwalk. He felt comfortably warm from the growing heat of the fire. Soon he would have to move, but for now he was content to lie there and rest.

CHAPTER TWO

Mrs. Henry Brand stood at the window of her suite in the Grand Central Hotel. It was not actually a suite in the eastern sense of the word. Instead, the management, impressed by the important visitor, had opened several adjoining rooms and curtained off a portion of the hallway on the second floor to make a fair approximation. Because of the press of gold seekers in Deadwood several guests had to be ejected. Judge Yount, however, found them other lodgings, and they were eventually placated.

"I heard," Mrs. Brand remarked to Julian Garner, "that there was great disorder in the town last night. I heard a lot of noise—shouting, gunshots. An Indian was beaten by a mob, so they told me, and there was also a fire."

The lawyer took the divan she indicated. It was of mahogany and flowered silk, and only yesterday had been in Judge Yount's own quarters in the hotel.

"Yes, it is very unfortunate. There are a lot of rascals in this city. Negotiating with the savages is difficult enough without such incidents. The poor fellow they set upon was not even a Sioux—an Arapaho, I believe, a harmless idiot. But the crowd maltreated him to show their anger against Walking Bull for refusing to touch the pen."

She looked up from a bouquet of flowers she was arranging in a vase. "Touch the pen?"

"It is a phrase the Sioux use. It means 'to sign a paper.'"

She put a flower to her nose, sniffed delicately. "And the fire?"

The lawyer looked uncomfortable. "Ah—that was what I came to see you about, ma'am."

"You may call me Abigail, if you wish. That was what my late husband called me, and my friends in Philadelphia."

"But—"

"You may as well understand, Mr. Garner; I am a modern woman. I do not stand much on ceremony. Man and woman, male and female, are both God's creatures; we should all communicate freely and easily."

"Well, then—Abigail—a fire broke out in a printer's shop. The place was just rented by an itinerant printer named Searles, who has declared his intention of starting a newspaper here in Deadwood. Searles is a hotheaded man, a malcontent, and has antagonized many of the townspeople—particularly the miners, who are waiting for the Indian lands to be opened up—with his stand on the Sioux question. Searles believes the Sans Arcs are being robbed by the Indian Commission, and intends to come out strongly against the government. He is, I am afraid, a disruptive influence, agitating against the normal order of things."

"And so they set fire to his shop? My goodness, why are such things allowed to happen? Is there no proper law here? Where were Major Toomey, I believe his name is, and the soldiers?"

Garner knew why Major Toomey had not interfered, but chose not to explain. Instead he said, "No one knows who set the fire. But the man Rollins—Jack Rollins, whom you met only yesterday —was found in a drunken stupor on the boardwalk before the printer's shop. He had a lantern in his hand that probably started the fire."

A hand crept to her throat. "Rollins? But why Rollins?"

"Judge Yount and others say that Rollins and Searles got into a violent argument yesterday. They were seen shouting and gesturing at each other; there was evidently bad blood between them. That is what is said."

"Where is Mr. Rollins now?"

Garner spread lawyerly hands. "In the town jail."

"But I need him! You know I planned to—"

"There is one more thing," Garner interrupted. "Rollins was searched, of course, and his weapon taken from him. But he had not one red cent on him, not one penny of the considerable amount you gave him yesterday to buy supplies. And it is said that last night the rascal gave a raucous party at the Paradise Card Room for several—ah—Cyprians, members of Mlle. Sophie's establishment there. There was champagne for all, and a bounteous buffet ordered up from the hotel."

"Cyprians," she mused. "I have not heard that word for a long time! You mean they were prostitutes."

He reddened. "Yes."

"Then," she decided, "you must get Rollins out of jail, and immediately, Julian. I am in a hurry. Autumn is nearly here, and there will soon be snow."

Upset, he rose and came to join her beside the window, working the brim of his hat between his fingers. "Ma'am, I can't do that! I have no authority in such matters. I am only the representative of the Indian Commission, and have no other status. Besides—"

She looked at him coolly; his gaze faltered.

"You are a lawyer! You know the law! If it is a matter of bail, I will pay it."

"Ma'am, I—"

"Abigail."

"Abigail, then. Please understand I warned you against this man. Jack Rollins is a drunkard, believes in nothing, and is dangerous into the bargain. He is rumored to have killed a man in South Carolina, where I understand he came from—a place called Honey Hill. He—"

With a sudden fierce movement she snapped off the head of a flower she had been arranging. "I do not care about his personal history! According to what you yourself told me—and I have substantiated it already by my own inquiries—Mr. Rollins is the only man who can help me! He is the only one in the Territory who is on good terms with Mr. Walking Bull, who 'speaks the lingo,' as he expresses it, and who knows the mountains sufficiently well to take me to Rainy Butte to do the chief's portrait!"

Garner's gaze was distracted by the pose with the red flower against her cheek. It was a masterly composition; the flower, the soft flush of her cheek, the raven-dark hair, lit in small soft blazes by sunlight streaming through the window.

"Well?" she demanded.

He started; in his confusion he blurted out a personal statement he was a good enough lawyer to regret immediately.

"In addition to everything else, ma'am—Abigail—how does it look? I mean—a lady of culture and refinement going into the mountains with a ruffian like Jack Rollins? Even—even coming out here to the Territory all alone, without an escort or chaperon—"

"I tell you," she cried, "I am determined to do this thing! I care not a fig for what you or Deadwood or the whole nation may think!" She stamped her foot. "I am not one of your namby-pamby delicate always-fainting females, with a bottle of smelling salts close to hand. I am as firm and resolute as any man, and I will not be denied!"

Under her onslaught he gave way, yet was stirred by her dedication, her eloquence, the way her bosom rose and fell under the ruching of Brussels lace.

"So I am forced to ask you again! Will you help me, or shall I wire East to get a proper attorney to help me?"

Still bemused, Julian Garner picked up his hat where it had fallen, and bowed.

"I will see what I can do," he promised.

Quickly she put a hand on his arm. He found the sensation delightful.

"I am sorry I lost my temper! It was very wrong of me, Julian. But there is a little of the devil in all of us, I am afraid. Sometimes Beelzebub triumphs over our better instincts."

Garner felt a little of the same devil burgeoning within him. Mrs. Henry Brand was a damned fine-looking woman.

On the veranda of the Grand Central Hotel sat Judge Yount, smoking one of the "wheeler" stogies he favored over more expensive brands. It gave him a certain common touch, which he found useful in dealing with people. He was a big man, with heavy shoulders and neck like a wrestler under the white linen suit he wore in Deadwood's blistering September heat. The judge was handsome in the style of a long-buried Roman coin; hooked nose, drooping full-lipped mouth, eyes heavy-lidded but with a penetrating gaze looking always into the future. Yount owned the Star Livery, the Paradise Card Room, and a half interest in the Grand Central Hotel. The rumor was that he had been a county judge back east in Ohio or Indiana, but no one really knew where he had come from, or when; he seemed to have been part of Deadwood from the beginning.

When he saw the recently released Jack Rollins inspecting the burned-out *Argus* storefront, he beckoned to him.

"Heard you were in the calaboose."

Rollins leaned on his carbine and said nothing.

"People—some people—believe you and Lew Searles had a little set-to, fell out. So you set fire to his shop."

Rollins' eyes narrowed. "Now you know that isn't true, Judge. Searles and I had no quarrel. We're good friends."

Yount shrugged. "People talk."

"But I was let out of jail kind of easy," Rollins said, "if anybody really thought I set that fire. Arson is a serious crime, isn't it?"

"Serious enough," Judge Yount said, sucking wetly on the stogie. He stared at the distant mountains. Huge clouds were forming over them, black and pregnant, lit round the edges with a thin braiding of gold. The heat was breaking.

"You made a deal yesterday with that pretty lady come into town yesterday. Mrs. Brand."

Rollins rubbed his finger over the worn action of the old Spencer. "News travels fast."

"Going to take her into the mountains. Something about painting Walking Bull's picture."

"That's right."

Judge Yount considered this, puffing the cigar. Then he said, "Well, long as you're out of jail now, you can do a little job for me up there at Rainy Butte."

The sun was in Jack Rollins' eyes; he squinted.

"What kind of job, Judge?"

"Walking Bull is a stubborn cuss. Half the Sans Arcs are ready to sign the land papers, but the rest are holding out to see what Walking Bull does. He's the one they all really look up to. Now it would be worth a nice bundle of cash to certain people if you were to talk to him while you're up there, persuade him to come back to Deadwood and dicker with Julian Garner and the Commission. You know the chief well—there's talk you once saved his boy Badger from floodwaters up on the Heart River last spring."

"There was talk," Rollins admitted.

"So I—we pay a good price if you bring him in. People don't really mean him any harm. It's just that they'd like to talk to him, that's all."

Rollins scratched his bristled chin. The money was the thing. Money was always the thing. "How much?"

Yount puffed for a while. "Say—fifty dollars. In gold."

"I guess I could have a fling at it," Rollins admitted. He had hoped for more; he was badly in debt. "But right now I'm a little short. If you could see your way clear, Judge, to advancing me a little on account—"

Yount laughed, shook his head. "Now you know I don't do business that way!" Chuckling, he went back to the stogie, and Rollins wandered disconsolately into the hotel.

Through the lace curtains, newly hung for the benefit of Mrs. Henry Brand, he noticed Judge Yount, rocking on the porch outside, motion to the man called Peach. For a moment the two talked together. Peach nodded, walked away. Leaning against a post, he began to blow softly, thoughtfully, into the instrument.

You son of a bitch, Rollins mused. *You hit me over the head last night and put that damned lantern in my hand!* Then Judge Yount had decided he would be more useful on an errand to Walking Bull. Rollins hated to be so manipulated, but he was a cipher in Deadwood, and ciphers were invented for manipulation.

When he reached Mrs. Brand's rooms on the second floor, he was in a mood, feeling himself badly used. He knocked on the door. She came, not peering around the door as most females would have done, but opening it wide and confronting him.

"I heard you wanted to see me," he said.

"I do." She stood aside, motioning him in. He was aware of silken cushions piled on a divan, of a pier glass framed in gold curlicues. "I see you are out of jail."

No one except whores received him alone in their rooms; he was ill at ease. But he supposed it was all part of Mrs. Henry Brand's unfeminine philosophy. Or could it be called unfeminine? She was certainly feminine enough for him, as feminine as even Mary Armistead had ever been. He guessed it was just the hard armor of confidence that made her seem a little masculine in her approach to things.

"They let me out," he said glumly. "They set me up and—"

"What does that mean—set you up?"

He gestured vaguely. "They wanted somebody to blame for the fire at Lew Searles's print shop. I'd been gabbing with Searles that day, and sometimes he gets kind of excited and waves his arms and yells. So someone seen me—"

"Saw you."

"That's right. So they said I had an argument with him, and blamed me for the fire because I just happened to be around at the time."

"Drunk," Mrs. Brand observed, sitting down and picking up a pair of knitting needles.

He flared into anger. "See this?" He lifted the shaggy hair to show a knob behind his ear. "I was stone-cold sober!"

Intent on her knitting, she did not look at him.

"It's true!" he insisted.

"Well, you're out of jail now, anyway."

"True also," he grumbled. "They changed their mind, and decided they needed me free to do a little errand for them."

The dark brows drew together in a frown. "You keep speaking of 'they,' Mr. Rollins. Who are these mysterious 'they' who persecute you?"

"That's neither here nor there," Rollins said. "I don't like to get mixed up in things. A man does better in Deadwood to keep his mouth shut much as he can, not look for trouble. They run things here in the Territory, and they don't like loose talk."

"Well—" She opened a tiny gold watch hanging on a chain at her bosom and looked at it. "Have you purchased the supplies yet, rented the animals you will need?"

He shifted from one foot to the other, thinking about what he could say, fumbling with the carbine, thinking it looked out of place in this boudoir. But with a quick movement she took the old gun from him and stood it in a corner behind a Boston fern. When his eyes widened in surprise and alarm, she laughed.

"My husband, the late Mr. Brand, taught me all about guns! I was a pretty fair shot. Henry bought me an expensive Italian gun with a carved stock and engraved cupids on the barrel. For the shooting, you know, in the New Jersey marshes." She rubbed her hands with a tiny square of lace. "Now about the provisions."

He swallowed. "Well, ma'am—the fact of the matter is that when I was struck down last night the bast—the man rifled my pockets. Took every cent of that hundred dollars."

He could not assess the small glint in her eye. Was she mocking him, making fun of him? He grew angry.

"I see," she said, gravely. Laying down the knitting, she began to rock.

"Well, it's true!" he grumbled.

She shook her head, a parent reproving a small and difficult child. "How much did you spend last night on that party at the Paradise Card Room?"

He felt a sinking sensation. Rubbing his chin, he stared at the Boston fern. "It seems to me, ma'am, you know one hell of a lot—excuse my French—for having arrived in town only yesterday!"

"I make it my business to know things, Mr. Rollins." She rose to face him. "As you know, I am a businesswoman. The Brand Iron Works returned a handsome profit last year. An employer must know her employees well, or they will steal her blind. You, I am afraid, are no exception."

"I'm not your employee!" he protested.

"Suit yourself, Mr. Rollins. But I know you are completely without funds, owe debts for which people are pressing you, and would be well-advised not to shout in my presence."

It was true. The money was the thing. It always was.

"I am going to give you more money," she went on. "I think you may by now have learned your lesson." Opening a flowered purse, she took out a roll of bills that made his eyes bulge. "Here is another hundred dollars—no more until I am satisfied you have spent this wisely! I want a written receipt for every penny! If you need more, come to me—with receipts. Is that understood?"

He nodded.

Quickly her mood changed. She paced the floor, excited. "I do hope you will hurry! I have heard so much about the beauties of the Dakota Territory, and cannot wait to see it at first hand. Imagine—riding in the clean fresh air, unpolluted by factory chimneys; seeing magnificent peaks, smelling pine forests, hearing the splashing of mountain streams!" She stopped, frowned, put a finger to her cheek in a delicate gesture. "I do hope there is a good tailor in town! I had forgotten—I must have a riding skirt made directly!"

He rubbed his bristly chin again; he must get a shave, and a haircut. The bristles were almost a beard.

"And a sidesaddle!" Suddenly, her face looked stricken. "Oh, my goodness! I never thought of *that!*"

Although he had not particularly thought about it, he had imagined her riding astride, like a Valkyrie. His voice was faint, and emerged with difficulty from his voicebox. "Ma'am, a—a sidesaddle?"

"Mr. Brand bought mine in England, several years ago. I could have brought it from Philadelphia, but I never thought!" Rummaging about, she found a sheet of writing paper and poised her pen above it, frowning. "Now we will just have to have a proper saddle made, Mr. Rollins! Is there a good saddlemaker in Deadwood?"

A sidesaddle in Deadwood, that raw and uncurried place? He made an effort to conceal his emotions. Mrs. Brand was very serious.

"There is a harness shop, yes, and they make saddles. Jake Van Meulen." He repressed a grin as he thought of the Dutchman's face at the prospect of making a lady's sidesaddle. Busy with the pen, she did not notice the aborted grin.

"Now here it is." She gestured for him to come closer.

Unbelieving, he stared at the sketch.

"It is like a regular saddle, you see, except that on the upper left side there is this curved and padded bar, like a horn, that sticks out—so."

"Yes, ma'am." He scratched his head. "But how—"

"The lady," she explained, "hooks her—well, her *knee* over this padded horn, and rides with both her—her limbs on this same side." Close to her, leaning over the neat sketch, he saw a delicious flush spread over the nape of her neck. As if sensing his gaze, she rose briskly and handed him the paper. "Is that in enough detail?"

"Ma'am," he said, folding it and putting it into his pocket, "I'm sure old Jake can cobble up something if anyone can." A sidesaddle!

"Now hurry, please, Mr. Rollins—I am *so* anxious to get out on the trail, as they say out here." Going to the marble-topped commode, she picked up the gold-lettered Bible. "First, however, as in all undertakings, we must ask for the Lord's help." She pulled him to his knees too quickly for him to have an opportunity to protest, and knelt beside him.

"Oh, Lord, we—Mr. Jack Rollins and I—are now making a

fresh start on this mission that is so dear to my heart. This time we ask thee to expedite his efforts so that we may all the sooner complete the journey and get about thy business of preserving the likeness of the noble savage, Mr. Walking Bull, in his camp at Rainy Butte."

Into a corner of Rollins' mind came a recollection of kneeling in prayer as a child in the old Blessed Redeemer Baptist Church at Honey Hill, in Berkeley County. That had been a long time ago. It was a hushed Sunday morning, himself in starched white shirt that was a prison, and new painful shoes, sitting between his uncle and aunt in the back of the carriage while old Enos drove his uncle's bays. Ned, one of them was named. The other was—

"—and we pray that this great sinner, who so transgresses thy Commandments, may now arise full of grace—"

The other bay was Billy Boy. Jack remembered Billy Boy fondly. He used to bring sugar and apples to Billy Boy, but the fractious Ned once bit him. He looked down at the white tracery of a scar on his knuckle.

"—that he will now go and sin no more—"

Rollins jerked suddenly upright.

"Now wait a minute!" he protested.

Abigail Brand opened deep-lashed dark eyes in surprise.

"I'm not going to be prayed over so!" he cried. "Maybe I'm your employee, as you say, for a while at least, but I'm damned if that gives you the right to maunder on like I was a corpse laid out with candles!"

"But I only—"

"Enough is enough!" Jamming the shapeless hat on his head, he clambered to his feet. "I've been humiliated enough this day, and I don't intend to take any more of it! Is that clear?"

Laying the Bible on the marble-topped table, she shrugged. "Clear enough, I should think. But perhaps I should remind you, Mr. Rollins, that great pride goeth before a fall. The Lord's eye is everywhere, even on the sparrow's fall. So you will have to settle up with your Maker someday. I was only trying to ease your way until that time."

Words failed him. The piety, the self-possession, the inhuman refusal to quarrel with him—all combined to reduce him to wordless fury. Desperate, he rushed from the room, forgetting his carbine in the corner behind the potted palm.

Judge Yount's man Peach was rumored to have been a box-fighter in the middleweights class, known professionally as "The Oswego Peach." He was short and burly, arms like a blacksmith, but with a catlike quickness. Jack Rollins did not mind the taunts and gibes of the hangers-on clustered about old Jake as the harness maker worked on the sidesaddle, pausing from time to time to stare unbelievingly through iron-rimmed spectacles at Mrs. Brand's sketch. The remarks of the onlookers were raucous, and rude, but in good humor. Peach, however, watched the proceedings silently, a glint in his pale eyes. His manner annoyed Jack Rollins.

Someone asked Peach, "What do you think of this contraption?"

Peach took out his mouth harp, tapped it on the palm of his hand. "I reckon," he said, "Jack Rollins can ride that pretty mare without a saddle."

There was sudden silence. Rough and violent as the men were, no one liked the Oswego Peach's remarks. Mrs. Brand was obviously a fine lady. Rollins straightened up and looked at Peach. He had, Rollins noticed, a V-shaped tear in his trousers that might have been made by the teeth of a small dog.

"You mean anything by that?"

Peach shrugged, implying that it was hardly worth his while to speak to a nonentity like Rollins. "Looks pretty plain to me! No proper lady rides out into the country with a tramp like you." He made an ostentatious hitching motion with his arm; the single-action Army Colt showed plainly. The gun nestled in a custom-made holster high under Peach's arm, and was ordinarily concealed by the coat. The style was new to Deadwood; they were not convinced it could be drawn as fast as a belted holster. But it suited Peach's style, and he claimed that soon everyone would be wearing the new holster. "You want to make something of it?" he asked Rollins.

Jack remembered his carbine, standing behind the Boston fern in Mrs. Henry Brand's suite of rooms.

"I haven't got a gun," he pointed out.

"I know you haven't," Peach smiled. "But then—I don't *really* want to get my hands dirty on you either, Rollins! You've got fleas in that mangy yellow beard of yours, and lice in your drawers."

The spectators drew back in pleased anticipation. Rollins flushed. Someone giggled, a high-pitched nervous sound. Jake Van Meulen paused in mid-stitch, spectacles tipped down toward the end of his nose. "Now, men—" he warned.

In two strides Jack Rollins' long legs took him across the clutter of the shop. Peach was waiting for him. With that deceptive quickness he rolled to one side and tried to trip Rollins. But Rollins knew tricks, too. At the last moment he raised his knee to catch Peach full in the stomach. The breath wheezed out of him in a great gasp but he managed to entangle Rollins' legs in a bearlike grip as he fell. Together they rolled on the littered floor, Rufus dancing about and yapping his war cry.

"God damn it—not in my shop!" Jake Van Meulen squalled. "Look what you're doing!"

They rolled into a bench. Needles, knives, hammers, tacks, balls of wax, and bits of leather rose into the air. Locked together, the two men rose, groaning, grunting, straining against each other for balance. Someone grabbed Rufus and choked him into submission.

Peach had his blacksmith arms in a vise around Rollins' middle and was squeezing the breath out of him. But Rollins expertly cocked both thumbs and poked them into Peach's eyes. With an oath, Peach dropped his grasp and stumbled back.

Winded and unsteady, Rollins watched Peach stagger about, clawing at his eyes. "I'm blind!" Peach protested. "I can't see!"

"Good!" Rollins panted.

He staggered toward Peach, reached into the armpit holster, drew out the man's Army Colt.

"Don't kill him!" old Jake quavered. "No murder here, Rollins, in my shop!"

Rollins took aim. With the butt of the gun he hit the Oswego Peach carefully and precisely behind the left ear. Peach's arms fell to his sides; trembling like a pole-axed steer, he dropped to the ground and was still.

"No hard feelings," Rollins gasped. "Just tit for tat, I guess you could call it!"

He swayed back to the proposed sidesaddle, sitting half-finished on a wooden trestle.

"Now about this padded horn thing," he said to Jake. "The lady didn't give me her measurements, but I think it ought to be" —shakily he held up two hands—"about this long."

CHAPTER THREE

Waiting for Mrs. Brand to emerge from the Grand Central, Jack Rollins talked with Lew Searles, the printer. The pack train of mules shuffled in the dust, snapped at flies, and also waited, along with the bay Rollins had rented for Mrs. Brand and his own wall-eyed and spotted Indian pony, a gift from Walking Bull. Rufus glared balefully from a pannier where Rollins confined him; the mongrel had been in three fights the last two days and was bloody but unbowed.

"Where did you get the tent you're set up in?" Rollins inquired.

Searles had managed to save the hand press and most of the type.

"Wah Chee. You know, that's one good Chink!" With a maul the printer drove the last of the pegs and straightened, wiping sweat from his face. "Now, Jack, if you'll just lend a hand with this damned press—"

Together they manhandled the Washington press into the hot dank-smelling tent.

"All right," Rollins said. "So you saved the press, and some type. So Wah Chee loaned you a tent. But day before yesterday you were flat broke, Lew. You were thinking about moving on to Cheyenne City, where they had a proper appreciation of a free press. But now where do you expect to get money for paper, ink—for that matter, beans and bacon? Prices in Deadwood are sky high, you know that!"

Searles grinned mysteriously. "I got money."

"From where?"

"Oh, there's money in this town, all right!"

Searles was an idiot. Deadwood was small enough so everyone knew what was going on; they didn't need a newspaper. For an-

other thing, only a fool would try to start a newspaper in Deadwood without the approval of Judge Yount. Rollins was about to
point out these factors when he saw Mrs. Henry Brand and Julian
Garner standing on the veranda of the hotel, deep in conversation.

"You know it wasn't *me* had anything to do with the fire,"
Rollins said.

Searles opened a lid to inspect a case of type. "Of course I
know it wasn't you! It was them!" He nodded toward the hotel.
"It's them—Yount and Toomey, and Julian Garner too. They're
the big bugs in the Territory, the ones that stand to lose the most
when the *Territorial Argus* stands on its hind legs and speaks its
piece!"

Mrs. Brand and the lawyer strolled toward Rollins and the pack
animals. She was beautifully attired in a pearl-gray riding skirt and
blouse, topped by an embroidered jacket which matched. Her
boots were polished to a mirrorlike finish, and she wore a Leghorn
hat with a scarlet ribbon. As she walked, she tapped a riding crop
into the palm of a gloved hand.

"Jesus Christ!" Rollins muttered.

A raucous crowd gathered around the mules, but as Mrs. Brand
approached they became silent. They had never seen a riding
habit, or a sidesaddle. Many had not for a long time seen a lady.
And a lady Mrs. Henry Brand certainly was, moving elegantly on
Julian Garner's arm.

"Rollins!" the lawyer called. "I hold you responsible for the
safety of this beautiful woman! See that no harm comes to her."
Garner's tone was mild, almost light, yet there was a serious content that did not escape Jack Rollins' notice. "Abigail," Garner
said, bending to touch her gloved hand with his lips, "I wish you
every good luck in your venture. I—we"—his hand swept out over
Deadwood—"we will await your safe return."

In another man the feeling in Jack Rollins' breast might have
been called jealousy. But he was certainly not jealous of this arro-
gant, uncorseted female.

Lew Searles was enjoying the show too. He started when
Rollins dug him in the ribs. "Eh?"

Rollins was morose. "I just said good-by, that's all."

The printer shook his hand. "Just as well you're leaving, I'd say. Gives Peach a little time to cool down."

Rollins cocked a weatherwise eye at the dark clouds on the horizon. Some weather was making up over Crow Peak.

"He been talking around?"

Searles shook his head. "You know Peach don't do much talking. That's why he's dangerous, like a rattler that don't give no warning."

Rollins held the bay, putting out a hand to help Mrs. Brand mount. But she flew into the saddle like a bird, fitting one knee expertly over the horn, slipping her small foot into the stirrup before he could help her. There was a murmur of delight from the crowd.

"There!" she cried. "You see, Julian? It works perfectly marvelously!"

She waved to the spectators; they applauded. As the little caravan moved out into the hot dust of the street, the drovers and bartenders and off-duty infantrymen from Major Toomey's command formed a procession behind them.

"Good Lord!" Rollins groaned. It was a spectacle.

"Did you speak, Mr. Rollins?" she asked, solicitous.

He shook his head. Behind them a fiddler scratched out tunes on an instrument with a broken string, children danced and howled. The girls at Mlle. Sophie's, over the Paradise Card Room, leaned from windows and waved, the fireman at the planing mill blew a shrill blast on the whistle. Rollins was red faced and embarrassed, but Mrs. Brand only smiled and waved her gloved hand.

"Such friendly people!" she marveled. "It's almost like the Mummer's Parade on New Year's Day in Philadelphia!"

At the outskirts, further humiliation awaited Jack Rollins. Wah Chee bustled down from his hillside eyrie and stood in the middle of the road, bland faced, hands tucked into his sleeves. When Rollins tried to ride around him, the Chinaman shuffled quickly to stand again in the way.

"Rollins," the Chinaman said, "you 'memba you owe me eighteen dollah?"

Avoiding Mrs. Brand's curious eye, Rollins spoke in low tones. "I told you I didn't *have* eighteen dollars!"

"You owe me money!" Wah Chee insisted. "Pay money before leave town!"

"Look!" Rollins muttered. "When I get back, I'll have plenty of money. Five hundred dollars, she promised me!"

Wah Chee shook his head, the pigtail swung obdurately. "How I know you come back? Some Sioux lift your hair—then where I be?"

Mrs. Brand kneed her mount expertly beside them. "What is this? Does Rollins owe you money, Mr. Wah Chee?"

"Eighteen dollah!"

Even riding, she carried a reticule in a strap over her arm. The sun was hot on the riding dress; she took out a tiny wisp of lace and brushed at her forehead.

"Eighteen dollars?" She extracted a wallet and counted out bills. "Is that correct?"

Wah Chee counted, carefully. "That right."

When she handed over the money, Rollins howled in protest, angry both at Wah Chee and Mrs. Brand. "God damn it, ma'am —excuse me—I don't want you paying my debts!"

"But is it not an honest obligation you incurred with this man?"

Furious, he smote the horn of the saddle. "That pesthole isn't *worth* three dollars a day! It's dark and full of bugs and rats—" In his indignation he almost lost his voice. "It's—well, it's unsanitary! There ought to be a law against Chinamen renting out such diggings!"

"Nevertheless," Mrs. Brand said, "nevertheless, Mr. Rollins. We must all pay our lawful debts, else where would this world be?" Seeing his speechless fury, she smiled. "If it will make you feel any better, I will make a point of deducting it from the five hundred dollars I promised you."

Her eye caught the latticework structure of the easel jutting out from a tightly roped pack. "Oh, my goodness, this will never do! If that mule ever scrapes against a tree, the easel will break. Please, Mr. Rollins—see if you can't find some way to protect it!"

Sullenly he dismounted. To Wah Chee he said through set teeth, "You damned old skinflint! I tried to pay you before, but you—"

Wah Chee only bowed, and chuckled, stuffing the bills into his sleeve. "Very nice lady!"

Before an interested crowd, Rollins took the easel apart and packed the pieces separately, wrapping them in scraps of canvas. A knitting bag, filled with colored wools, was drifting astray, too, and he jammed it into a canvas sack.

"There!" he growled, hot and red faced and dusty. "Does that satisfy you?"

He was already weary of the expedition to Rainy Butte. From the way it was starting, it was bound to end in disaster.

At the foot of the mountains they rode through horse-high grama grass, so rich from thousands of generations of buffalo droppings that the mules obstinately refused to pass by until they filled their bellies. Rich-leaved willow and box elder marked the flowing streams. The sun shone beneficently on them in spite of the ominous clouds that skirted the horizon. The air smelled fresh and clean, without the stench of frying grease, horse droppings, stale beer, seared hoofs, and human sweat that lay like a miasma on Deadwood. They saw deer, and once a shaggy black bear crossed their trail, staring at them from a distance. Mrs. Brand was delighted. She propped a sketch pad on her knee and drew constantly with a charcoal pencil.

"And what is that?" she asked, pointing.

"Bullberries," Rollins muttered.

"What?"

He was still piqued. "Bullberries."

"Are they good to eat?"

He shrugged. "You can boil them. They're good for the scurvy."

"Scurvy?" She was puzzled. "I thought only sailors got scurvy! You know—when they were on a long sea voyage without fresh fruit and vegetables?"

"A man can get scurvy in the mountains," he said. "If he eats only animal meat—and a lot of the trappers do—they can get a prime case. Their teeth fall out. That's when they know they need a mess of bullberries."

She learned to identify wild plums, and he picked some for her, reluctantly. Together they sat on a slab of sun-warmed rock, eating plums, while Rufus chased prairie dogs.

"What are those trees over there?" she asked, pointing to a mass of gray-green leaves fluttering on slender stems.

"Cottonwood," Rollins said, wiping plum juice from his chin. "Good winter feed for horses. They eat the branches." He pointed. "Along the stream, there—that's box elder and willow. The Sioux have a dance in the spring called the Willow Dance. They make flutes out of the wood and play tunes."

She was sketching again, glancing covertly at him and then back at the pad. "You're a different person out here, Mr. Rollins —on the trail, I mean."

He shrugged, wiped his hands on his shirttail, clucked to the paint. "I'm the same, ma'am. It's the country that's different."

Occasionally he dug his heels into the paint's ribs and rode casually off the trail into a screen of bushes, rejoining her without explanation. In the afternoon, after one such absence, she watched him amble out of a thicket.

"Mr. Rollins," she said, "women too have an occasional need to relieve themselves." She urged the bay off the trail. A few moments later she returned, looking serene. "Let us go on now," she said.

It was only reasonable that women too should be confronted with such problems. Perhaps he should have realized the situation, spoken to her about the practice of the country, but he would have been embarrassed to speak about such things to a female. Yet he felt somehow offended by her easy talk of "relieving" herself. Somehow, he thought, she should have had the grace to dissemble—hemmed and hawed, perhaps blushed, certainly stammered and been uncomfortable and awkward. Yet she had come right out with it, almost as man to man. It was unsettling. In his confusion he cut a switch and slashed it across the rump of a malingering mule.

"Hi, there!" he shouted. "You goddamned son of a bitch! Get now—get along there!" He did not even apologize for the language, feeling himself put upon by her attitude.

"I hope," she said, wincing as he whipped the mule, "you do not treat your little dog so roughly, Mr. Rollins."

He watched the errant mule scramble up the back and onto the trail again.

"Rufus ain't no God—" He checked himself. "Rufus isn't a mule, ma'am. A mule takes special attention."

That night he pitched a tent for her on a grassy knoll under some scattered pines, and cooked supper. Hesitantly she dipped a spoon into the tin plate he offered her.

"What is it?"

Rollins ate noisily. "Beans. Bacon."

She ate a small mouthful of the beans. "They're a little—a little *strong*, aren't they?"

"That's the bacon," he explained. "I got a bargain on a chunk of it because it was coming green." Hastily he added, "I scraped the green off!"

She tried to drink the coffee, but finally turned her head away and disposed of it. "It tastes like lye!"

"I prefer it strong," he said cheerfully.

She was concerned when he wrapped himself in a blanket, head on his saddle, to lie down where the paint pony was grazing.

"Do you mean—well, what I was wondering about—are you going to lie down there and just—sleep?" It was the first time he had seen her at all discomfited. "I mean"—her gaze turned toward the tent—"I guess I thought you'd have a tent, too."

"I don't hold with tents," Rollins said. "Out here I can just look up at the stars, hear the wind, smell the pine trees. They haven't got a perfume in Paris, France, that can compare to a pine tree."

After he was assured she was asleep, he rose and tiptoed to the pile of packs. Lifting a flap, he pulled out a bottle. It was one of many carefully packed in straw. Feeling the fierce thirst assail him, he wrenched out the cork and tipped the bottle high. Afraid she would hear his frantic gurgling, he lowered the bottle and wiped his mouth. All was quiet. The pony went on nibbling grass, the mules sighed, nuzzled each other, and broke wind; a rind of moon sailed high against scudding clouds. Bad weather was coming. He hoped it held off till they got to Rainy Butte and the Sans Arc camp.

Holding the precious bottle carefully, he skulked back to his blanket and lay down. Staring in a friendly manner at the stars, he took another pull at the bottle, and then another. Sometime during the night he must have emptied it, but did not remember. Anyway, he had presence of mind enough to throw it far from him, into the grass, before he passed out completely.

In the morning he was wary and uncommunicative, telling Mrs. Brand of a headache due to the altitude.

"Always get one," he explained, "when I leave Deadwood and go into the mountains."

She was unsuspicious, offering him quick solicitude and a draft of powders from her purse, which he refused. "Medicine don't—doesn't do any good," he said sadly, explaining that it was a constitutional weakness that had always plagued the Rollinses.

During the day they rode higher and higher into the foothills of Pa Sapa. Larger stands of pine and fir and some spruce and juniper began to replace the more familiar cottonwoods and willow. A leisurely grizzly sat on a rocky ledge and watched them approach. When they came near, the animal shuffled away with amazing speed.

"They're fast, spite of their size," Rollins said. "Don't never try a foot race with one."

At times they had to pick their way carefully through fields of broken rock, occasional boulders the size of a room. The bay stumbled, its hoofs striking fire among the rocks. Once, after a particularly frightening scramble, Mrs. Brand turned a white face toward Rollins.

"Don't worry, ma'am," he reassured her. "That bay is sure-footed as a cat!"

Finally they passed through the rockslides and paused under a stand of twisted junipers, grateful for the shade.

Dark clouds ringed the horizon and moved inexorably toward them, swollen with the threat of bad weather. The air was still and hot, and black flies bit maddeningly at them and the animals. Rollins handed her cold bacon and a piece of bread hacked from the loaf with his knife.

Dutifully she tasted the bacon. "It's a little—greasy, I think," she said, wiping frosted grease from it with her handkerchief, then throwing the cambric square away. Doggedly she chewed at the bread, and smiled when he looked curiously at her. "My goodness," she said. "The bread isn't very fresh, is it?"

"Dries out fast up here," Rollins said. "The wind and all."

She looked at him. "And the altitude, too, no doubt."

He nodded. "That, too."

"Haven't you—I mean—isn't there any different kind of food?

Surely, in all those packs, there must be—perhaps a little butter to go with the bread?"

He hooted. "Butter'd melt in a minute in this heat! Besides, the nearest milk cow is probably in Omaha or someplace like that! There's precious little butter in the Territory, and those that eat butter pay a high price for it!"

"But I gave you such a lot of money! I should think that—"

"Time to go," Rollins said, rising and whistling for Rufus. "We've still got a long way to go, ma'am, and best be on our way."

That night, exhausted, Mrs. Brand went to bed early. Her hair had come down. Resignedly she braided it and wrapped it around her head. Famished, she managed to eat some beans and a piece of bacon, made a face but drank a cup of Rollins' coffee. She was too tired to protest.

"How much farther is it?" she asked.

Remembering the store of bourbon bottles in the packs, he was cheerful. "Not far now. Tomorrow we ought to come on my mine."

"Your what?"

He gestured up the dark bulk of the mountain. "Got me some diggings up there. Found a bit of color. Hope to take out a few ounces or so before the miners get here."

"But I thought the Indians didn't want anyone digging up here! They say they have ancestral graves, and spirits, and things!"

He shrugged, rolled himself in his blanket. "Walking Bull gave me a kind of totem when I pulled his boy out of the Heart River that time." He showed her the rawhide bag, ornamented with beads and feathers, hanging around his lean neck. "It's Walking Bull's own private medicine—like a ring an old-time king might give a courtier as a sign of his favor. This little bag says Rollins can do what Rollins wants in Pa Sapa."

In the firelight her face was pale and haggard, accentuated by the dark braids. "I am so hungry! Mr. Rollins, couldn't you *shoot* something tomorrow to eat? A deer, maybe—even one of those bears!" She got unsteadily to her feet and walked toward the tent.

That night he drank another bottle of whiskey, and part of a second. He was not worried, though; there was plenty more in the packs. In the morning, when he came near to hold the bay for her, she sniffed, looked curiously at him, but said nothing.

The trail was rough, he would give her that. By now, a less determined female would have turned back. At first he secretly hoped she would do so; he would earn the five hundred dollars by default. But Mrs. Henry Brand went gamely on, earning from him a grudging respect. It was all right, he was anxious to have another look at his New Ophir mine anyway. Winter rains and snow and ice might have broken open a new ledge, rich with gold. In spite of the steep trail, Rollins felt renewed, began to whistle.

"You're musical," she observed.

He shrugged.

"Do you know what that melody was?" she asked. "It's Italian opera. *Rigoletto*."

He nodded. "The duke's song. Third act."

Silent and thoughtful, she rode quietly for a while. There was no sound but the wind in the trees, the music of mule shoes among the rocks, a shifting and creaking of packsaddles. Then she said, "Mr. Rollins, you're an amazing man."

In good humor, thinking about the New Ophir, he said, half-mockingly, "You may call me Jack."

She took him seriously. "And I suppose you must call me Abigail, also." Gesturing, she said, "Out here, in all this beauty, social distinctions seem a little—well, *silly*, don't they?" Breathing deep of the cool air, she closed her eyes. "It's so different! In Philadelphia, when I made my plans, I didn't realize. I knew the Indians loved their country, and gave them credit for that, but I don't think I really understood. Now I—" She broke off, took out her sketching pad. "Look at those huge black clouds! I know so little about the west, the weather and all."

He cocked an eye skyward. "Going to pour soon, ma'am."

"Abigail."

"Abigail, then. But let me warn you—when it rains out here, this time of year, it's apt to be a real gullywasher! None of your namby-pamby eastern rains, like in Philadelphia."

She was sketching again, looking covertly at him.

"Jack, what do you think—really think—about the Indian situation? I mean—Walking Bull and his people, their fight to keep the Black Hills, the Pa Sapa?"

He laughed, shook his head. "I'm not going to be drawn into any talk like that! I've got good friends on both sides."

"But surely you have an opinion!"

"It don't pay a poor man like me to have opinions. Opinions are for the rich, and the powerful. No, I'm not going out on a limb for anybody. Deadwood is the only real home I've had since —since—"

When he paused, abstracted, she asked, "Since—what?"

He shook his head, refused to answer. After a while she said, gently, "I don't mean to pry, believe me. But I am interested in you. You didn't seem to have any money, back there." She nodded far behind them, to a distant Deadwood. "How on earth do you survive?"

He shrugged. "I pick up a few jobs here and there. In the winter I unload beer, swamp in a saloon, cook some for the Busy Bee Restaurant. In the summer I do odd jobs—a little carpentry for Judge Yount at the hotel, help out at the planing mill."

Abigail was thoughtful. "Judge Yount—he seems very powerful."

"He is." Rollins kneed the paint, and the Indian pony swerved to avoid a grayish coil in the dust.

"Why didn't you kill it?" Abigail cried. "Wasn't that a rattlesnake?"

He grinned. "Got the same right here as you and me!" He went on, eyes fixed on the trail ahead. "No, there are a lot of powerful men in Dakota. Yount's only one of 'em, though maybe the biggest. Major Toomey draws a lot of water, too, and your friend Julian Garner."

"Powerful men," she said, "always have an objective. They all have a craving for something, I find."

"That's right enough."

"So what does Major Toomey want, for instance?"

"Toomey? Well, he wants to smash the Sioux for once and for all; he wants a treaty signed, Walking Bull pacified, and his braves safe on the new reservation they're building on Whitewood Creek. Then Toomey's free to go back to Washington and the cushy War Department staff job he's always wanted, with silver leaves or maybe a pair of eagles on his shoulders."

"And Judge Yount?"

"He's aiming for governor. If he can bring off a treaty with the Sioux, open up Pa Sapa to the miners, he's got a ready-made constituency when this Territory becomes a state. He's a cinch for the first governor. Mind my words, Yount will be a national figure some day if everything goes right for him."

"What about—Julian Garner?"

He had seen Garner making calf's-eyes at her.

"All he wants is to get the hell—I mean, go back east, return to civilization. This is a rough country for a tailor's dummy like Garner. He isn't used to it. He's accustomed to tea in the afternoon and finger bowls and the theater and a clean shirt every day. He's all wrong for Dakota." He said this with a certain pride.

"They all want something," she sighed. "Something material, something of this world. But they have forgotten."

"Forgotten what?"

"Love!" Her eyes were dark and luminous. "Love is the answer! To everything—love is the answer! And love is what we all should concern ourselves with. Love of our fellow man, even of the savages!"

Rollins' voice was curt. "I don't believe in love any more. As a matter of fact, it's hardly a virtue. There aren't any virtues any more—real ones—except one."

"And that is?"

"Courage! Personal courage!"

"Whatever do you mean?"

"Look back at the ancient cultures! Love was considered weakness. Compassion was thought unmanly. Loyalty depended on the tribe you ran with. Thrift was stinginess. Magnanimity was foolishness." He shook his head. "But they all recognized a man's courage as a virtue, a real genuine virtue."

"But the war!" she cried. "Just look at the war! So many fine men died! Was it just a matter of personal courage for them? Is that why they went?"

He looked bleakly at her. The drooping yellow mustache trembled with emotion.

"Of course that's why!" he said. "After all, what other reason? Each side had good arguments, fine-sounding phrases! But it was all smoke—vapors and smoke! What did it finally come out to? Men fought and died because they were brave, because they didn't want to let their comrades down! No, ma'am, I don't believe in prattle about virtue any more! I don't believe in much of anything any more. Not even love. Courage is all there is, courage to bear us up in our passage through this world. After that—blackness, nothingness. So I am not moved by love, or anything else."

That night Rollins felt weary and spent, more from the unexpected emotion of their discussion than from physical fatigue. He had not realized how it would hurt to touch on these things, this talk of virtue, of love, of God. Sighing, he straightened up from pounding in the last tent peg.

"You are tired," Abigail said. "Perhaps it is you who should sleep in the tent tonight, and I outside, under the stars. I am beginning to love the night skies. And you will be more comfortable in the tent, can rest better."

He shook his head. The dark clouds covered almost all the heavens; the sky was streaked only here and there with a last shaft of sulphur-colored light. The air was cold; the tops of the pines thrashed in an upper wind.

"You won't see much tonight," he warned. "There's going to be a storm."

"But you—"

"I've been in lots of storms."

A jagged streak of white fire lanced the clouds. A moment later a crash of thunder assaulted their ears, rolling away in the fastnesses of the mountains, echoing and echoing until lost in the distance. She trembled. The air smelled as if something were burning.

"Probably hit a tree up the slope," Rollins observed.

He fried the last of the bacon and mixed in the remaining beans, stirring them well into the grease. Tomorrow, he figured, they should reach the mine, where he had cached a small store of tea and flour. Shortly after, they should arrive at Walking Bull's camp. But Abigail Brand refused to eat anything. Perhaps her stomach was unsettled by the approaching storm. Rollins ate all the beans and bacon himself and rolled in his blankets, confident she would fall to sleep quickly and allow him to get at the whiskey.

Almost immediately it began to rain. Hastily he snatched up

the blanket and saddle and withdrew to the protection of an
overhanging ledge of rock that formed a shallow cave. Though
wind blew rain in on his blanket-wrapped form, he managed to
keep fairly dry. God, how he wished he had a drink to warm him!
Once he started toward the pile of packs, but a great white flash
drove him back, and thunder rolled. He cast an anxious eye toward the tent. The lantern he had lit for her was turned low. Everything appeared to be all right. He had dug a trench to divert
water, and the pegs held in spite of the wind rippling the canvas.

His thirst, denied, grew to new bounds. In sudden resolve he
sprinted to the packs, drew out an armful of the precious bottles.
Who knew—lightning might strike the packs, immolate the precious bourbon! Back in the shelter of the ledge he squatted on the
sandy floor and drank long and deep. Ah, it was good stuff! Nothing like whiskey! What was it the Micks called it? *Usquebaugh*—
water of life.

In a short time he became pleasantly drunk. He passed through
several stages—happy, maudlin, then sorrowful. *Mary*, he thought.
He tilted a nearly empty bottle. *Where are you tonight? I am
here, but where are you?*

He was just draining the bottle when he became aware of a
phantasm beside him under the ledge, leaning over him, holding a
guttering rain-splashed lantern to his face.

"Mary!" he cried. "Is it you?"

His eyes began to smart. He realized he was weeping. It was a
long time since he had shed tears. He clung to the hem of Mary's
skirt. "If you knew how I've missed you all this time!"

Abigail Brand raised the lantern higher. "Whatever is the matter with you? Are you—ill?" Her dark brows drew together.
Sniffing, she wrinkled her nose. "Have you—my goodness, have
you been *drinking?*"

He dropped the empty bottle and staggered toward the pile of
packs. "I'm going to have another one. Jush—just a little one."
On hands and knees he scrabbled among the sodden packs. "Now
where are those damned bottles?"

Holding the lantern high, Abigail followed him into the rain,
wind whipping petticoats around her ankles in a welter of lace.
Her feet were bare, and she winced as she stepped on the rubble.

With wide eyes she watched him rifle the packs and sway triumphantly to his feet with an armload of whiskey.

"Mary!" he said in sudden recognition. "I hardly knew you! It's been so long!"

She snatched a bottle from him and hurled it into the blackness. "You're drunk!"

"No!" he protested, trying to protect the bottles. "No, I was cold! Jush—just to warm me, that was all. I—"

"No wonder there was never any proper food to eat, Mr. Rollins! No wonder I gagged so on weevilly beans and moldy bacon and stale bread!" She grabbed another bottle and smashed it against a rock. "No wonder I lost my proper weight and became haggard and ill and will probably catch the consumption in my weakened condition!"

Even Rufus was cowed, running back under the ledge to burrow in Jack Rollins' blanket, whimpering.

Rollins looked at the splintered glass, quailed at the odor of spilled whiskey—prime whiskey.

"Mary!" he protested blearily. "You're not Mary!"

"I am indeed not Mary!" she screamed, and slapped his face. When the rest of the bottles fell from his nerveless grasp, she snatched them up and hurled them far down the mountain. The beautiful hair, rich and thick as an Arabian's mane, had come down and lay dank and wet around her face. Her clothing was sodden with rain, and her face shone palely, like a banshee, in the night. "Whiskey, indeed, you rascal! You spent all my money on *whiskey!*"

Like a tigress she faced him, breasts heaving under the taut rain-wet lace.

"I am tired and wet and saddlesore and hungry—yes, *saddlesore*, Mr. Rollins! I have come two thousand miles by carriage and steam car and railroad and stage and horseback on an errand of mercy and compassion! Now I find myself lost in this wilderness with a simple-minded drunkard! I will probably be punished for the blasphemy, but I hope God strikes you down with a bolt of His heavenly fire right this instant, for the deceiver and sinner you are!"

Searching through the depleted packs, she found the last bottle and hurled it into a chasm. "I—I *hate* you!" she cried, and ran weeping into the tent.

"Jesus Christ!" he wailed, almost completely sobered by the destruction of the bottles. "God damn it, look what you've went and gone and done!" Furious, he searched among the rocks with the lantern. But she had broken every bottle; the aroma of wasted liquor, forever gone, laced the rain-wet night.

"That's a fine way to act!" he shouted at the tent. "Now where's all that love you were talking about? Love is all, you said! God damn it—looks to me like you haven't got very much love in *you!*"

Glumly he went back to sit under the ledge with Rufus. The rain had slackened, but rivulets of water leaked into the cave, running down the walls and wetting his chilled buttocks. He shifted his weight, uncomfortable. In the lull in the rain he could hear a muffled monotone, and realized she was praying in the tent.

In sudden resolve he got to his feet. Carrying the lantern, he walked with great purpose toward the tent. Bending over, he pulled out the pegs one by one. When the tent collapsed, he cried out in sheer pleasure at the despairing wail that arose from within.

CHAPTER FOUR

Dawn leaked gold through the retreating clouds. Abigail lay in the ruined tent, looking out. Everything was wet; raindrops sparkled in the grass, on pine needles, hung like jewels on spider webs. Clear water splashed and bubbled across rocks on its path down from the mountain, and the birds sang. The rising sun was bright and hard in a cloudless sky, and there was a tang of autumn in the air.

It seemed she had awakened from a bad dream. For a long time she lay still, trying to remember the dream, listening to the sounds about her. Jack Rollins was moving about the camp. He started a small fire and boiled coffee; the smell nauseated her. She liked coffee, but only with a good breakfast. Now she was famished, and she knew there would be no breakfast.

Here and there she heard him moving, muttering to himself. He was roping the diminished packs onto the mules, she thought. When he clucked to the wall-eyed paint, it moved across her view through a rent in the wind-shredded tent and shambled up to stand meekly before Rollins. Their shadows were black against the sunlit canvas.

"Sho, now!" Rollins murmured to the paint. "Stand easy for a minute, old boy." There was a creak of saddle leather and the jingle of hardware as he cinched up the girth. "God damn it, pull in your belly!" he ordered. "There, now!"

Unwilling, she got to her feet and stumbled into the brilliant slanting sunlight. Rollins didn't look at her, only went on tightening ropes on the sullen mules.

"Didn't take too long to pack," he muttered. "We ain't—I mean, we haven't got much to pack any more."

"No food," Abigail said faintly.

"And no liquor." He went over to the tent and knocked it

down; it sprawled in a tangle of wet canvas and cordage. "One good thing—I don't have to pack *it* any more! The storm ruined it."

After the tent fell down in the night she had managed to prop it up again with her easel. Or *had* it fallen down? She shook her head, not wanting to talk about it, or even think.

"Well," she sighed, "we are near the end of our journey, anyway."

For the first time Rollins looked directly at her. Suddenly he let out a whoop of laughter. He slapped his thigh, leaned against the paint for support, still chuckling.

"And what is so funny, pray, Mr. Rollins?"

He pointed at her, still weak from mirth. "You!"

She had slept in her clothes; the riding habit was torn, muddy, disheveled. The once-elegant Leghorn hat was shapeless from the wet, and dye from the red ribbon was, she realized with a pang, running down her cheek. Angrily she scrubbed at it with her hand.

"If you could only see yourself!" Overcome, he collapsed and sat on the ground like an Indian, holding his head in his hands. "I swear—you look like something the cat drug in and couldn't eat!"

Furious, she ran to the tent and brought out the rolled-up sketch she had been working on while they rode.

"Look at that!" she snapped. "You don't look any better!"

He stopped chuckling. "What is it!"

"Look at it!" she insisted.

Still chuckling, he unrolled the damp paper. He stared at it for a moment, then pursed his lips. "God in heaven—do I look like that?"

"You do, indeed—and I may have even softened the effect a little!"

He stared at the sketch. It was a fair approach to Don Quixote —a ragged scarecrow astride a shaggy pony with fantastically blotched hide. The rider's bony arms stuck out akimbo, and he rode with shortened stirrups like a jockey so that his knees splayed sidewise. A long toe protruded from a boot, and there was a kind of haystack of hair insufficiently confined by a drooping felt hat.

"Well, you certainly don't give a subject much mercy!" he grumbled, getting to his feet and hitching up his pants. "If you make poor Walking Bull look as bad as me, he's going to run both of us right out of camp! He's got quite a temper!"

"Well," she said, "it's what you look like! I can't help what you look like!"

Ruefully, he offered his hand. "Let's call it quits, eh? Seems to me we came out about even."

"All right. But I can't"—she looked down at the ruined clothes —"I can't go into Walking Bull's camp looking like this!"

"By noon we'll be at my mine," Rollins promised. "I've got stuff cached there—a little flour, and salt and tea. You can open one of your trunks and get out fresh clothes. There's a nice stream with big rocks where the crick flows into a kind of basin, and the sun warms the water. Maybe you could take a—a—" He hesitated. "Well—a bath, change. From the mine, it's only a couple hours or so to the Sans Arc camp."

He put out cupped hands to help her mount the bay. She wanted to refuse his help, but she was so weary and bedraggled that she meekly placed her booted foot in them and climbed into the saddle. In her whole life she had never been so unkempt, so dirty and discouraged. Even the dog, Rufus, seemed to look askance at her. When she left Philadelphia she had not counted on anything like this.

"All right," she agreed. "I suppose I can last another few hours. Tea, did you say?" The thought of hot tea with sugar almost brought tears to her eyes.

The trail became precipitous, winding through rockslides, thick timber, across ice-cold streams. At times the bay climbed like a goat, scrabbling up so steeply she was forced to bend far forward, clinging to the animal's mane for support. The sun soon dried her wet clothing, but now she was damp with perspiration.

"I—I don't know how much farther I can go!" she gasped.

Rollins turned in the saddle. "You'll make it," he said. "A woman determined as you is bound to finish anything she starts." His remark was really not unkind. Pointing far up the slope, he showed her a scar on the broad flank of the mountain. "That's my diggings. The New Ophir, I call it."

Winded, she could only cling to the saddle. According to her calculations, it must have been long after midday when they broke out onto a flat shelf of granite several hundred yards long.

There was a lot of rubble, some rusty iron devices, and a small cabin of rough-hewn logs.

"Here we are!" Jack Rollins said proudly. "The New Ophir mine, ma'am."

He helped her down; from weakness, she almost fell into his arms, but quickly withdrew.

"At last!" she gasped.

In a daze she stood finally on firm ground, freed from the pitching and tossing of the saddle. Her fingers went to her hair. She had thrown away the ruined hat; for a moment she struggled with the wet unruly mass, then gave up. "I—I am very hungry," she whispered, even her voice failing her. "But first—I would like to bathe, and change."

"Sure," Rollins said, cheerful.

He unpacked the trunk she pointed out and dragged it to a screen of bushes. Behind was a shallow sun-warm pool. "Just you go ahead," he said, "and freshen up. I'll start a fire and mix some biscuits." He picked up the ever-present carbine. "Maybe I can find us a brace of quail. This time of year they're nice and fat."

Forgetting modesty, she stripped off the ruined clothes as soon as he was out of sight. In this mountain fastness, the only prying eyes would be the noisy and ever-present jays. In the trunk she found perfumed soap and busied herself with it, working the lather into every pore of her body.

The sun was warm, the water warm, relaxing. The emptiness in her stomach was still unpleasant but she began to feel happy again, almost sure of herself. It had been a bad dream, but soon she would be in the Sioux camp, focus of her ambition, and get about her appointed task. She hummed a chorus of "Jesus Fills My Heart With Love," starting briefly when she heard Rollins' gun go off. Finishing her rinsing, she lay back in the tepid pool, wet dark hair spread over a rock to dry, looking with satisfaction at her body. Neat, trim, purposeful—its accustomed pink and white again—comfortably she wriggled her toes and luxuriated, eyes closed against the sun, naked body half-submerged.

At first she thought she had fallen to sleep and was dreaming again. The bushes rustled; a savage face, daubed in red and yellow paint, stared down at her. It hung specterlike in the greenery, disembodied.

"Oh, my goodness!" she quavered.

Could he—could it be Jack Rollins trying to frighten her? Was this some mischief he had planned—painting his face and violating her sanctuary for some frightful obscene purpose? She remembered words, distantly. *I'm not sure this is very wise, Mrs. Brand. He's a rough and violent man—a drunkard, too. He—*

"Jack?" Her voice rose to a wail. "Jack, where are you?"

She stumbled to her feet, slipping and falling in the pool. "Jack, where are you?" She placed one hand across her breasts, the other between her legs. "Jack!" she screamed.

The painted face stared, the eyes blinked. There were unintelligible words, muttered ejaculations. Quickly the face disappeared, leaving behind only fluttering leaves, a twitch of branches. Dust stung her nostrils as horses pounded away, up the rocky slope.

"What the hell—" Jack Rollins parted the leafy screen, stared down at her. "What's going on?"

In panic she blundered toward him, cowered against him, flung arms beseechingly about his waist. She had forgotten her nakedness. "An Indian!"

He put comforting arms about her, stared up the slope at the retreating horsemen. "Yes," he said. "Yes."

"He—he poked his head through the bushes! Oh, Jack—he frightened me so!" She burst into tears.

For the first time he seemed to realize he was holding an unclothed female in his arms. His face grew pale and concerned, and he tried to disengage her grasp.

"It's—it's all right!" he stammered. "I know them. They're from Walking Bull's camp. One was Hatchet Man, and I think the other was Bad Smell. You probably scared them as much as they did you."

Still in the grip of panic, she clung to him. But he pushed her away, and not gently.

"It's all over," he said. "You haven't been hurt! How in hell do you expect to live in an Indian camp if you're afraid of Indians?"

Averting his eyes from her shivering naked form, he stalked away. Through the bushes he called to her.

"Get some clothes on! Dinner's almost ready."

◄━◆━►

When she emerged from the bushes, dressed in a clinging red gown, slippers on her feet, dark hair brushed back and secured with a ribbon, Rollins would not look at her. He had been greatly shaken by the experience. The Sioux visit, of course, was expected. Ever since the business with the youth Badger, up on the Heart, the Sans Arcs had been his good friends. They allowed him the New Ophir, when they would not permit any other white man to enter that country. They kept a watchful eye on his diggings while he was absent. They were, however, amused at the idea of a man digging for wealth in the ground when there were so many riches on the surface: the wind, the stars, the trees and rocks, fish in the streams, buffalo grazing the rich grass.

It was not the visit of Bad Smell and Hatchet Man that made Rollins silent and uncommunicative. It was only that this woman resembled Mary Armistead so much. His eyes burned with the vision, his head swam, heart pounded in his chest. The same statuesque beauty—skin warm marble, the flowing dark hair, the same thoughtful eyes, mobile mouth, the delicate structure of womanhood he had thought never to see duplicated again. *Mary*, Rollins thought. *Mary! Ah, there has been no life without you!*

She misread his silence.

"I am sorry." She knelt beside the small fire where he was broiling the birds, split wide on green twigs. "I suppose I should not have cried out so. You are right—I must learn to see the Indians as others of God's creations, like you and me. But I was so frightened."

He looked at her briefly, then back at the partridge. When he did not speak, she tried again.

"It—it was an awkward situation." She flushed. "I—I have shown my body, before, only to my husband, the late Mr. Brand. But I am not ashamed of it. It is God's creation, as is yours, and was also Mr. Brand's. We should not be ashamed. The body is God's temple."

He made an impatient gesture. "That wasn't it! That wasn't it at all!"

"Then why—"

Gruffly he handed her one of the birds. "Just pull it apart. It's very tender. Eat it with your fingers; I never laid in any forks.

There's tea in the pot, and the biscuits are a mite burned, but inside they taste pretty good."

Greedily she attacked the breast of the partridge. Though there was no sugar, the tea was hot and refreshing. She even relished the scorched biscuits. He watched her eat, then silently handed her a piece of his own bird. Shamelessly, she devoured that also. Never had she been so hungry.

After dinner, she expected him to saddle up and move on. But he delayed, seeming content to loll in the sun, drinking tea, staring at the resinous smoke of the fire. After a while he threw out the leaves from his tin cup and muttered, "Well, it isn't good old bourbon whiskey, that's for sure! God, how I'd like to have a jigger or so."

She adjusted the folds of the red dress. "You're much better off with tea."

He grunted. "Matter of opinion."

Emboldened by this brief comment, she asked, "Who is Mary?"

He stiffened, looked wary. "Mary?"

"Last night, when you were so drunk, you kept fumbling at me and calling me Mary."

There was a glint of old pain in his eyes. "A lady," he said. "A lady I once—knew."

"You must have known her very well."

"Why?"

She shrugged, plucked a long stem of grass. "When you spoke her name, there was great emotion in your voice. I do not think it all came from the liquor."

He was silent, staring into the dying fire.

"If you want to talk to me about her," she offered, "I"—not knowing how to phrase it, she hesitated—"I mean, at the Brand Iron Works, after my husband died, I talked to the men, on payday. Many of them had problems, personal or financial. I got to know them, their difficulties, and counseled them. Perhaps I could help you."

He snorted. "I can just see you—Goody Two-shoes herself—holding a perfumed handkerchief to her nose while she told some smelly Mick to go right home and not stop at the saloon on the way!"

She flushed. "You can make fun of me if you want, but—"

"Let me ask you some questions! After last night, maybe *you're* the one needs counseling!"

Evading his eye, she split the stem of grass and made an unsuccessful attempt to whistle through it, as she had done when a child. But her hands trembled, and she lost the stem in the thick grass.

"What—what do you mean by that?"

Hands clasped behind his head, he lay back against a rock. "You're not so damned holy as you try to make out! When I pulled the tent down around your ears—"

She was shocked. "You did *that?*"

"You deserved it! You used language to me that would embarrass a mule skinner!"

Paling, she fumbled at the brooch at her bosom. "I suppose you are right. I *was* wicked! The fact is, of course, that I was greatly distressed. But I admit that was not an excuse for taking the Lord's name in vain. So during the night I prayed a great deal, hoping that He would again restore peace and serenity to my troubled mind."

"And did He?" Rollins gibed.

"He did." She tossed her head. "Though you are still such a ruffian, you see that I am able to speak courteously and kindly to you again, Mr. Rollins. I am restored, completely restored!"

He changed his tack. "What, exactly, is the 'mission of mercy' you were talking about?"

"My what?"

"Last night, when you were reviling me so, you said you had come two thousand miles on an errand of mercy and compassion. Now what in the hell did you mean by that? I thought you just come—came—to paint Walking Bull's portrait for your collection. Do you call that an errand of mercy and compassion? There's something a little strange here!"

"Did I say that? Really? Well, I—I didn't mean it. Not exactly."

The blond eyebrows, bleached by the summer sun, drew together; the pale blue eyes stared accusingly at her.

"Now, perhaps, Mrs. Henry Brand, you'd like to talk to *me*— bare your Christian soul, so to speak! Just why in hell did you come all the way out to the Dakota Territory with your traps and trunks and stuff?"

"I—I have told you," she stammered. "I explained it all to you, and to Mr. Garner and to Judge Yount. Why should you imagine that I have any other purpose?"

He got up, whistled to the paint.

"Smoke!" he jeered. "Vapors and smoke—that's what you're peddling, ma'am! No substance to your remarks at all, none whatever! You're not telling the truth—at least not the whole truth. But it's none of my business, long as you pay me what we agreed on."

Stung, she caught the bridle of the bay, refusing his help to get into the saddle. The red gown was awkward but she tugged violently at it, managing to drape it so it would not catch the wind and embarrass her further.

"Yes!" she cried angrily. "Smoke! Vapors and smoke, as you say, Mr. Rollins! Vapors and smoke from that private hell your thoughts seem always to inhabit!" She beat a slippered foot against the bay's ribs. Breaking into a gallop, the brute almost flung her from its broad back. Behind her she heard Jack Rollins guffaw.

"You aren't completely restored—not yet!" he bawled.

———◆———

Lying near the South Fork of the Grand, Rainy Butte soared above the lower Pommes Blanches to the west. The great massif was propped on splintered cliffs of granite, approachable by scattered and devious trails known only to the Sans Arcs and a few of their friends who could be trusted. The mountain was topped by thick stands of pine, juniper, and fir. Rainy Butte itself formed a high watchtower; the western slope descended into a wooded valley with abundant springs of sweet water, rich grass, and game.

After the exhausting climb to the saddle linking the butte with the wooded valley, they were both tired. It was late afternoon; the sun had sunk low in the west. Only scattered rays pierced the gloom of the coniferous forest. Though the ground was now level, they had to pick their way carefully through dense brush, thickets of wild plum, and clinging grapevines.

Rollins was still angry. He had not wanted to be reminded of

Mary Armistead—not ever again. For eleven years he had shut out the memory. In Deadwood he was sure he had blotted out every vestige of recollection. Now, covertly looking at Abigail Brand, he felt again a gnawing sadness.

"That's a hell of a rig you've got on," he grumbled, watching her fend off a clinging thorny bush. "Wasn't there anything more suitable in all those trunks?"

She shook her head, her voice level and composed.

"I hoped the Indians would like it. I have heard they fancy bright colors."

The composure annoyed him. He was certainly the aggrieved party, yet she was patronizing him again; he did not like her air of forgiveness.

"Well, it's holding us up, going as slow as you got to go with that damned thing on!"

Her glance was almost amused. "I know you do not think very much of me, Mr. Rollins, but a lady can hardly wear—pants!"

Now he was embarrassed, and that added to his discomfiture. It was amazing how Mrs. Henry Brand made him feel guilty and ashamed when he hadn't done a thing. To relieve his feelings he whipped the mules soundly, and kicked at a puzzled Rufus, who had lately chased a skunk.

"Get away from me, dog!" he snarled. "You smell like a privy!" Then, suddenly holding up a finger, he paused.

"Hark!"

Abigail reined up.

"Listen," Rollins whispered. "Did you hear it?"

"I heard a bird whistle."

He pursed his lips and whistled, three tones in a descending pattern, ending in a whorl of grace notes. He closed his eyes, listening. A moment later a similar call sounded from the trees ahead.

"That's it!" he cried, pleased.

"That's what?"

He grinned. "Bird talk. The Sans Arcs are expecting us."

"But where are they?"

"All round us." Rollins clucked to the paint and the little train moved off again in the dying day, picking a careful way between the columns of trees. "Don't look right nor left! Just sashay along

—sing, if you've a mind to. Never does a person any good to let a Sioux see you're concerned about anything."

Fearfully she followed after him. She tried to think of a hymn, but her throat was dry and constricted.

"Are—are you afraid, Mr. Rollins?" she asked.

He chuckled. "You can call me Bone Man now."

"Bone Man?"

"That's what the Sans Arcs named me. Guess it was because I'm sort of long and desiccated, like the leg bone of a deer." He whistled again, a short flutelike run, and said, "No, not exactly *afraid!* They know me and I know them, and we're kind of beholden to each other. But this is a rough country out here, and occasionally some hair gets lifted. So it's well to keep an eye out, always."

Now she saw the Indians, half-hidden behind the trunks of trees, peering from bushes, watching from high rocks that bordered the trail. Their silence unnerved her. Kneeing the bay, she rode up to remain near Jack Rollins.

"They *do* fancy that red dress," he said, not turning his head. "Maybe it was a good idea after all."

The trail debouched into a clearing. At the sight of the Sans Arc camp she caught her breath in wonder. In the twilight, the lodges glowed like giant tapers. Cooking fires were lit, and a haze of woodsmoke lay in the valley. In the distance a herd of horses grazed in a pole corral, and children played a game of stickball. As they rode into the camp, Walking Bull's people left their activities and came to stand beside the trail, hushing the children as the caravan passed.

"There's old Bad Smell!" Rollins said from the corner of his mouth. "He still looks flabbergasted at seeing you naked at my diggings!"

Bad Smell was a big man, straight of back and bowed of leg, clad only in a clout and a necklace of fierce-looking teeth—bear, she guessed—with a red trade blanket thrown over his shoulders like a cape. His stolid face showed no emotion as he watched her.

"I suppose," she whispered, "he doesn't bathe often. Is that why he is called—"

Rollins' laughter was strangled. "No," he said. "Not exactly! But no need to go into it now."

As they rode toward the giant lodge in the center of the ring of tipis he kept up a running commentary.

"That one in the fur jacket—that's Buffalo Talker. He's the big medicine man. You can always tell because they wear the jackets with the fur outside. The rest always has the hair inside."

"Buffalo Talker? Is that his name?"

He nodded. "That's where he gets his magic. He talks to the buffalo, and they tell him secrets." Rollins pointed to a youth sitting a spotted pony atop a ledge of rock. "That's Badger, Walking Bull's boy."

"The one you—"

"There's Crow King," Rollins said. "And Kills Often. Running Man, and Bear Teeth; Walks On The Sky."

At the huge lodge he reined up, motioning her to wait. "Keep an eye on the mules. Don't let them wander."

She was alarmed. "Where are you going, then?"

He paused before the doorflap and scratched on the taut skin of the lodge.

"Got to pay my respects."

When he slipped inside she felt panic-struck, abandoned. Motionless and mute in the saddle, she dared look neither right nor left. Rollins had said never to show fear or emotion before them. One of the mules strolled toward a juicy-looking patch of grass and wildflowers. Fiercely she hissed at it.

"Come back here! Oh, come back! Lord, *make* him come back!"

In wide-eyed wonder a small naked boy stared up at her. A girl joined the boy, and they both giggled. A woman, fat and very old, approached, carrying a leather waterbucket. The crone pointed to Abigail's brooch, and made an inquiring sound.

"This?" Abigail fingered the brooch. "Do you want it?" Desperately she tried to unpin it. "Here—take it if you want! Only just— just go away and leave me alone!"

She was near a catatonic state when Rollins lifted the flap and emerged again. He had been gone a long time. She remembered Indians did not like to be hurried. First they always wanted to smoke a peace pipe or something.

"What happened?" she asked. "Is everything all right?"

He helped her down from the bay. This time, limbs weak from

the long ride and from the fear welling in her bosom, she was grateful for his steadying hand.

"You can stay here tonight," he said.

"Tonight? Just for tonight? But—"

"I had one hell of a time getting that much out of him! He's in a bad mood, anyway; he gets like this at times."

"But—"

"He says women in camp cause a lot of trouble. But a white woman—that's *really* bad luck. He says his pony herd will get the glanders or something, and the game will disappear."

She clutched his arm. "But did you tell him about the portrait? The one I came all this way to paint of him?"

"I know," he said, "that that's the line you've been pushing all along, but—"

"Line?" Indignant, she pushed him away. "What 'line' are you talking about? I am a portraitist! There are examples of my work hung in museums in—"

"I know all that," Rollins sighed. It had been a hard day; he had developed a headache that sat on his skull like an iron crown. A drink would relieve it instantly, he knew; it always did. But Walking Bull was a teetotaler, and demanded abstinence in his camp. "It's just that I think the portrait business may be a cover for something you're not telling me."

In spite of weariness she drew herself up full-length, looking him in the eye. He began to doubt his theory.

"A cover for *what*, pray? Whatever can you mean?"

Defeated, he nodded toward a small lodge on the fringes of the meadow. "You can sleep there tonight. There's an old woman that will take care of you, fix a bed, give you something to eat."

"But—"

His head seemed on the verge of exploding. "Will you *go*?" he howled.

Her chin trembled, but she stood her ground.

"Don't treat me like one of your Indian women!"

His face changed, a kind of resignation came into it.

"I haven't got any Indian woman," he muttered. "Or any other kind! Now will you go?"

She went.

CHAPTER FIVE

That night Abigail Brand dreamed of a long-ago winter holiday. She was in a sleigh—Uncle Dick Massie's handsome cutter with the team of matched blacks—gliding through Fairmount Park. The trees were festooned with white, runners hissed over hard-packed snow, the breaths of the horses emerged in steamy clouds. Passers-by in fur coats waved, and the harness jingled. But Abigail was cold. Shivering, she turned to her aunt for warmth. But Aunt Sylvie only looked straight ahead, eyes fixed on the bobbing black rumps. She tugged at her aunt's sleeve but there was no response. About to weep from cold and despair, she was surprised when someone threw a great furry robe over her. Gratefully she burrowed into it, snuggling down, face pressed deep into the fur. She slept, profoundly.

When she woke, she did not know the time of day. She lay still for a long time, watching branches make leafy patterns on the wall. Or was it a wall? And where was she? Frowning, she sat up, brushing her hair back with an anxious hand. Near her bed burned a small fire; an iron pot bubbled, a smell of brewing tea came from a battered tin pot. She stared about, feeling disoriented but not at all frightened. She lay on a strange bed—a slatted platform of willow rods interlaced with strips of rawhide. Over her legs was a heavy fur robe. In wonder she touched the long hairs. Someone had covered her in the night.

Recollection flooded back. She was in the camp, the Sioux camp—Mr. Walking Bull's camp. Still in the wrinkled red gown, she walked to the doorflap of the tipi. For a long moment she stood there, staring out at a strange new world.

Sunlight, early sunlight, dappled the camp. Smoke-stained lodges were scattered among the trees. Before each were stacked the travois, the litterlike arrangements she had read the Sioux

used to transport their goods when they traveled. Each lodge had
a racklike structure of peeled poles, on which hung what she supposed were cuts of meat, drying. The camp was veiled with woodsmoke. Women busied themselves cooking the morning meal in
outdoor kitchens of willow boughs. People called back and forth
in the crisp sunlight, laughing and joking. There was singing, too
—a pleasant chanting like a musical backdrop to the bustle of the
camp.

In a patch of sunlight she saw a group of young men with her
bay—the one Jack Rollins had rented for her. While one youth
held the animal by the halter, others passed her sidesaddle from
hand to brown hand, examining it carefully. One boy grasped the
protruding leather horn and wrenched at it, apparently attempting to pull it off. But Mr. Van Meulen had done a good job.

"Oh!" She started. Behind her someone emerged from the tipi.
It was the old lady who had so admired her brooch—a very old
lady, she now saw, face stitched with thousands of incised lines.
She had no teeth, but her smile was wide. The night before, in
her weary and disoriented state, Abigail was only dimly aware of
figures moving about the lodge, handing her food, making small
soothing noises, preparing a bed for her. The lodge had been dark
and smoky, lit only by a small cooking fire. Now she realized the
crone must have been in the tipi all the time, must be the old
lady Jack Rollins said would take care of her.

"Good morning!" Abigail smiled.

The old lady bobbed her head. She had a tin spoon in one
hand. Making sipping motions and rubbing her stomach, she invited Abigail to come back into the lodge.

Grateful, Abigail knelt on a mat and watched the old woman
dish out a broth filled with unidentifiable vegetables. They appeared to be roots of some kind, and she thought she tasted wild
onions. She ate ravenously. The crone, pleased, dished out another
cup of the soup. It was not the kippers Abigail favored at home,
nor yet the deep-fried scrapple with butter and maple syrup. But
it was satisfying, very satisfying.

Licking her fingers, she spoke to the woman. "You, then, are
the lady who covered me with the robe last night, when I was so
cold!"

She supposed the old lady could not speak English, but Abigail managed to sign her gratitude to her. The woman went over to the willow-rod bed and patted the heavy robe, grinning and bobbing her head again.

"Yes," Abigail said. "Thank you very much."

She turned when a shadow darkened the doorway. Jack Rollins stood framed in a V of sunlight.

"Had breakfast?"

Still licking her fingers, she nodded. It was not proper manners, but the juice was delicious. "It was good."

He came in to kneel beside her. His manner was constrained; he retained some of the waspishness of the night before. He suspected her, she knew. She would be well advised to win back his confidence.

"This is Ugly Woman," Rollins said, indicating the old lady. "She's been told off to do for you, keep an eye on you."

Ugly Woman touched Rollins' cheek in a gesture of affection, and he pulled her braids. In mock anger the old woman doubled a fist and banged him on the arm, chuckling.

"I think it is very wrong, to name people so," Abigail protested. "If she is ugly—and the case has not necessarily been made—then it is cruel to remind her of it."

He shook his head. "You've got a lot to learn. There's no cruelty intended, none at all. Indians are just honest, matter-of-fact about these things. She's ugly—she knows it, her husband Crow King knows it, all the Sans Arcs know it. But there's no stigma attached, the way there might be back in your Washington, D.C."

"Philadelphia!"

"Philadelphia, then. But among the Sans Arcs she's an honored old lady. She's called Ugly Woman just like someone else might be called Wind Runner or Big Heart or Walking Bull or whatever."

It still did not seem right to her. Nevertheless, as he said, she had a great deal to learn about the Sioux. She changed the subject.

"What about Mr. Walking Bull? When will I be permitted to see him, to show him my work—to persuade him to sit for his portrait?"

He poked the diminishing fire with a stick.

"I'd advise you not to get your hopes up. Walking Bull says women are always trouble, and white women in his camp are *bad* trouble." He grinned his twisted, mocking grin. "Don't know but what I agree!"

She did not think it amusing.

"Now don't get mad, Abby," he advised. "We'll see him this morning. It's just that these things are delicate, and have got to be approached with care."

She had not given him leave to call her Abby, and was annoyed. Besides, Abby was a contraction she disliked. Her father always insisted on Abigail, and required her mother and uncles and cousins to do the same. But Jack Rollins did not notice her displeasure, or ignored it.

"Whenever you're ready," he said, "we'll go by to see Walking Bull. But let *me* do all the talking—understand?"

First she insisted on a brief toilette. Ugly Woman brought a basin of warm water. Abigail washed her hands and face while Rollins waited outside. The trunks had been neatly arranged near her bed. She found a comb, brushed her dark hair the customary hundred strokes while Rollins fidgeted. Finally, with rice powder on her cheeks, a dash of cologne on wrists and temples and between her breasts, along with an ineffectual smoothing of the slept-in red dress, she was ready.

Rollins stared at her. "I never thought you were really pretty," he admitted, "but this morning you're passable." He noticed the roll of canvases under her arm. "What are those?"

"Samples of my work, of course."

He looked doubtful. "I wouldn't take them along—at least not this first time."

"But why not?"

"Indians don't like to be hurried! This morning we'll just pay our respects, you and me."

"But I must!" she insisted. "There's so little time! You've already mentioned how the snow is coming soon!"

"Are you going to listen to me? I'm only telling you the facts, the honest facts! I've lived with these people long enough to know how they think!"

She set her chin firmly. "That is all very well, Mr. Rollins. In most matters, I am content to be guided by your decisions. But I am a painter, and a good one. I cannot help but feel that the chief will be intrigued by the work I have done, and desire to have his own likeness also preserved."

Rollins groaned. "Walking Bull is a young buck yet! He gets mad quick, and takes offense! When he's roused, he's meaner 'n a skilletful of snakes!"

"I will not blame you," she promised, "if things come out wrong. But painting is my field, you see, as the wilderness is yours. So this time you must let me prevail."

As they walked toward Walking Bull's tipi, Rufus sprang into a thicket in pursuit of an impudent squirrel. Jack Rollins, cursing, ran after him. Head hanging, the small shabby dog ambled back.

"He's just enjoying life!" Abigail protested, woolling Rufus' ears. "He smells that marvelous tang in the air, too!"

Rollins grunted. "He won't be enjoying life very long if he runs about like that!"

"What do you mean?"

"Sioux like dog meat."

"What?" She was shocked.

"They like dog meat! I'm partial to it myself. Something like goat—bland, and a little stringy, unless you get a nice fat bitch."

Involuntarily her hand went to her bosom. "Oh, my goodness!"

"You'll learn a lot of things in this Sans Arc camp," he grinned. Looking at the red dress, he said, "Sioux love the color red. *Sha* in Sioux means red, like your dress. And *sha sha*—the reddest of reds, you might say—means good, excellent." As they walked he showed her the hand language for *sha*, rubbing his whiskery cheek with the palm of his hand. "That sign comes from the custom of painting their faces with red paint, do you see?"

"I see," she said, very gravely. But she did not really understand why she need be concerned with such things. All she wanted to do was paint the chief's portrait.

Still, when she noticed Rufus bounding off to join a pack of Indian curs, she called sharply after him herself. The dog came slinking back, looking first at Rollins and then at her. Rufus, Abigail thought, was another friend; she did not want him to be a Sioux entrée. In spite of the color and activity of this Indian camp, the sweep and vigor that made her fingers itch for a brush and bright colors, it was still a potentially dangerous place for a Philadelphia matron.

When they approached the great central lodge, Rollins
scratched again on the doorflap. Someone called out, bade him
enter. He was not at all polite to her, stepping quickly inside himself and motioning her to follow.

As her eyes became accustomed to the dim light she saw a fire
smoldering in the center. Painted rawhide trunks lay about the perimeter of the lodge. There was an incongruous chest of drawers,
much like the burl-chestnut one in her own bedroom in Philadelphia. Furs were scattered about, and cooking pots; an old brass
alarm clock which did not tick, a portable harmonium, such as
traveling missionaries carried. She wondered about the fate of the
missionary who had owned it.

Walking Bull lay on a pile of robes, smoking a pipe decorated
with feathers and ribbons. He was powerfully built, and the
firelight glistened on his skin with a coppery sheen. Around his
neck was a silver medallion depending from a chain. In the gloom
at the rear of the lodge sat two women—probably his wives—
chewing at hides, apparently to soften them. One was young and
rather pretty, even by Philadelphia standards. The other was gray
and middle-aged, with a heavily seamed face and a bosom that
sagged like a bag of grain. The wives looked up in alarm, and hid
their faces, but Walking Bull did not move. Puffing at the long
pipe, he eyed Abigail Brand. A jewel of perspiration sparkled on
his forehead; it was smoky and stifling in the tent.

"Sit there," Rollins commanded her, indicating a blanket near
the doorway, "and don't come between him and the fire, whatever
you do. And don't *speak* unless I tell you to—understand?"

"I understand," she said.

Rollins sat cross-legged across the fire from the chief. For a long
time neither spoke. Abigail began to feel faint in the close atmosphere. The women—wives—uncovered their faces and stared at
her. The pretty one made a small gesture that might have been
the Sioux equivalent of crossing one's self, a protection against
evil.

After a while Walking Bull passed the pipe to Jack Rollins,
who bowed his head in acknowledgment of the courtesy. He
puffed a small ring in each of the four cardinal directions, followed by a fifth that shimmered into the smoke-blackened upper
reaches of the lodge.

Again they sat motionless. Abigail twitched. Her leg cramped, and she was in agony. Finally she managed to shift her weight a little, and furtively rubbed her calf. Outside, she could hear children playing in the meadow, the gurgling of the brook that laced through the camp, the shrill neigh of a pony.

Rollins handed the pipe back to the chief and started to speak. It was the first time Abigail had heard the language. Though she had always been good at Greek and Latin at Miss Fitts' School and Female Academy, she could make nothing of it. Rollins spoke rapidly, fluently, in the strange sibilant tongue, supplementing his words with graceful sweeping motions of hands and fingers.

Walking Bull's face was stolid and impassive. Once he looked at her, a searching gaze that made her flush and avert her eyes. Rollins talked on, long-fingered hands fluttering in the gloom like pale birds.

She did not know how long they had been there, but it seemed an eternity. Beads of perspiration broke out on her forehead, stitched maddeningly down between her breasts. Her clothing seemed dank and restricting. A fly lit on her cheek but she willed herself not to stir. Whatever could take so much talking about?

Walking Bull had not uttered a word. When Rollins finally paused, there was again a long silence. One of the wives—the plump, gray-haired one—crawled forward with a pouch and stoked the chief's long pipe. Neither Rollins nor Walking Bull appeared to notice the woman; it was as if she did not exist. Abigail resented their lordly manner. Could they not at least show the woman a little courtesy? She would allow no one to use *her* so.

Walking Bull finally stirred from his indolent pose. He sat up, cross-legged, staring at her, his face grave. Suddenly he belched, which made her start, then patted his lean stomach placatingly.

For the first time she noticed the jagged scar that ran from eye to thin-lipped mouth, another that stitched crazily across his sweating naked chest. The fierce eyes held her; she felt hopeless to avoid them. The orbs were black and shiny, with glints of the firelight in their depths.

Finally Walking Bull signed to Rollins and began to speak in the same guttural sibilant tongue. *Sha sha*, she remembered, meant good, excellent. Would she hear that word spoken? Would Walking Bull, hereditary chief of the Sans Arcs, come to think it a good idea, an excellent idea, to have her paint his portrait? Straining her ears, she listened intently. But although she did not understand a word of the palaver, she suddenly realized she had lost her case. Walking Bull was even now refusing to sit for her. In fact, his voice turned bitter and challenging. His gestures became dramatic and violent. Finally he slashed the air with both hands in a gesture unmistakably final.

Rollins turned to her. "It's no go," he muttered. "He won't hear of it. He thinks you're an evil spirit sent to trick him, maybe deliver him into the white man's hands."

"But that's foolish!" she protested. "I only want to help him! I want to paint his portrait, that's all! I wouldn't be in the way! Can't you tell him I'm his friend?"

"I told him all that!"

Angry, she jumped to her feet. "But I can't tell you how important this is to me—and to him, too!"

Rollins shook his head. "He's gone for a long time without anyone painting his picture. Guess he figures he can go a few more years." He tugged at her skirt. "Now sit down, will you?"

Frustrated, she almost wept. "Listen to me! Listen! Does he speak any English at all?"

The two wives were appalled at such effrontery before their master. They chattered like magpies, pointed accusing fingers. One made an obscene gesture that even Abigail Brand recognized. Rollins rose, snatching at her arm in an effort to dissuade her.

"Be quiet!" he hissed. "For Christ's sake—"

Angrily she pulled her sleeve away, picked up the roll of canvases. "But—"

"You're only here on sufferance!" he warned. "And you're not doing me any good, either!"

"I don't care!" she stormed. "Let *me* talk to him! After all, *you* didn't do any good!"

Walking Bull said something short and hard to Jack Rollins. Rollins released his hold.

"Speak little English," Walking Bull said. "Speak little. Maybe understand. What you say, Red Dress Lady?"

She pushed Rollins aside. Kneeling beside the seated chief, she unrolled the sheaf of canvases.

"I will speak very slowly, sir," she said, "and hope you understand me."

The first portrait was a study of her husband, the late Mr. Henry Brand, sitting at his desk in the Iron Works. Abigail had caught his likeness rather well: the iron-gray beard, steel-rimmed spectacles, the placid and conservative mold of face. Near Mr. Brand's shoulder was a great window; through it could be seen the belching stacks of the foundry he had built.

"You're being a damned fool!" Rollins protested.

The second canvas was of Mrs. Letitia Bettencourt, the dowager empress of Main Line society. If a couple had not been invited to one of Mrs. Bettencourt's soirées, they simply did not exist in Philadelphia, no matter what their status in lesser places such as New York or Baltimore.

Walking Bull was unimpressed. "I not know these people."

With a sinking feeling she showed him what she conceived to be her best work—the portrait of President Grant, done from photographs and a brief audience when she and Henry Brand had been asked to the White House. To her surprise Walking Bull proudly showed her the silver medallion around his neck. Indeed, there was the President's likeness on one side and an engraved legend on the other that spoke of some Indian treaty.

"How very nice," she murmured.

He let the medallion fall. Then he shook his head.

"Rollins," he said, pointing. "Rollins—Bone Man—friend. I owe him. But Sioux have gods. Rock. Thunder. Buffalo—all the rest." He made a peculiar gesture. "Iktomi, too."

"Iktomi?" she asked.

"Bad god. Trickster. Send trouble, Iktomi. Must watch him, always." Walking Bull rose, arms crossed over the jagged scar, and stared down at her. "Maybe Iktomi send you, Red Dress Lady! So you go away, today. Go quick! Bone Man take you!"

Then she had lost! The red dress had not helped. Her canvases had not won the case. Rollins had not helped her; perhaps he had even managed to damage her case. The long tedious trip had been for nothing. Abigail was furious. Angrily rolling the canvases together, a square of sketching paper fluttered out. She knelt to retrieve it, but something on the paper caught the chief's eye. It was her sketch of Jack Rollins on the trail, the grotesque representation of Rollins as Don Quixote—shambling loose-jointed figure, straggly beard with long hair tucked into the battered hat, feet in split and broken boots dangling without stirrups. There was about the figure an air of infinite disrepair, a manikin held together, as she had said, only by the dirt of his clothing.

Walking Bull stared somberly at the sketch. He held it at arm's length, scrutinizing. Then he maneuvered it for better light into a patch of autumn sun entering the smoke hole of the tipi. She wondered whether he were about to show the temper Rollins had told her about, and was afraid. But suddenly he laughed in pure delight. He stamped the skin floor of the lodge with moccasined feet. The silver medallion around his neck danced and clattered against a necklace of sharp claws.

"What—what—" Pale and startled, Abigail turned toward Jack Rollins. "What is he laughing about?"

Walking Bull motioned to his wives. They approached, mystified also, and fearful. But when they saw the sketch of Rollins, they too burst into laughter. The great lodge was filled with un-Indian merriment. She had not known that Indians ever laughed.

"I don't think it's as damned funny as all *that!*" Rollins protested.

"*Sha sha!*" Walking Bull chuckled, pointing to the sketch.

His wives were in full agreement. *Sha sha! Sha sha!* Screaming with laughter, they poked each other. One of them—the attractive younger woman—walked about the tipi in imitation of Jack Rollins' long-legged shambling gait.

"Well," Abigail said, "I guess it *is* pretty funny, at that, though at the time I was doing the sketch, I remember being very put out with him."

"Come on!" Rollins growled, seizing her arm.

She resisted. "What about my portrait?"

"I don't give a good goddamn about your portrait!" he snarled.

Walking Bull ceased his laughter long enough to wipe his eyes, pat Abigail affectionately on the cheek.

"You stay!" he said. "Stay, all right, you!" He pointed to Rollins, and again was convulsed with laughter.

"Will you come?" Rollins howled.

She had won, it appeared. She would be able to do the portrait. Feeling almost charitable toward Jack Rollins, she allowed him to drag her through the meadow, past the long file of lodges, through the onlookers who had been mystified by the gales of laughter from the chief's lodge, ordinarily a scene of somber and weighty confrontations.

He deposited her before the tipi where she had slept the night before. Ugly Woman was cooking a stew in an iron pot before the doorway.

"You made a fool out of me!" Rollins protested. "Whatever possessed you to show him that damned silly picture?"

"I thought it a good likeness," she said, coolly. "A caricature, I admit, but it did catch you to the life!"

Making a growling sound, like a bear, he flung her arm away. Angrily he stalked away, Rufus tagging at his heels.

Jack Rollins was miffed at her, but she didn't care. She had succeeded in the first part of her mission. And after all—who could possibly care about the opinion of such a crude and unspeakable person? She looked forward, after all this was over, to seeing a real gentleman again; someone like Julian Garner.

For Abigail, the days that followed were glorious. Rising early each morning, she helped Ugly Woman prepare breakfast for Crow King, the old lady's husband. She and Ugly Woman ate later. From Ugly Woman, Abigail learned the Sioux names of the common foods. Corn—they had sweet corn—was *waka maza*. Coffee was *pazuta sapa*; eggs, tiny quail eggs, were *witka*. Sugar, which the Sioux loved, was a jawbreaking *chahumpiaska*.

Depending on circumstance, she was allowed for an hour each day to take her easel and canvases and paints and brushes into the great tipi and work on the portrait. Walking Bull was a busy man, as busy as her husband had been as chief executive of a great commercial enterprise. There were councils of war with Buffalo Talker, the shaman, and representatives of various warrior societies—the Foxes, the Silent Eaters, the Badger People, the rest. There were emissaries from other Sioux tribes—Miniconjou, Brulé, Hunkpapa—concerned at the threat to their own lands, trying to establish a common front against the white man. The Rees traded with the Sans Arcs, bringing corn and beans in exchange for meat and fur, moccasins and robes. There were problems of deciding how many sacks of grain to put aside for the winter, how much food should be eaten during the celebration of the Willow Dance, how much dried in the sun and stored against a time of need. Abigail could not, of course, presume on the chief's time, but he always managed to find a short recess when he could summon her.

"I am grateful for the time you give me," she told him.

After the merriment in his lodge over Jack Rollins' picture, Walking Bull had lapsed again into the noble gravity she had associated with Indians.

"Where you red dress?" he asked.

"It was dirty. I washed it in the creek, and Ugly Woman hung it out to dry."

"Wear tomorrow," he ordered. "Wear red dress."

Much of her information about the Sans Arcs came from Crow King, Ugly Woman's husband. He was an elderly man with graying braids and the remnants of a white man's ruffled dress shirt. Somewhat of a dandy, he sat before the lodge in the thin sunlight each morning, painting his face and squeezing hairs from his chin with a clamshell. At first, Crow King did not deign to notice Abigail Brand. But he had seen the beginnings of her portrait of Walking Bull, and wanted her to paint him too. Crow King spoke a little English, learned from contacts with white fur traders along the Big Cheyenne and the Belle Fourche.

Surprisingly, Ugly Woman had a little English, too. She taught Abigail to say *hie hie* for "thanks," and the gesture for "glad," the sign Abigail thought so beautiful. The Sioux made a small heart by curling thumb and forefinger together, placing them over the left breast. Then they held their two hands, palms down, before the chest and swept them forward, at the same time turning over the palms. Literally, the completed sign meant *sunshine in the heart*; first, the small heart—then the sweeping gesture associated with the coming of dawn, the rising of the sun, an unfolding of day. Abigail wished there were a way to paint that sign, to fix it forever in its beauty.

Rollins, still angry, avoided her, but she did not care. She had the freedom of the camp. When she was not working on the portrait she took her sketching pad and strolled about. Young men raced prize mounts in the meadow, the camp crier rode a spotted pony here and there, calling out the day's news. Feathered warriors, magnificent-looking men, rode in from the night's sentry duty on the cliffs that overlooked the tortuous trail up Rainy Butte. Old men cut up tin frying pans and made arrow points, women washed clothing in the stream—the Sans Arcs were very clean, bathing and changing clothing every day—children played a game by rolling a willow hoop downhill and trying to throw stick spears through it.

The Sioux clothing especially interested her, crying out to her feeling of color. The men dressed in garments that might have looked foreign to Sunday strollers on Market Street in Philadelphia, but had a dignity and beauty and style of their own. There were scarlet trailing breechcloths, a foot wide, reaching from the belt to the ground. Some wore leggings of buckskin, a bead stripe down the leg, with a twisted fringe from knee to ankle. Many wore shirts of mountain-sheep skin, shoulders and chests decorated with what Ugly Woman told her were dyed porcupine quills, and tassels of hair in rows on either side. Human hair? Abigail was queasy, and shuddered.

Unable to resist the lure of the savage colors, she got out canvas and paints one afternoon and set up shop near the tipi. Badger, the chief's stripling son, came shyly to watch, sitting on a grassy hummock nearby. He was a slender youth, about sixteen, she judged, with long braids wrapped in otter fur. She wondered which of Walking Bull's wives was the mother. Perhaps it was neither of the two, but another woman. These people, colorful and interesting as they were, knew little of morals.

At first, Abigail did not speak to the boy, fearing to make him uncomfortable. Instead, she reached for her sketch pad, never far away. In a few moments she had drawn him, quiet and pensive, staring into the distance with that withdrawn look. When she showed him the sketch, he smiled at first, apparently pleased. He was a nice boy, she decided; it was difficult to imagine this gentle dreamer the offspring of a fierce and warlike Sioux chieftain.

Suddenly he frowned, drew back. She tried to hand him the drawing but he hurried away.

"Here!" she called. "Take it! It's yours!"

In the twilight—she had painted later than she thought—she

did not see Rollins. He came silently beside her, and took the sketch from her.

"Not bad." He peered at it in the failing light. "You've caught his likeness, right enough." Seeming to want to make conversation, he handed the sketch back to her. "That's what worries Walking Bull—the gentleness in the boy! If Badger's ever going to amount to anything among the Sans Arcs, he's got to develop some grit, some orneriness. Got to stand up for himself, for his people!"

With surprise she noted the change in Jack Rollins' dress. Gone were the sagging breaches, the threadbare shirt, the split boots. He wore a leather vest, ornamented with beads and quills and bits of colored glass, along with high Sioux leggings. The amulet given him by Walking Bull hung against his naked chest. Tufted with yellow hair, the bare skin showed immodestly through the vest, and she averted her eyes. His long hair, she noticed, had been trimmed; a red cloth was tied around the shorn locks. He had, she was sure, recently bathed, and smelled clean and fresh.

Carefully she picked up a still-wet canvas, and put brushes and paints away in their leather case.

"What happened to your old clothes?"

He grinned sheepishly. "I tried to wash them in the crick, but they fell apart!"

"I should think so," she said.

He followed her into the lodge. Ugly Woman sat in a corner, knitting industriously, tongue caught between her few remaining teeth.

"What in hell is *she* doing?" Rollins demanded.

"Knitting socks for her husband. I am teaching her."

Rollins examined the bold plaid pattern. "By God, old Crow King ought to have a plug hat and a gold cane to go with these!"

"They will keep his feet warm," she said. "He has very cold feet."

He grinned at her, a sly grin. "How do *you* know?"

"Ugly Woman gave me to know that is the case."

"All right," he soothed. "Don't get your dander up!" Ugly Woman handed him a fat roast rib and he chewed reflectively on it. "As a matter of fact, I finally decided it was silly—us disagreeing so. After all, we're the only two white folks in about a hundred miles."

"That's right," she said.

His nails, too, were neatly trimmed; gone was the black rim she so detested. Bathed, divested of the filthy clothes, John Fitzhugh Rollins was not unhandsome.

"How's the portrait of the chief coming?" he asked.

"Rather well."

He looked through the doorflap at the twilight. "We've got to keep the season in mind. At these high altitudes, snow can come fast. First snowfall is generally light—a kind of warning—and we'd better be ready to travel. We don't want to get snowed in."

"But I am working as fast as I can! He is very busy, as you must know. If he could only spare me more time—"

Rollins seemed not to have heard. Squatting on his heels, he poked absently at the fire. "I must admit I sneaked a look at your portrait. Pretty fair, far as it's gone. Good draftsmanship, an eye for color. You're talented, all right. But—"

Ugly Woman, seeing them in serious conversation, went tactfully away on an errand. The autumn twilight dwindled, the fire painted shadows on the skins of the lodge.

"But what?"

He shrugged. "I was just thinking. Francis Bacon. Did you ever read any of Bacon?"

"A little," she admitted, "in school." In an amicable gesture she poured him coffee from the battered pot. "I found him very dry."

"He wrote profound things. He said, 'That is the best of beauty, which a picture cannot express.' I mean—now don't get riled, Abby—I mean you have to live with these people a long time to be able to paint them well, to do justice to them and the life they lead. Their lives have got to be your life."

"I don't know what you mean," she said, with some asperity.

"I mean a picture can never show what makes a Sioux a Sioux." His voice lapsed into a murmur; she had almost to strain to hear him in his reverie. "The long blue days, the lightness of the air—meat cooking on a willow twig. Children playing, the women singing—peace, contentment. Then, all of a sudden—blood! A raid on the Crows, women wailing, gashing their arms for the dead." He stirred the fire. "Then blue days again, plenty of chokecherries and fat meat." He broke off, turned to her. "Do you know what I mean?"

Moved by his mood, she said, "I—I think so."

"They are rich," he said. "Rich in their ways, and customs. Do you know—when they shoot a deer, first they say a little prayer, because all animals are a part of *Wakan Tanka*, their Great Spirit. They say, 'I need you. Please come into my lodge. If you do I will give you red paint.' Then they shoot the animal. Afterwards, they put a daub of red paint on its head to carry out the agreement." He smiled, gazed into the fire. "Isn't that remarkable?"

She poured him more coffee. "It's beautiful."

"They have a lot of gods; Rock, the war god—Earth, Buffalo, Sun, many others. But there's always the one great god, like yours in Philadelphia, I suppose. *Wakan Tanka*, the head god. He's in their food, they think, in their clothing, their weapons—in the sunlight and the water and the air—in the faces of children, in the voices of old people, in charms, amulets, rituals, their dreams. They use *wakan*"—Rollins made the sign—"to describe anything mysterious, beyond their understanding. When the Spaniards came, a long time ago, the Sioux were frightened. They had never seen a horse. The closest they could come to a name was *shonka wakan*—God's dog, I guess you could call it."

She was moved by his eloquence. "You must love these people very much. When you speak of them you are almost a poet, Mr. Rollins."

His mood changed. "Who was speaking of love? Love is a lot of smoke!" He threw the dregs of his coffee into the fire. "Vapors, smoke!"

"But you said—"

"Listen," he said. "Listen to me! I don't make out a case for anyone! I was just telling you how the Sioux are to help you understand them, make a better painting, maybe. They're good people, all right—brave people, a spiritual people. That's fine. But there are a lot of good folks in the Territory. Poor people, people who left steaming tenements and ruined farms to come west, hoping for a chance to make a better world for their children. Deadwood is full of miners—Welshmen who came from the old country to get away from filth and poverty and rascally landlords. They, all those people, want the Sans Arc lands. They dream about gold, their heads are full of visions! And who am I—or you —or Walking Bull himself, for that matter, to say their cause isn't just? Who's to say they won't make a better use of the land than ignorant savages just hunting and fishing? No, I've been poor myself, and you haven't, so maybe you can't even understand what I mean!"

"I know what you mean," she said. "You've told me often enough. You don't believe in causes any more. You've seen too many men kill each other for causes."

"That's right!"

She clasped her hands before her. "Nevertheless, there is an answer."

"What's that?"

"Love! Love is the answer! It is the answer to all things. A man need not burden himself with perplexing decisions about causes. It is only necessary to—to love! There is no need for philosophy or ideology or rationales."

"Love?" The laugh was scornful.

"I know!" Abigail said defiantly. "You do not believe in love, Jack! Sometime, somewhere, you were terribly hurt—I can tell. You gave your love, and it was rejected. But perhaps you have asked too much of love."

"And what should I ask of love?" he jeered.

"Love," she said, "is simply—well, it is simply wanting to do things for others. As I teach Ugly Woman to knit, as a mother cares for a sick child, as our Lord Jesus died to save sinners!"

In the firelight his eyes were hard and challenging.

"How about love of a woman for a man?"

She flushed, lowered her eyes. One hand played nervously with a jeweled brooch at her neck.

"What does a woman want to do for a man?" he insisted.

Her voice was low, almost inaudible. "She wants to—to love him."

"Circular reasoning, Red Dress Lady! You'll have to do better than that!"

"She—she—if she loves him—"

"Then she wants to sleep with him, doesn't she? Isn't that what your prattling about love comes to?"

Embarrassed, she jumped up. "You are a very devil, Mr. Rollins, to twist my meaning so!"

As quickly as she, Rollins sprang to his feet. When she drew her arm back as if to strike him, he seized it and pulled her to him. He pressed his lips hard against hers; for a moment they stood motionless, locked together. She thought the wild beating of her heart would tear it from her bosom, but she could not move.

"No!" she tried to say. She drummed her fists against his naked chest. "Stop it, I tell you!"

When he had his fill, he let her go.

"Morals," he told her dryly, "are a matter of geography, Mrs. Brand! I guess you'd better learn that—you're a long way from Philadelphia now." His lip curled. "And speaking of religion, the way you were doing, I think your brand is just plain mental confusion!"

"You—you scoundrel!" She drew back, rubbing her cheek where his brushy mustache had pressed.

"All this talk about love—" He snorted. "Love is what animals do, too, isn't it? I mean—they enjoy it without a lot of hypocritical fine talk. They get right to the point, like I did just now. And you enjoyed it!" He pointed his finger at her. "Admit it, now —you're not so damned holy as you make out!"

Shaking with anger, she screamed at him. "Get out of here! Oh, get out of here at once! How can you talk so? Get out!"

For a long time she remained near the dying fire, arms held tightly about her as if to imprison some deadly impulse. Ugly Woman crept back into the tipi, looking curiously at her troubled face. Abigail felt lonely, humilated, discouraged. All were feelings new to her. When Ugly Woman made a sympathetic clucking sound, Abigail rushed into the old woman's arms and wept, great wrenching sobs that racked her body. It took a long time for Ugly Woman to comfort her.

CHAPTER SIX

Jack Rollins sat in a sun-warmed pool of the creek, soaping himself. Rufus lay beside him, eyes closed against the autumn sun. Though the pool was tepid and pleasant, there was fresh snow on the peaks above the camp. In the morning the meadow had been heavily frosted. At Honey Hill, now, in Berkeley County, the chinkapins would be falling. The baying of coonhounds would sound clear and bell-like in the night. Leaves would turn orange and red and brown, and fall—

"Eh?" Rollins asked. "What?"

He had not seen the approach of his old friend Bad Smell. Bad Smell grinned at him.

"Friend," he said, feigning surprise, "when you washed away that dirt, you were white! I did not know!"

Rollins looked at him sourly, working a piece of *champa* root between his palms to produce lather.

"Look at her!" he growled, pointing a soapy finger. "Just look at her, sashaying round the camp! You'd think she owned the place!"

Bad Smell's gaze followed the finger to where Abigail Brand played the hoop game with a band of shouting children.

"The children like Red Dress Lady," Bad Smell observed. "And Crow King says his toes are not cold any more, since his wife made him those funny-looking things for his feet. Ugly Woman is fond of her, too. Red Dress Lady taught Ugly Woman to sing a song. It is called 'Jesus Fills My Heart With Love.' What is a Jesus?"

Rollins glowered. Ugly Woman and he were old friends, but he did not care for the old woman's rendition of the hymn.

"When are you going to pay me back the money you borrowed?" Bad Smell demanded.

Rollins jerked his head toward the hoop game.

"I asked her to advance some of what she owes me for bringing her up here, but she wouldn't. Said I hadn't earned it yet." He spat, muttered an oath. "Lord deliver me from female women like that!"

Bad Smell grinned slyly. "We have a saying."

Rollins went on soaping himself, appearing not to have heard.

"We say, 'When a man is angry with a woman, it is to show his love.'"

Rollins picked up a rock and threw it, but Bad Smell was out of range.

"I go now," he called back, grinning. "Tonight there is a meeting of the Strong Hearts Society. I must practice beating my drum!"

Though neither had spoken of it, it was now common gossip that Walking Bull sent away his two wives, Yellow Bird and Twin Woman when the white woman was in his lodge, painting the picture. Tongues wagged, though all were careful to speak of the development in hushed tones. Walking Bull was rash, and had a bad temper. Rollins decided he would speak to Abigail Brand. As soon as he could get her alone, he would put a bug in her ear about her conduct. Did she not realize how it looked—a lone white woman in a Sioux lodge? Sluicing a leather bucket of water over his head, he stood up. A crowd of children peeked from behind a jumble of boulders, giggling at his long white nakedness.

"Get the hell away from here, you little heathen!" he shouted, waving his arms.

They only giggled the more. Despondently he wriggled his way into shirt and leggings, poked his toes into the new moccasins Ugly Woman had sewed for him, whistled to Rufus. "*Hopo!* Let's go!"

Shambling back to his own lodge, his thoughts were gloomy. Once life had seemed simple; food, drink, whores. He had been closely, intimately, connected with nothing; that had been good. But now, things had gotten immensely complicated. He felt an invisible skein of circumstance trapping him.

———————◆———————

Already it was October, the Deer-rutting Moon. The Sans Arc camp lay under a blanket of frost; aspen leaves quivered yellow.

The fresh mantle of snow crept farther and farther down the peaks of Rainy Butte. Women sat in the mellow sunlight of afternoon. Softly they sang as they pounded chokecherries fine to mix with tallow and fat for the winter pemmican. Jack Rollins, summoning his courage, went looking for Abigail Brand. He found her sitting on a blanket in a cove among the rocks. Crow King, splendid in checkered socks, was teaching her how to grind rocks to produce a red pigment.

Casually she spoke to Rollins, as if they had not last parted angrily, very angrily. She would give him no money, she had told him, until he completed the contract—at least, no money for gambling. Rollins had wanted to bet on a horse called Red Pet, belonging to Buffalo Talker, at the races in the meadow.

"I have quite run out of the bright color I need to do justice to the chief's ornaments," she remarked. Regarding him coolly, she pushed her dark hair up with both hands. "Did you want to speak to me?"

He indeed wanted to speak to her, and that firmly, but could hardly find his tongue. This afternoon she looked fresh and clean and pretty. A red ribbon bound her dark hair; her cheeks were pink in the wind, her eyes bright, and the uncorseted body slim and supple in her balmoral traveling costume.

"Where's the red dress?" he asked gruffly. "The one Walking Bull's so fond of?"

"Ugly Woman is washing it out for me. It had gotten quite soiled. But I think it will launder well. Surely you did not seek me out to ask about a red dress?"

The way she looked at him, he felt like a penniless immigrant applying for a job at the Brand Iron Works. Hesitating, he dug a moccasined toe into the dirt.

"Did you want to speak to me?" she asked again.

He gestured toward the snow. "It's getting late in the season. We should start for Deadwood before the passes are blocked."

"How many days would you say we have left?"

"We ought to leave no later than—well, the end of this week. And that's cutting it pretty fine."

Watching Crow King mill a rusty-looking rock between two larger ones, Abigail sifted the growing mound of red powder through her fingers.

"I have quite lost track of time in this wondrous experience! What day is this, pray?"

"Wednesday."

"Then you would say—three or four days?"

"No more."

"I will be ready by then. It will hurry me, especially since I have important discussions going on with Mr. Walking Bull, but—"

"Discussions?" He frowned. "I thought you were painting his picture!"

She dusted her hands. "I want some ethnological data to go along with the portrait. Material about the Sans Arcs, you see— their customs, their language, their religion." Suddenly she was preoccupied with the grinding process. "Now, sir," she said to Crow King, "you must let *me* try it!"

She did not pay him any more attention, and Rollins stalked away. But in a last effort to make amends, he called back.

"You know that money you wouldn't let me have?"

She turned, a smudge of red dust on her cheek.

"It's just as well," he said ruefully. "Red Pet lost." He shook his head. "Never bet with a medicine man!"

"So I predicted!" she said. "Gambling is an invention of the devil! Perhaps you have learned your lesson, Mr. Rollins."

At least he had established a deadline. If Mrs. Henry Brand did not meet it, she would have to find her own way back to Deadwood as best she could—first, of course, paying him the whole five hundred dollars. Certainly he would not hang around a godforsaken Sans Arc camp all winter just to please *her!*

He was crossing the meadow when Buffalo Talker emerged from the great lodge, called to him.

"Bone Man! Come and smoke a pipe with us!"

Rollins went into Walking Bull's lodge, careful not to step between the chief and the fire. It was part of the chief's medicine. If a person stepped between him and the fire, the hunting would be bad and his pony herd would die. Taking the proffered pipe, Rollins blew the prescribed ceremonial puffs to the four winds, a final one skyward for Wakan Tanka. The Great Spirit loved the smell of tobacco.

"I want to talk to you, Bone Man," Walking Bull said.

In the firelit gloom at the rear of the tipi Rollins noticed the easel with the portrait. Abigail Brand was a damned fine painter, whatever else she was—or was not.

"I am ready," Rollins said. He noticed that Yellow Bird and Twin Woman were indeed not in the lodge. At this time in the late afternoon they might be expected to be cooking a stew for the chief's meal.

"Buffalo Talker does not like Red Dress Woman," Walking Bull said. Cross-legged on a fine robe, he puffed reflectively at the beribboned pipe. In the gloom of the lodge his face was sober, concerned. "Buffalo Talker is my old friend. He was medicine man"—Walking Bull made the sign, holding first and second fingers outstretched from his fist, rotating the closed hand upward and outward—"for my father. He is very wise. I must always listen to what he says."

Buffalo Talker shifted his ancient bones. He spoke in his faltering husky voice, like dried seed pods in the wind.

"A woman like that is a danger, I say! Send her away, quick, before she can do us harm!"

Rollins spoke. "What has she done? What does my father see in her, that she means danger?"

Buffalo Talker waved his ceremonial rattle, a turtle shell filled with pebbles and ornamented with feathers.

"Can you not see her shadow? Have you not watched the shadow of her passing about the camp?"

Rollins was puzzled. "How should I notice her shadow, father?"

The old man leaned forward; his eyes glittered.

"The shadow takes on strange shapes as she walks about in the sun. Once I saw it look like a goat! Everyone knows *Iktomi*, the trickster god, takes on the shape of a goat at times! Another time, it was told to me that a woman—Kills Often's woman, who never has been known to lie—saw the white woman's shadow leave her, and go floating off"—he gestured with his rattle—"to the top of Rainy Butte, where a crow took it in his mouth and flew away!"

Walking Bull pointed the stem of his pipe at Jack Rollins. "You know I have told you I will not go back to Deadwood—not when bad men like Judge Yount and Major Toomey and the rest are there! I want honest men to talk to, honorable men, men who can be trusted to be fair and keep their word, once they have given it!" He touched the silver medallion. "This thing is heavy and pretty, but it did not mean anything when they gave it to me. Their word meant nothing." He got up to pace the confines of the lodge, the bells on his moccasins tinkling. "But I am worried about what is going to happen now. Snow is coming soon. The Winter God will freeze everything dead until the spring comes. Before winter the white men will want to act, to force me to do something. I know that." He nodded toward Buffalo Talker. "Last night my friend had a dream, a powerful dream. He saw the white men coming against us, coming up the mountain with a thunderbolt. The Thunder God, Buffalo Talker says, has turned against us. He has given the white men his thunderbolts because of something bad I have done."

Buffalo Talker waved his rattle. "Send her away! Send her away now! That is the reason the Thunder God has hidden his face from us! It is that Red Dress Lady!"

"Bone Man," Walking Bull said. He stopped his pacing, looking at Jack Rollins. "You are one of them. You lived with them, in Deadwood. You know the man Yount, the soldier Toomey, the miners who want our land. It is true that at times I do not trust you. You would do anything for money. But I think in your heart you are a friend of the Sans Arcs. In your heart you do not want us to become slaves, farmers, poor people with no home but a white man's jail on Whitewood Creek. What do you tell us, Bone Man?"

Rollins sucked a long draft from the pipe. He did not want to be drawn into anything. He had enough trouble already.

"Friend," he said, "my thoughts are all mixed up. I do not know what to say. It is true I am a friend of the Sans Arcs. They sheltered me when I was cold, fed me when I was hungry, took me in as a friend when I had none. When I saved the boy, Badger, from the waters of the Heart River it paid only a little part of what I owe the Sans Arcs. So I will speak the truth." He puffed smoke, watching it curl higher and higher into the smoky apex of the tipi. "Wakan Tanka! Hear me! Send down punishment if I do not speak the truth!" He made the sign for truth, holding index finger close to the lips, then moving closed fist forward; *straight tongue*. "This is Pa Sapa, the Sans Arc land. It has always been so. The Sans Arc dead are buried here. It is a sacred place."

Pa Sapa. The sacred land. Buffalo Talker began a small chant, eyes closed, swaying to and fro as he crooned. *Our people are buried here. From a long time ago our people are buried here.*

"In the old days," Rollins went on, "the Sans Arcs took this land, this Pa Sapa, from the Mandans. The Winter Calendar tells us that. It was a long time ago. There was a hard fight. Many of the People were killed before the Mandans were driven away. Now the white men are coming to try to take Pa Sapa away from the Sans Arcs. But they do not want to fight for the land. They want to buy it." He shrugged. "Who is to say? Is it better to sell the land, move to Whitewood Creek? They will give you beef every day to eat, a warm place to stay. Or is it better to stay here and fight? A lot of the People will be killed if you fight. The white men are strong over the Sans Arcs now, as the Sans Arcs in the old days were strong over the Mandans. Friends, I do not know." He blew a last puff high into the air from the expiring pipe, and made the sign for *finished, all done.*

Angry, frustrated, Walking Bull kicked at the fire. Burning embers scattered. A coal lit on Buffalo Talker's mountain-sheep shirt, and the shaman brushed hastily at it.

"I am tired of all these things I have to decide!" Walking Bull protested. "In the old days, the days of my father, it was not hard to be a chief! When a man went on the warpath, it was enough to look out for the enemy and do something brave. I studied everything and tried to understand it. I had good will to all people. I did not tell lies. Anyone who tells a lie is a weakling! I always kept an even temper, and never was stingy with food. That was all a man had to do for his name to become great. But now!" Walking Bull raised clenched fists above his head and howled like an animal. "Now that is not enough! A man must be magic to know what to do, what is the best course! The white man is coming all around us. Some of our own people want to take money for the land. Some have gone away already to that place the soldiers have made on Whitewood Creek. And the white men threaten me with guns if I do not give in to them!"

"Fight!" Buffalo Talker raised his cracked voice in a whoop.

"Let us fight the way we always did—the way we fought the Mandans!"

Jack Rollins shook his head. "I do not know. The white men have a lot of guns."

"But sell the land?" Walking Bull's voice choked with emotion. "Dollars—what are they? A man spends them for paint and bullets and corn and knives. What then? The paint is used up, the bullets shot, the corn eaten, the knives get rusty and break. But the land—the land is always here." He shook his head in perplexity, the long braids swung. "This land is my blood and heart and bone and flesh! If I sell these things—sell my body, the body of the People—then am I not a slave, like the black people were to the whites before the Big War?"

Buffalo Talker shook his rattle. "That is so! In my dreams the buffalo tell me, 'Do not sell the land; never sell the land!' That is what the buffalo say!"

Walking Bull sighed, squatted again on the robe. He stared at the smoking remnants of the fire. "I do not know what to do," he said, and put his face in his hands.

Someone scratched timidly at the doorflap. A moment later Abigail Brand entered, carrying her leather box of paints and brushes.

"Oh!" she said. She looked at the chief, at Jack Rollins. "Am I intruding?"

Rollins started to speak but Walking Bull held up his hand. He looked at Abigail Brand. She was pale, apparently embarrassed at her intrusion into a state council.

"Send her away!" Buffalo Talker signed, clawed fingers darting like a rattlesnake. He glowered at Abigail Brand, muttered a malediction.

Walking Bull continued to look at Abigail. A slanting shaft of late sunlight entered the lodge, lit the clouds of tobacco smoke. It beamed golden across the unfinished portrait, illuminated Abigail Brand's raven-black hair, the firm bosom, the slender, intense body, cast a pool of shadow at her feet.

"No," Walking Bull murmured. "No. I will not send her away. Not—now!"

Buffalo Talker scowled, got creakingly to his feet. "You are the one to decide," he said. "But your father would have sent her away quick!" He paused at the doorflap. "Your father did not want white people in his camp, even traders who came with beads and blankets and red paint! The People will suffer for your rashness. And you will suffer for it, son of the father!"

That night Rollins' lodge was the scene of a draw poker session. Bone Man had taught them the game. Fanatical gamblers, the Sans Arcs loved to sit on a blanket and wager knives, tobacco, sometimes a horse, even greenbacks and gold coins when they came into possession of any.

Rising winds whipped the skins of the tipi, but inside they were warm and comfortable. Walks On The Sky was there, and Bear Teeth, along with Running Man and Crow King and Badger. Walking Bull's son was young for such a stiff game, but he already had his own string of ponies, a store of colored blankets, and an English repeating shotgun. Since Jack Rollins had pulled him that day from the rain-swollen waters of the Heart, Badger had been fond of his savior.

"Three of these things," Walks On The Sky grinned, showing his hand. "Aces, they are called?"

With an oath Rollins tossed down his own greasy cards.

"Wins!"

The Sans Arcs were carrying him on jawbone—he had nothing any of them really wanted—and already he owed Walks On The Sky thirty-eight dollars. While Badger dealt the next hand Rollins listened morosely to the chatter of the players. Before females the Sioux were wooden-faced and uncommunicative, but in a male gathering they gossiped like old ladies at a quilting bee.

Running Man spoke of his wife's persistent illness and Buffalo Talker's attempts to cure her with airs made favorable by burning sweet grasses. So far, it had not worked. Walks On The Sky owned a fractious new pony; Crow King advised him to break it by tying a heavy rock to its neck with a rope, forcing the rebellious animal to drag it about until its spirit was broken. Bear Teeth complained about the poor hunting, Crow King told a scabrous joke which made even Jack Rollins blush. All in all, it was not much different from a poker game in the Paradise Card Room at Deadwood.

Badger was not to be outdone. In this circle of elders, he too had a juicy tidbit.

"My father is very worried."

Running Man agreed. "The white men are angry with the People because we will not sell our land."

Badger picked up his cards and fanned them out. "I do not think it is exactly that."

"Then—what?" someone asked.

Rollins glowered at his own hand—a jackrabbit straight; six, seven, ten, jack, queen, in as many different suits as possible.

"I do not know," Badger said, "but I think it has something to do with that Red Dress Lady. I think my father likes that woman."

"Give me three cards," Rollins grumbled, "and don't talk so much! Just deal the cards."

"I think," Badger said, proud to be the center of interest, "she wants my father to do something. I do not know exactly what. But I have seen him before, when a woman is trying to get him to do something and he is not sure if it is a good or a bad thing. Right now my father is thinking very hard about something. Maybe we will find out soon."

Badger, for all his youth and his dreaming ways, was a sharp observer. But it was really none of Jack Rollins' business. All he wanted from Abigail Brand was his money. The money, that was the main thing. Her intrigues no longer interested him.

After another busted straight he threw down his cards in disgust and left the game. Outside, there was a hint of snow in the air, an iron-hard quality to the rising wind. Low in the west, the moon scudded through a wrack of cloud. He shivered, pulled the blanket tighter about his shoulders. In the pole corral the Sans Arc ponies milled restlessly, turning their rumps to the wind. Rufus, following Rollins from the tipi, leaned against his legs and whined.

"Going home soon, old boy," Rollins muttered. "No matter what *she* does! Your own box, a piece of steak, maybe a saucer of whiskey once in a while. With that five hundred dollars you and me will live high off the hog!"

Arranging the folds of the blanket about his lean frame, he saw a glimmer of light at the doorflap of the lodge Abigail Brand shared with Ugly Woman and her husband Crow King. For a moment Abigail was silhouetted against the glow of the fire within. It was late, the camp quiet except for an occasional cry of triumph from his own lodge, where the Sioux still played poker. They would gamble until dawn, or until one of them had won everything.

The doorflap dropped. In the moonlight he watched Abigail Brand pass through the sleeping camp, his only gauge of her progress the momentary shadow when she passed the other lodges, shining pale in the moon. Rollins squinted. Goat? Deer? What did her shadow resemble? Buffalo Talker claimed Abigail was sent by Iktomi. But where was she going, this time of night?

He had not long to wait. Abigail went directly, shamelessly, to the great lodge in the meadow. For a moment she paused at Walking Bull's doorflap—in the shadows he could not see her well. Then, very certainly, she slipped within. He saw the firelit aura as the doorflap opened and closed.

He was shocked, knowing Walking Bull's wives had been banished from the lodge; there could be no one there but the two of them, in scandalous liaison. But had he truly seen her—seen Abigail Brand—go unescorted into a Sioux tipi in the night season? Mrs. Henry Brand, wife of the late industrialist Henry Brand, of the Brand Iron Works and the Brand Patent Plow? Mrs. Henry Brand, leader of Philadelphia society, pillar of the church, virginal in her Christian faith?

Suddenly he was angry. Tossing aside the blanket, he walked swiftly toward the big lodge, frozen grass crunching under the stride of his moccasins. Whatever could she be thinking of? He remembered the light in Walking Bull's eyes when he looked at Abigail Brand in her red dress.

Pausing near the tipi, he listened for a moment. Whatever was going on was being conducted in silence; he became more suspicious. Abigail could hardly be painting at this time of night. Listening, he closed his eyes for greater concentration. Nothing. Nothing but the faint keening of the wind, a faraway chorus of yips and yaps from prowling coyotes.

Eyes still closed in intense concentration, he tiptoed closer to the doorway, hoping to hear some incriminating sound, some scrap of conversation to confirm her brazen conduct. But one furtive toe caught a pole supporting the meat rack. Flinging out his hands for protection, he sprawled headlong through the doorflap.

A female cry pierced his ears. Scrambling to hands and knees,

Rollins saw Abigail Brand in the arms of Walking Bull, hereditary chief of the People, the Sans Arcs of Pa Sapa. Both stared in amazement. Walking Bull's brows drew together in a scowl.

"What are you doing here, Bone Man?" He snatched up an ax. "Why do you come into my lodge this way, in the night, without leave?"

Abigail Brand caught the chief's arm to stay the brandished ax. "Yes!" she cried. "Yes, indeed! Mr. Rollins, what right have you to —to burst in this way?"

Perhaps the breath had been driven from him by the fall. Perhaps he was only so astonished that emotion sucked the air from his lungs. He got to his feet, speechless, staring at the licentious pair.

"I am waiting!" Walking Bull shouted. "I am waiting for you to speak, Bone Man!"

Rollins made an agonized gasping sound. He pointed at Abigail Brand.

"*Me* speak, eh? Well, it seems to me, Mrs. Henry Brand, *you're* the one should speak, explain yourself, explain what you're doing in here all alone at night with—with a man!" Snatching at the easel, he turned the portrait to catch the light from the fire. "Painting, is it? A portrait, is it? Maybe you find the night light better for your daubing—is that it? Jesus Christ!"

Outside there were anxious voices, people awakened by the tumult. Someone called, "What is going on in there, friends? Is there trouble?" No one dared enter without an invitation.

"I will pick my own time for my daubing, as you call it!" Abigail cried. She stepped away from the chief, pushing her disheveled hair back into place. Around her neck was a quilled collar, bright with beads and bits of shell, that Rollins knew Walking Bull himself had commissioned for her.

"Vapors!" Rollins shouted. "Vapors and smoke—all to confuse me and make me forget my point! To think of such a thing! You —a lady of formerly good reputation, though I must admit too independent and freethinking for my tastes—"

"Blast your tastes!" Abigail seethed. "I care not one whit for your tastes! And tell me, pray—who are you to judge me anyway? A godless vagabond—a man who himself lives only for pleasures of the flesh—whores, booze, low dives, and a brutish existence!"

Rollins took a deep breath to steady himself. It had been a long time since he felt so deeply about anything—or anyone. God, how he needed a drink! If he only had a good stiff belt of whiskey! His head hurt, abominably.

"Speaking of pleasure of the flesh—" He leered at her.

Striding forward, she slapped him hard. "You are mouthing filth, pure filth! You do not even know the circumstance that brought me here tonight!"

He goggled at her. "What circumstance—what *possible* circumstance?"

"My errand tonight was innocent! I had merely—"

"You were in his arms!"

Her eyes flashed. Under the bodice her breast heaved. "That is so—I do not deny it! But you should also know that Mr. Walking Bull has made me an honorable proposal of marriage!"

Rollins' mouth fell open. "Marriage?"

She tossed her head. Walking Bull watched her with admiration.

"Perhaps you might as well hear the whole story, since you so rudely blundered into the middle of the matter!" She pointed to the almost-completed portrait. "I am, as you know, an accomplished painter. Modesty forbids me to dissemble about that. But I must admit that the portrait was only an excuse to visit this Indian camp of the Sioux peoples."

Rollins, dazed, was trying to follow her argument.

"I have been for a long time sympathetic to the Sioux cause. I saw our American Indians enslaved, oppressed, pushed from their rightful lands by an insensitive government and greedy speculators. For a long time, as a Christian lady, I sought to do something to better their condition. Finally, a thought came to me."

She turned to Walking Bull. Gently she touched the chief's arm. "As Secretary of the National Indian Defense Association, an organization dedicated to the relief of the exploited Sioux, I was voted their full approval to travel to the Dakota Territory, to persuade Mr. Walking Bull to accompany me back east on a lecture tour. We hoped thus to win support for the Sioux cause against the government and the miners."

Rollins blinked, wet his lips, spoke in a cracked voice. "You mean you—you—"

"And Mr. Walking Bull has at last accepted."

"You mean—"

"Yes, indeed—I deceived you all! Judge Yount, Major Toomey, even Julian Garner himself! Knowing I stood little chance to meet with the chief if my true purpose were known, I gave it out I only wanted to do his portrait. They humored me, thinking me a silly female. But now that the portrait is almost finished—I have caught his likeness rather well, don't you think?—we can now all return to Deadwood, where the chief and I will take cars for the East, and—"

"No!" Rollins felt suddenly released from his paralysis. "No! You tricked him!" He pointed to Walking Bull. "And me, too, I've got to admit! I thought all the time you were up to something, but I couldn't quite put my finger on it. Now it all comes out!" His brain churned with the remembrance of her embrace of the Sans Arc chief. "And now you propose to cap the climax by marrying him—hoodwinking him into coming east with you?"

Her voice was icy. "The proposal of marriage is a private matter, and does not concern you, Mr. Rollins! What disposition I make of it is only between the two of us, and is none of your damned business!"

"I didn't ever think," Rollins jeered, "that you were nearly as holy as you pretended! Using your favors to beguile an innocent savage! Abby Brand marrying an Indian—even *thinking* of marrying an Indian! Why, he's already got two wives!"

In her anger she was illogical. "In Salt Lake City," she flared, "I understand the men have five or six—perhaps more!"

He was beside himself at her effrontery. Besides, there were other things to consider.

"This will make me a lot of trouble in Deadwood! They'll think I had a hand in this from the beginning! But I was duped—hornswoggled, right along with Yount and Major Toomey and all the rest!"

She came to him, holding out her hand. "I will explain to them all, when we return. I take on my own shoulders whatever blame there is. But please do not judge me harshly, Mr. Rollins. There are great issues at stake here, larger than you or me, or indeed Mr. Walking Bull and the Sans Arcs. It is a matter of—"

Roughly he pushed away her hand.

"Then, if we cannot be friends, let me pay you the money I promised you, right now! I am sure the chief and his warriors can escort me safely back to Deadwood."

He was illogical also. "I don't want your damned money! Money isn't everything!"

She was exasperated. "Well, then," she said, putting her hands on her hips, "I must tell you that I think you are acting like a child! But you may as well understand, Mr. Rollins—and the people in Deadwood and the rest of the Territory—that I mean to help these unfortunate people! To do so, I will conduct myself as I think best, not in accordance with their thoughts—or yours! I am sorry you were disillusioned with me, but you have often disappointed me, also. A man of your gifts, squandering your life as a ne'er-do-well, a drifter, a—a common drunk!"

He almost beat his skull with rage and frustration.

"I haven't had a drink since you—since you—"

His voice failed him. With a howl of animal rage he rushed from the tipi, shouldering his way through the crowd that had gathered. In a few minutes he saddled his surprised paint pony and galloped down the mountain. Gradually the clatter of hoofs was lost in the large wet flakes of snow kiting down from the heights of Rainy Butte.

CHAPTER SEVEN

The Oswego Peach practiced quick draws from his new shoulder holster, banging away at rabbits as they emerged from dens to watch the column.

"Put that damned thing away!" Judge Yount growled. "You don't have to shoot every damned thing you see!"

Major Toomey tugged at the judge's bearskin sleeve. "Look!"

At first Yount thought the solitary descending figure was an Indian, perhaps one of Walking Bull's scouts, observing them march up the mountain toward Rainy Butte. But the horseman did not flee to give the alarm. Instead, he continued to pick his way down the slope through scattered boulders and wind-blown drifts. Peach whistled in surprise.

"That's Jack Rollins!"

Major Toomey stared through his field glasses, then handed them to the judge.

"Damn if it isn't!" Judge Yount said. "And decked out like a Sioux himself! Blanket, leggings, everything."

The major held up his hand, the crawling column halted. Glad for a respite, the infantrymen fell out. The miners opened lunchpails, the muleskinner whose charges pulled the twelve-pounder howitzer took out nosebags and grain. Dickybird Conway, incongruous on the mountain trail in bowler hat and checkered waistcoat under a linen duster, reined up beside the judge and Toomey.

"What are we stopping for, Judge? The men are anxious to get up there and settle this matter for once and for all!" His Welsh tenor was rich and resonant. Conway had a knack of making the most casual statement sound important.

John Toomey pointed. Conway's eyes narrowed against the snowblink.

"Who is it?"

"Jack Rollins," Judge Toomey said. "I wonder if he ever got my message to Walking Bull? And where is Mrs. Brand?"

Conway drew a pasty wrapped in grease-stained newspaper from his saddlebag. "Too late for messages to Walking Bull," he said. He winked at Toomey. "That cannon is going to do all the talking now—right, Major?"

Judge Yount shifted his weight uncomfortably in the saddle. "We'll see, Conway."

They waited while the horseman continued to approach. It was indeed Jack Rollins, wrapped in a blanket, face red and frostbitten. "Well, it's you, Judge!" Rollins grinned at Dickybird Conway. "And the Welsh flannelmouth, in all his finery!"

Conway said something obscene; Rollins did not appear to notice. His eyes swept the trail, took in the lounging soldiers, the miners with their collection of clubs and ancient firearms, focused on the mules and the brass howitzer.

"Got quite an army, it looks like! Where you all bound for?"

Major Toomey started to speak but the judge cleared his throat. "We were worried about Mrs. Brand. You should have brought her back to Deadwood by now. What's going on up there?" He nodded toward the great spire of Rainy Butte.

Rollins licked chapped lips, shifted the carbine across his thighs. "I tried to convince Walking Bull to come down from there, Judge—I really did. But he's a hothead, you know that. He said no."

"I thought as much," the judge sighed.

"But what about Mrs. Brand?" the major demanded. "She's an important person—we've had telegraph messages from the War Department, asking her whereabouts."

Rollins laughed, a mirthless rasp that seemed to hurt his cracked lips. "I wouldn't worry about *her!*"

Yount was puzzled. "What do you mean?"

"Mrs. Brand seems to have made her own private arrangements with the chief."

Dickybird Conway protested. "Rollins, you're talking nonsense!" He pointed with his shotgun at the snow-peaked bulk of the mountain. "It's late already, and we've got a far piece to go!"

"Shut up, Conway," Judge Yount said heavily. "Now, Rollins,

what do you mean—Mrs. Brand has made her own arrangements?"

"Just that! She's sweet on Walking Bull; he's proposed marriage to her."

The judge's face was incredulous. "You mean Mrs. Brand—Mrs. Henry Brand? She and—"

"Told me so herself! She'd just about finished her picture of the chief, and I said I'd bring her back to Deadwood. But she told me the chief was in love with her, wanted to marry her. She said Walking Bull and his people would take care of her, bring her back when she was ready." Rollins' eyes became shrewd, calculating. "Seems strange to me, though, you need an army and a twelve-pounder to inquire into Mrs. Brand's situation."

"Well," Judge Yount admitted, "there *is* more to it than that. Actually, we've been very patient with Walking Bull and his Sans Arcs. Now we find ourselves forced to take action. There is a federal warrant out for his arrest."

"Arrest? What for?"

"Offenses against the laws of the Territory."

"What offenses?"

The judge's voice was measured, heavy with the force of the law. "There are charges, filed in Deadwood. Last week a pack of Walking Bull's braves, drunk on whiskey, shot up a wagon train in the Short Pine Hills. Killed a teamster on contract to the Army, as well as most of the mules—they like mule meat, you know. They looted the wagon, and set fire to what was left."

"How do you know it was Walking Bull's people?"

Conway kneed his mount forward. "From the descriptions! It couldn't be anyone else! They identified Crow King and Walks On The Sky and Running Man. They're all known to be hell-raisers!"

"That's a damned lie!" Rollins' voice was cold. "Crow King and Walks On The Sky and Running Man have been in camp for the last three weeks. I ought to know, oughtn't I? I've been there all the time, trying to get Mrs. Brand to hurry with that damned picture and leave Rainy Butte before the snow comes!"

Judge Yount shrugged. "It's a matter to be decided by the courts."

"But it's a put-up job on the face of it!" Rollins protested.

"Listen," Yount said, looking at Jack Rollins with grave pouched eyes. "Listen to me! I just got my commission as U. S. Marshal for the Territory, Deadwood District. In the lawful discharge of my duties, I swore in a *posse comitatus* of the good men you see here, along with a detachment of Toomey's Ninth Infantry, to arrest Walking Bull and return him to Deadwood for trial. Now understand this, Rollins—I call on you as a citizen of the Territory to assist us. You can be of value in finding a good way to approach the Sans Arc camp. From a military point of view, I understand it's a hard nut to crack."

Major Toomey grunted assent.

Rollins scratched his chin, looked at Toomey, then back at the judge. "What about Mrs. Brand? She's still up there."

Judge Yount spread his hands in a deprecatory gesture. "I hope no harm comes to the lady, since she seems to be an important person. But I must say she is a meddler by nature, and meddlers must accept the consequences of their meddling. Naturally, we'll make every effort to rescue her, shield her from violence. But I am afraid this time Mrs. Henry Brand has put her dainty fingers into something more important than she knew."

Rollins looked again at the mountain gun. He seemed in a quandary. When he swallowed, the cords on his lean neck stood out like bowstrings.

"Well, sir?" Judge Yount demanded.

Rollins stared at the judge, almost unseeingly. Raising his quirt, he slashed the paint's rump. Squalling with surprise and indignation, the pony bounded away into the cover of the snow-capped boulders.

"He's going to warn the Sans Arcs!" Major Toomey yelled.

Deer-legged, the pony bounded among the drifts like a fantastic mechanical toy. Peach reached inside his coat and fired as the judge tried vainly to knock down his arm. Toomey signaled the infantrymen, but they had laid down their weapons and were enjoying hardtack and coffee.

"What in hell got into him, do you suppose?" Major Toomey blurted, watching the disappearing horse and rider. "I never saw Jack Rollins get excited about anything before—unless maybe it was a bottle of booze!"

Judge Yount pursed his lips between his fingers and stared up the forbidding path.

"I don't know," he murmured. "But where there's a pretty woman—"

"I think I hit him!" Peach grinned, ejecting the empty shell and reloading. "I know damned well I saw him twitch when I fired! The pony give an extra kick, too!"

"You hit him all right!" Dickybird Conway exulted. "Damned Indian lover! Did you see that medicine sack hanging around his neck?" He laughed. "Didn't do him no good, though! I *know* you hit him, Peach!"

Major Toomey nodded to his bugler, a brassy throat summoned the column forward again. Judge Yount settled his bulk deeper into the bearskin coat. He had hoped not to use the howitzer. Now, with the Sans Arcs alerted, there would be no alternative. Damn drunken Jack Rollins! Damn meddling females like Mrs. Henry Brand of Philadelphia! Damn intransigent savages like Walking Bull and his Sans Arcs! Damn *everyone* who stood in the way of progress!

———◆———

Walking Bull's proposal of marriage had been as startling to Abigail Brand as to Jack Rollins. Armed with a notebook and neatly sharpened pencils, she had gone to the big lodge that evening on the chief's promise to tell more about the history of the Sans Arc Sioux. They kept, Walking Bull told her, a historical record, written on thin-scraped deerhide—a thing they called the "Winter Calendar." Each year in Sioux history was identified by an important event. There was the Winter When Many People Died, a smallpox epidemic, apparently. There was the Winter When the War Bonnet Was Torn, commemorating a fight with their enemy, the Crows. There was the Winter When the White Woman Was Rescued; Abigail was not yet sure who the white woman had been, or who rescued her. But Walking Bull promised to have Buffalo Talker, custodian of the record, bring the Winter Calendar and explain it to her.

She was elated. It was all so colorful, such a dramatic backdrop to the nearly finished portrait. And it would make fine copy for the eastern newspapers; the *Press* in Philadelphia, the *Daily*

Chronicle and *National Intelligencer* in Washington, the Baltimore *Sun*. How could the Indian Defense Association lose this fight, with such publicity? And the chief himself—Mr. Walking Bull in his Sioux finery—would be on the lecture platform with her, as he had already agreed. Too, it would be a feather in her own cap. Other women could follow her shining example, enter into business, politics, perhaps even international relations, showing that the vanity of males had blinded them to the intelligence and capability of their women!

When she had scratched at the doorflap, as she had learned, and been bidden to enter, Walking Bull sat alone. Buffalo Talker and the promised Winter Calendar were not there. Abigail, at the chief's invitation, sat down cross-legged on a buffalo robe, modestly arranging the folds of her skirt.

Walking Bull lay at ease, hands clasped thoughtfully behind his head. This night he seemed to be dressed in ceremonial garments, and her curiosity was aroused. His body was covered with a long robelike shirt of whitest and finest deerskin, belted at the waist, and ornamented with shiny multicolored beads that glowed in the firelight. Instead of the usual buckskin leggings he wore a fine pair made from heavy blue woollen cloth, with coin-yellow piping down the side seams. His feet were in new moccasins, freshly sewn, and over his shoulders was thrown his best red blanket, the kind Jack Rollins told her was a four-point Northwest blanket, probably bartered from some French-Canadian fur trader. The silver medallion with President Grant's likeness winked in the firelight.

"I—I—" She stammered, one hand nervously touching the brooch at her throat. "I understood Mr. Buffalo Talker would be here, tonight." She cleared her throat. "To show me your Winter Calendar, I mean."

Without taking his dark eyes from her, he reached for the soapstone pipe and handed it to her.

"Fill pipe, you please."

Since his wives no longer inhabited the tipi, she usually filled his pipe for him as a gesture of goodwill for his kindnesses to her, his co-operation in the projected lecture tour. Pouring trade tobacco from the pouch into the bowl, she tamped it with her finger, handed it back. At first she had been queasy about the pouch, thinking to recognize it as a gruesome trophy of some raid against the Crows, but it was so blackened and leathery she had grown accustomed to it.

"Light! You light, please—Red Dress Lady," he demanded.

Using a split twig to draw a coal from the fire, she dropped it into the bowl. He was acting strangely, she thought, looking at her in an appraising way over the rim of the bowl. She fussed for a moment with her hair.

"Will he be here soon? Mr. Buffalo Talker, I mean?"

Walking Bull shook his head. "No."

"But why—" She broke off, confused. It was one thing to stand in a corner of the great lodge, busy with paints and brushes and canvas while messengers came and went, emissaries from other tribes argued and wrangled, endless decisions were made about gambling debts and affronts to honor and the fair rotation of guards at the approaches to the camp. It was still another thing when Walking Bull sent his two wives away, and she was sometimes alone with him, during the day, in the lodge. While she had been nervous about that, she bore it. Walking Bull was a noble savage. She could imagine nothing gross about him, nothing of the flesh. He was spirit incarnate. But this night—

"Well," she said briskly, "perhaps you can lie there, just so, while I put a few finishing touches on the portrait! The light is not very good, but I understand Mr. Rollins is in a hurry to reach Deadwood before bad weather." Professionally she stood back, eying the nearly completed canvas on its easel. "Now—a touch of vermilion here—perhaps a bit of yellow there—" Intent, she picked up her brush. "When do you think we will all be able to leave, so that we may take the cars and travel east?"

He did not answer. She worked swiftly and nervously.

"I am sure you will enjoy Philadelphia! They have a street railway there, with horses pulling iron cars. We will go to Washington, too! At the Observatory, near the foot of New York Avenue, they have a giant telescope. We will go out there—I know Professor Drumright, he is an old friend of my late husband. You will look through the telescope and see more stars than were ever imagined!"

At first, she hardly noticed the eerie sound. It was small, wavering, somehow sweet yet melancholy. Eyes still judging the portrait, she asked, "My goodness—what is that?"

He had cast aside the long-stemmed pipe, and now held between his lips a flute, fashioned from a willow shoot. She stared at the long tube, olive-green with splashes of white where the bark had been cut away to form finger holes. Slowly, playing the plaintive melody, he rose and drew near her.

"What—what is that you are playing?" she murmured.

He did not need to answer; it was a love song. Jack Rollins had explained that to her, grinning as he pointed out Running Man's stripling son playing just such a flute to Deer Girl, the shaman's niece. Abigail had smiled pleasurably, having a heart tender for young love. Boys and girls were no different in Philadelphia. But now— Her heart thudded in her bosom. Trying not to hear the plaintive melody, she closed her eyes. Five notes, rising and falling, played in endless permutations and combinations. She laid the brush down, fumbled at her bodice. He touched her arm; she trembled.

He spoke softly, insistently, into her ear.

"You be my wife?"

When she did not answer, he touched her arm with his brown fingers. "You be my wife, Red Dress Lady?"

She forced herself to look into his eyes. They were shy, with a moist luminosity.

"But—but you already have *two* wives!"

His cheek brushed lightly against hers, and she trembled as if experiencing an electric shock. His cheek was soft; the smell of him was sweet grass and smoke. One hand gently stroked her breast. He was indeed rash; Jack Rollins had so characterized him. She pushed the hand away, and felt faint. "Please—"

"No wives," he said. "Nothing. They nothing. Cook, sew. You see—" His hand swept around the lodge. "I send them away. But you—me"—he touched her breast again—"we be together, all the time."

Her body was rigid, fists clenched at her sides. Feeling giddy, she swayed a little. The cheek pressed once more against hers, the lean body molded itself powerfully to the contours of her own. It had been a long time since Mr. Henry Brand, the Brand of the

Iron Works, her husband—her late husband. And Henry Brand had not been a passionate man, either.

"Please—" she faltered. "Please—I—"

His grip on her tightened. With a start she saw that he was looking beyond her, into the darkened perimeter of the lodge.

"Someone—" he muttered.

Dazed, she followed his eyes. Her own hand was unaccountably against the smoothness of his cheek, and she saw her fingers as if they belonged to someone else, engaged in a business she did not recognize.

"What?" she whispered. "What do you hear?"

It was at that moment that Jack Rollins chose to fall full-length through the doorflap to confront them.

After the *contretemps*, after Rollins flung himself from the lodge and rode pellmell away on the spotted pony, Abigail felt almost ill. People peered curiously through the doorflap, Crow King and Running Man came in, and everybody talked at once. Walking Bull must have seen her deathly pallor. He spoke to Ugly Woman, who was hovering outside in the falling snow. The old woman hurried away. In a few moments she returned with a handful of pungent herbs. Grinding them quickly between her palms, she held them under Abigail Brand's nose.

Gasping, she turned her head away from the acrid fumes. Smelling salts—Sioux smelling salts! But she felt better, the giddiness left her. Slowly she got to her feet, leaning on Ugly Woman's arm. At the doorway she paused, looking back at him.

"I don't know," she murmured to Walking Bull. "I just don't know! I don't know what to tell you."

Shaken, she spent the next day in Crow King's lodge, reading her Bible. No verse seemed to comfort her. Again and again she went over in her mind the strange circumstance that had happened. Certainly, when she came out to the Territory, she had expected no such development as this! She had been confident in her knowledge of business, of men, of her abilities in any and all circumstance. Now—

She went to the doorway to look out at the snow. Perhaps, from his manner, she should have expected Walking Bull's fondness for her, perhaps even the proposal of marriage itself. The flakes spiraled down gracefully, silently. Already the meadow was covered, the ponies in the corral wore mantles of white on backs and manes. Children played in the stuff, molding snowballs and flinging them with shouts of glee just as they did in Fairmount Park at home. Was Walking Bull bargaining with her? Did he mean to barter his offer of visiting the East against her favors? No, she decided; it was more than that. With a twinge in her breast she remembered the shy gentle look in his eyes. He truly loved her!

But what did she feel for him? Her thoughts were confused. Men were such a puzzle. She remembered the enigma of Jack Rollins—his unbelieving stare when he had come upon them, his anger, the cruel words he had hurled. Did he, perhaps, love *her*? Oh, it was all too perplexing! Why were men such a problem? Mr. Brand had been such a simple and uncomplicated man, whatever his other shortcomings. Bewildered, she sat across the fire from Ugly Woman and put her head in her hands. For a moment the old woman watched. Then she picked up Abigail's horn comb and knelt beside her, combing out the tangled hair.

"I thank you," Abigail murmured. Oh, Lord; what was she to do?

Late in the afternoon, a red disk of sun setting in a saffron-streaked sky, she heard a commotion. Both she and Ugly Woman hurried to the doorway. People were running this way and that, calling out, "*Hopo!* Let's go!" The men were armed, heavily armed. Some made for the corral, calling out to favorite war ponies.

"What is it?" Abigail asked.

Ugly Woman shook her head. Signing to Abigail to wait, she hurried away, lifting her gingham skirt as she waddled through the already knee-deep snow.

Darkness deepened. Men and horses plunged about. Women called out in alarm, children hung at the edges of activity with wide-eyed faces. Someone touched a sulphur match to a pile of twigs and boughs; the fire caught and roared. Orange rays painted great shadows across the snowy meadow. It was like a Breughel picture, she thought; some atavistic winter carnival. Crow King rushed into the tipi, almost knocking her down, to seize his rifle and hatchet and war rattle.

"What is it?" Abigail cried. "What is happening?"

Intent on shoving cartridges into a belt, he did not answer.

Wearing the checkered socks Abigail had taught his wife how to knit, he ran away in the snow, moccasins leaving deep inky prints.

Pulling the doorflap closed, she knelt over the small fire, rubbing nerveless hands together. She had not realized she was so cold. Drawing a blanket over head and shoulders, she tried to contain the meager heat from the fire. But she was still cold. It was not from the snow, she knew; she was afraid. What was going on?

Bible clutched in one hand, she finally heard Ugly Woman return.

"Thank God!" she cried. "You're back! What has happened?" Throwing aside the blanket, she turned.

Jack Rollins stared down at her. The deerhide vest hung torn and awry, his long leggings had a great rip down the thigh, the blue eyes stared with mad intensity.

"Get ready to leave!" he ordered.

"But—"

He caught her wrist, pulled her erect. "There's no time to explain!"

"But what—you—I mean, what is happening out there?"

He snatched a handful of her clothes, drying on a rawhide thong near the fire, stuffed them quickly into a bag. "We've got to get out of here! Judge Yount and Major Toomey and a whole damned army are on their way here!"

"But why?" She took the bag away from him. "Will you please tell me what this is all about?"

In the firelight he was very pale. Beads of perspiration shone on his forehead, wetly, greasily. The red headband was askew, and he pulled it off and flung it down.

"Listen! Listen to me! They've trumped up some ridiculous charges against Walking Bull and the Sans Arcs—a wild story about how they attacked and ransacked a wagon train in the Short Pine Hills! It's a put-up job from the word go, but that doesn't count! What counts is they've got a federal warrant—a cannon, too—and they mean to arrest Walking Bull and take him back in chains to stand trial in Deadwood!"

"But—he won't go, surely?"

"Of course not!" Rollins shouted. He clung to a lodgepole as if for support. "He'll fight, that's what he'll do! This place will look like the Bloody Angle at Spotsylvania! We've got to get out of here right now, before all hell breaks loose!"

"I won't go!" Abigail protested.

"What do you mean, you won't go?"

"I am not a coward! The least I can do is to stay here and try to persuade the judge and Major Toomey they are mistaken!"

He groaned; there was real pain in the sound.

"Did you hear me? I said they had a *cannon!* A twelve-pounder mountain howitzer!"

"I know nothing of cannons, but—"

He grabbed the sack again. "I *do!* The Yanks had that same gun at Petersburg! We were on the Old White Oak Road, thought we were safe under a ledge. But they set up that cursed thing and the sky rained shells for days! We lost half the regiment!"

"I intend to stay!" she insisted. "As a woman, I can surely not fight. But you—" Her voice was accusing. "You told me once there were no real virtues except physical courage! Can you not show me that you possess at least one virtue? Will you let a woman shame you into bravery, Jack Rollins?"

"Then you won't come?"

"I will not. The Sans Arcs are my friends!"

She was unprepared for the sudden onslaught. Seizing her, he threw her over his shoulder like a sack of meal fresh from the miller. In a free hand he caught up the sack with her clothing, tossed the Bible into it.

"Put me down!" she screamed, drumming his back with her fists.

"Stop it!" He grunted in pain, and she was glad she had hurt him.

"Put me down!" she cried again, and kicked wildly at his thigh. He winced, cursed under his breath, but bore her relentlessly from the tipi.

Outside, behind the lodge, were Rollins' own paint, her bay— the one he had rented for her in Deadwood and she had not ridden since—and some of the pack mules. He flung her upside down over the saddle of the bay and flicked a loop of rawhide string around her wrists. "Couldn't find your damned sidesaddle, but maybe you can ride this way!"

"What are you doing?" she wailed. "Let me go!"

He passed the thong under the bay's belly and tied it to her ankles, pulling it so taut she cried out in pain.

"You *will* go!" he muttered. "For once in your life, you spoiled female, you're going to do what I say!"

She tried to scream, to call for help, to summon Ugly Woman or Crow King or whoever would answer. But the commotion in the meadow was still moiling and boiling; no one heard her. She screamed again, a piercing shriek that startled even the placid mules, nuzzling the snow for shreds of winterkilled grass.

Rollins stuffed a rag into her mouth, bound it in place with another rawhide string. "Yell your head off, Abby Brand! A hell of a lot of good it will do you!" Clambering stiffly on to the paint, he took the bridle of the bay in his hand.

"Get on with you!" he called to the mules.

Upside down, giddy, frustrated, humiliated, she lurched to and fro as the bay ambled down the trail. Once more she tried to scream, but nothing came out but a strangled sob. When they were some distance from the camp Rollins finally stopped and untied her. There was a scallop of moon; in the distance a pack of coyotes caterwauled. An owl flitted on hushed wings through the falling snow.

"You can scream all you've a mind to!" he growled. "We're far enough away so no one can hear you anyway." He took off the gag and peered at her. "You all right?"

Quickly and expertly she scratched his face.

"I'll tie you up again!" he warned, holding a hand against his lacerated cheek.

Speechless with fury, she at last contained herself. He helped her back on the bay, and she rode silently behind him, uncomfortably astride, her limbs indecently showing. But she no longer cared.

CHAPTER EIGHT

All night long they rode through falling snow, lit to a ghostly luminance by the moon. She did not understand how Rollins ever found his way. For a while they were in the forest; she could hardly make out his form on the paint pony ahead of her. Several times she rode the bay into a cul-de-sac and called out frantically, afraid she had lost him. When they emerged onto the rubble-littered slope, where the moon might have been expected to aid her vision, the snow fell even thicker and wetter. Now she was sure he was gone.

"Jack!" she called. "Mr. Rollins! Where are you?"

Snow fell on her cheeks and eyelids so she had constantly to brush it off.

"Are you there? Oh, where are you?"

Startling her, he loomed out of the white nothingness. He wore the shapeless felt hat he wore when they had left Deadwood; it was covered to the brim with snow, and resembled a giant mushroom. "What's the matter now?"

"I—I thought I had lost you."

"No such luck!"

"I'm cold!" she protested.

"Better cold than dead." He pulled a blanket from a pack and tossed it around her shoulders. From the smell she decided it was a horse blanket, stiff with dirt and smelling of sweat. But it was thick and warm. Gratefully she drew it around her. He turned away, but urged the pony back again.

"What about your head?"

"My head?"

"Something to cover it."

She was unwilling to accept more favors. "No. My hair is so thick, you see—"

He was gone again, into the whiteness. Anxiously she clucked to the bay, afraid she would fall behind.

The night was still, the mantle of snow muffling all sound. A ghostly caravan, the pack train bore southward, down the slope toward a far-distant Deadwood. The only signs of their going were the hoofprints that seemed to fill with snow and disappear as soon as they passed.

Abigail dozed in the saddle, dreamed of Mr. Brand. Her late husband had been a kind man, a Baptist who did good works and never raised his voice or his hand to her. Henry Brand had been much older than Abigail Massie, but both families thought it a good match. The widower had always been kind to the girl, bringing Abigail presents even when she was small, and was a long-time friend of the Massies. Abigail was not sure she loved him as he loved her, but her mother had been explicit about that. *Love, Abigail, is not a thing that is turned on immediately like a gas light. It will come, dearest; it will come. Mr. Brand is a fine man.*

Love had not come. She respected Henry Brand very much, of course. It was impossible to do less. But he was not a passionate man. Her schoolgirl dreams at Miss Fitts', and later at the Female Academy, were of a romantic prince, carrying her away to a perfumed bower strewn with roses. On the few occasions when her new husband visited her bedroom—from the beginning they slept in separate chambers—he had been very nervous, and unavailing. The visits became less frequent, ceasing when he became so busy with the management of the Iron Works during the war.

She did not blame Henry for his shortcomings as a lover, but with characteristic good sense and hard work threw herself into various activities. When he died suddenly, she took over the management of the Iron Works herself. The same hard work and good sense continued to make a handsome profit for the shareholders. She worked hard also at her painting, for which she had always shown a talent. When she joined the National Indian Defense Association, more hard work and common sense brought her quickly to the post of secretary, and the opportunity to go out to the Territory on the mission to Mr. Walking Bull, chief of the Sans Arcs. If she succeeded, it was likely Mrs. Henry Brand would be elected president at the next national meeting.

Henry would probably have been proud of her record of accomplishment. In fantasy she saw him clearly—the high brow, the noble face, the sweeping dundrearies that made him impressive. But in her dream, Henry was not in the usual long sateen coat and sleeve protectors he habitually wore. Instead, he was dressed in nightgown and cap and looked severely at her, as if something were her fault. His arms were folded, his feet were bare. Unaccountably, she was on her knees on the polished floor of her bedroom, pleading with him. But for what? She did not know. He had given her everything, had he not? Henry Brand had been a faithful and generous husband, a friend, a rock of strength and solicitude.

Henry! she called. *Please! Help me!*

He turned his face away. For some reason he was angry and upset. But how could that be? They had never had a disagreeable word.

Henry! She began to weep. Holding out her arms, she moved entreatingly toward him on her knees. *Help me!*

Henry regarded her with fear and loathing. What was it? What could the matter be? She felt crushed. When she tried to reach him, touch his hand, he moved away. The manner of his moving was odd, unreal. He did not change his pose. Instead, hostile and distant in his snowy nightshirt, he dwindled into the distance like a child's toy pulled by a hidden string.

Henry, wait! Bare feet slipping on the mirror-polished hardwood floor, she ran after him as the pull-toy faded and glimmered out in the darkness.

"Henry!"

"What the hell's the matter with you?" Jack Rollins growled.

Dazed, she opened her eyes. It had been a dream, the same awful dream that pursued her since Henry died. She was sitting cold and cramped on the bay. The crust of moon was far away now, low on the western horizon. The snowfall had stopped.

"I—I guess I was dreaming."

"Well," he said, "it must have been a bad dream! You were yelling something fierce. I thought—" He broke off, screwing his eyes shut in what seemed to be pain.

"Is something the matter?" she asked.

He took a deep breath, wincing. "Nothing." Taking off the battered hat, he shook snow from the crown. "Ought to be there in about an hour."

Deadwood—a warm room in the Grand Central, a hot bath, something to eat. But Deadwood was a long way off. Had they already come so far?

"Deadwood?"

"The mine," he said.

"The—mine?"

"The New Ophir. We'll hole up there till the excitement simmers down. Then I'll see that you get back to Deadwood."

She remembered the bleak granite ledge, the scattering of rusty buckets and shovels, a cabin of unpeeled logs.

"Can you make it?" he asked. "You all right?"

Numbly she nodded.

"I'll make hot tea soon as we get there."

Even that prospect did not lift her spirits. She did not think she could ride another foot. But again, common sense and a willingness to undertake hard tasks spoke for her.

"Go ahead. I—I'll follow."

Guiltily, she recalled that not once, since leaving the Sans Arc camp and its beleaguered people, had she thought of Walking Bull and Badger and Crow King and Ugly Woman and the rest. Had Judge Yount and the soldiers yet come upon the camp in the meadow? Was there fighting? She hoped not. In Deadwood, Judge Yount had seemed such a kind and wise man, and she knew that Julian Garner had great respect for the judge.

Firmly she made up her mind. Good thoughts would always dispel bad ones. There would certainly be a palaver of some kind—that was what Jack Rollins called it—and then reasonableness would prevail. Onerous as the accusations were, the chief would allow himself to be escorted back to Deadwood, where a proper court would establish the falsity of the charges against him. Abigail felt better.

Eyes smarting from lack of sleep and fatigue, she imagined the gradual lightening an aberration due to her physical condition. But dawn had finally come, almost without her noticing. The cold luminance in the east was streaked with rose. As she watched, a thin ruching of gold bordered the serrated edge of the mountains. The revealed landscape was harsh and bare, only the mantle of snow softening the rugged mountains. Rollins pointed. "Down there."

For a moment she could not make out the New Ophir. Then, under a blanket of white, she saw the bleak cabin, the rusty tools, the ledge with its scattered mounds of ore-bearing rock. She saw something else, too; a furry animal that stood on its legs like a man and peered at them. Rollins swore, drew the carbine from its boot. But as he lifted the weapon the animal dropped from the roof of the cabin and waddled away in the snow.

"Damned grizzly!" Rollins swore. "I think I left a can of sugar in the cabin. They love sweets."

He slid off the paint and helped her down, hobbling because of stiffness. Opening the door of the cabin, he lit a fire in the rusty stove. He put a teapot on. Wrapped still in his Indian blanket, he shuffled about the cabin, finding flour and tea and a chunk of stale bread frozen hard and nibbled by rodents. In mid-activity he stopped, put a hand to his head, swayed on moccasined feet.

"After while—" he murmured.

"Yes?"

He shook his head as if to clear it. "After a while, when I feel a little better, I'll shoot some birds. We can make stew, with a little flour to thicken the gravy, and dip the bread in it."

He was acting queerly, she thought. His eye was bright and sparkling, his face flushed. From the cold?

"Are you ill?"

He looked at her, a long grave look.

"What is the matter? There *is* something wrong! You have never acted like this before!"

Rollins' knees trembled. Long and thin, his blanket-wrapped body collapsed—slowly at first, then gathering speed so that he lay finally on the dirty blanket.

"Jack!" She knelt beside him. "What's wrong?"

For the first time she saw the ghastly wound along his thigh, and felt a wrench of agony and compassion. Through the rent in his Sioux leggings showed a jagged tear, plowing its way into the buttocks. The wound was crusted and foul, with an edging of pus. Seeing her stare, he tried feebly to rise.

"That damned Peach!" he murmured.

She lifted his head in her arms. Already the wound smelled horrible.

"Who is Peach?"

He grimaced. "Man I had a little dustup with in Deadwood. Judge Yount's man—the Oswego Peach."

Frantically she looked around. Bandages? Ointments, disinfectants? The teakettle began to steam, the lid clattered as vapor lifted it. "Why did he shoot you?"

"They figured I was coming back to warn the camp. And they were right. So that damned Peach let off a wild shot and hit me as I rode away—right in the butt!"

She was a strong woman; getting him under his arms, she half-lifted, half-dragged him to the bed, a crude affair of peeled saplings in a heavy log frame.

"Here!" he said in alarm, trying to keep her from spreading the ragged coverlet over him. "What's going on?"

"Just you lie there!" She pushed him down. "You're in no shape to be on your feet!" Anxiously she rummaged through the cabin—a rude cabinet, a few rough shelves festooned with spiderwebs. Nothing that would help; a sack of flour torn open and spilling grayly on the dirt, a box of cartridges for the carbine, a butcher knife stuck into a post, some dirty rags.

"And you rode all night without telling me! You were hurt when you came to the camp to kidnap me!"

This time Rollins did not speak. He lay silent under the torn coverlet. His forehead beaded with perspiration, in spite of the chill of the cabin. She had no watch, but lifted his wrist. His pulse was fast, very fast. Queasy, she forced herself to lift the coverlet and examine the wound again. Ugly, so ugly! It was a good eight or ten inches long.

He must have felt her hand, sensed her fascinated gaze.

"Ball went right between me and the saddle," he whispered. "Plowed right along, cut hell out of my saddle. Guess it ended up somewhere in my ass!"

She disliked uncouth language—surely there was a better word for that part of the body—but dropped the coverlet and went to the teakettle. Hot water, wasn't that what they needed to treat injured people? But what did they *do* with it, the hot water? *Jesus,*

she prayed silently, *tell me what to do! This man is sore afflicted,
and I, Thy servant, must help him.*

At the Sans Arc camp she had berated him for his lack of courage. Now she hated herself for the angry words. Gravely wounded,
with that frightful lead ball in him, Jack Rollins had ridden all
the way back to the camp to warn Walking Bull and the People—
and to save her from what he regarded, rightly or wrongly, as imminent peril. She loathed herself. But there was no time for loathing now, nor anything but action. She was the one in control. She
would have to be the mover and shaker, she would have to help
him. She felt a dimension of fear she had never known.

Gratefully, she came to the conclusion that he was now sleeping. Sleep itself was a great healer. His breathing was stertorous—
deep and slow. Abigail felt a surge of hope. The Massie family
doctor once explained to her, when her pet kitten was mauled by
a dog, that the body of a living thing was a marvelous mechanism,
often healing itself when physicians failed. The kitten died, but
she prayed that Jack Rollins' lean body, so like a weathered rawhide thong, would find within itself the defenses Dr. Merridew
had spoken of.

Leaving him, she went outside after tucking the blanket and a
furry robe around his still form. The sun was already high, the sky
a bowl of breathtaking blue without a single cloud. The storm
had passed. She did not know what to do about the animals, but
they seemed to be making out well enough, drinking from melted
pools of snow water and wrenching patches of dry grass with their
big stained teeth. The mules, free to roam, grazed on the rubbled
slope below the cabin, eating small branches of stunted trees.
Rufus came to her and whined.

"It's all right," she comforted. "He's going to be all right,
Rufus." But she did not believe it.

Searching the saddlebags on Jack Rollins' paint pony, which
ambled up when she called, she found meat—Indian pemmican,
mixed with fat and berries, and a sack filled with withered-looking
vegetables. Going back into the cabin, she put wood on the fire,
dumping the meat and a handful of the desiccated vegetables into
a smoke-blackened pot. Adding a little flour from the torn bag,
she soon had a creditable ragout.

"Jack!" she called.

Her heart began to pound. Was he dead?

"Jack! Wake up!"

He opened an eye to stare at her. She bent over him, spooning the stew into a cracked bowl.

"Here's something hot and nourishing."

Weakly, his head rolled on the pillow. "Sleep. I want to sleep."

"But you must eat!"

He tried to avoid the spoon but she held him tight. "Now, another swallow!" she cajoled. But the blond head rolled obstinately away. "No more! I—I'm sick."

Afraid he would vomit what she had already fed him, Abigail ate the rest of the stew herself, wolfing it down but remembering to save a little, mixed with pieces of the dry bread, for Rufus.

Scouring out the pot with sand and snow water, she caught a glimpse of herself in a cracked mirror tacked to the log wall. Dark-rimmed eyes stared at her, the hair fell in snarls and tangles, her face was haggard and grimy. The collar of the balmoral traveling dress was stained, the lace torn half away. But with food in her stomach, Abigail felt better. There was a rudely fashioned chair of rough boards in a corner of the hovel. Sinking back in it, she pulled a robe of some sort over her, and slept.

———————◆————————

Jack Rollins did not improve. His fever burgeoned, so that his forehead seemed to burn her fingers. She fed him from the small store of food remaining, tended to his needs, helped him stagger occasionally from the bed to the tin bucket. But his condition steadily worsened. He became delirious, singing bawdy songs that made her blush, talking aloud to old friends in the Army, telling jokes and laughing loudly. At times he pleaded with Mary. *Where are you? Mary? I had to do it, Mary! But why did you—you—* Then he would fall into a feverish sleep, lying silent and unmoving for hours.

His face became waxen and pale, with a yellowish cast in the small light from the stub of candle she found on the shelves. It was very cold in the cabin. It had not snowed again, but the temperature dropped so that pools of water around the cabin were icy mirrors. The animals stood close to the cabin, rumps turned against the wind, silently asking her to do something to improve their condition. But she did not know what to do. He was going to die, Jack Rollins was going to die.

One morning she heard the distant booming of a cannon. She started, clutching at her throat. The mountain gun! Judge Yount and the soldiers had at last reached the Sans Arc camp. Perhaps they had—what was the word—palavered. Perhaps they had palavered, but the talks had failed. The sound of the cannon was faint but perfectly clear on the still cold air. Involuntarily she began to count. Three. Four. A long pause. Five, six. Distraught, she paced the floor of the cabin, wringing her hands. If she had stayed, perhaps she would have been able to step between the soldiers and the Indians, bring about a workable compromise the way she had always done with unhappy workmen at the Iron Works. To shut out the distant booming she pressed her hands against her ears, but the sound filtered maddeningly through.

"Lord Jesus," she prayed, "make them stop! Protect the Sioux, because they were made by Your hand also, though they are heathen and worship a strange god! Save and defend them from harm, from that awful cannon!"

The cannonade went on and on, pausing for a few minutes, then resuming with purposeful intensity. Distracted, she had to do something.

"Jack!" she called. She shook him. He opened his eyes, then closed them.

In her panic she was not gentle. She shook him. "They are shelling the Sans Arc village! They—they—the People are being killed! Do you understand me?"

The poison was seeping into his vital organs, he was surely near his Maker. She wrung her hands, desperate. Her gaze fell on the butcher knife stuck into a post that supported the sod roof. Unspoken, kept from her mind by her own resolve, the thought finally demanded consideration. But—could she do it? Oh, how horrible!

She drew back the sweat-stained blanket, staring at the wound, one long jagged fissure of evil yellow-green pus under a transparent scab. The smell sickened her. Dropping the coverlet, she rushed to the door to breathe the cold air. Rufus whined, pressed close to her legs.

"Do you know how to pray, dog?" she murmured. It was a silly thought, yet it gave her comfort. "Then pray, in whatever dog fashion you think proper. Because"—she looked again at the knife, gleaming dully in the candle glow—"because we are going to cut out from your master this deadly thing that—" Her voice caught in her breast; it was almost a sob. "We are going to cut it out, do you hear me?"

It was dusk, but the cannon kept up the deadly drumbeat. Now that she had made the resolution, she felt better. Quickly she rushed about the cabin. Finding the stub of another candle, she lit it for better light and placed it on a wooden box near the bed. She piled wet branches into the stove, hearing it creak and hiss steamily as the wood caught. Filling the teapot with snow, she put it on to boil. She tore her own petticoat into long strips, and wished it were cleaner. Wrenching the knife from the post, she went outside and stabbed it repeatedly into the earth to clean the rust from the blade. Then, kneeling beside Jack Rollins, she wiped it clean with the hem of her skirt and took a deep breath.

Lord, guide my hand aright! Don't let me hurt him, but—

Carefully she pulled aside the Sioux leggings, ripping them down to give a better field of view, so that at last he lay naked in the candlelight, blond beard poking stiffly upright, resembling a picture she remembered from her art studies at the Female Academy; "The Anatomy Lesson," or something like that. A cadaver was stretched on a table. The naked body was stark and marblelike in appearance; a bewhiskered medieval surgeon, scalpel in hand, lectured to a group of fledgling physicians. Rollins' body, too, was long and white, like marble, except where sun and wind had weathered and roughened it on his forearms and in a deep V at the neck. The small feathered bag—the "medicine" his friend Walking Bull had given him—still hung around his neck. She touched it with an inquiring finger. Then, yielding to impulse, she placed her hand gently on the rise and fall of the chest, covered with a golden fleece. She had wondered how it would feel, that golden hair. It was not dry and springy as she imagined, but soft and silky. Mr. Brand had almost no hair on his body.

Slowly her hand tightened on the cord-wrapped haft of the knife. Biting her tongue in concentration, she looked down at the wound. It was cold in the cabin, very cold. Even the fire could not combat the metal-hard chill leaking through the chinks, around the sagging leather-hinged door, through the translucent deerhides covering the window holes.

"I will do it," she murmured. "Lord, I *will* do it! Keep Thou steady my hand!"

With one long sweeping movement she slid the knife in, gutted the wound from knee to hip. Jack Rollins screamed in agony, tried to rise from the bed. She threw her body over him, forcing him flat again. In the guttering light a gout of pus flowed from the wound. The stench of putrefaction filled the cabin, and she became nauseated. Clamping her lips hard together, she forced back the gall rising in her throat.

"It's all right!" she cried. "Jack, it's all right! It's done! You'll feel better now."

He struggled feebly. Exhausted more by emotion than by any effort, she continued to lie across him, feeling the emaciated body quiver and tremble. It was a very awkward position for her to be in, but she felt strangely comforted. Gradually his body relaxed, his struggles ceased. "Mary," he murmured. "Oh, I am so tired! I want—I want—"

Feeling him sag, she got cautiously up. He lay motionless. She had a feeling a climax had been reached, a corner turned. Perhaps he would live. Of course, perhaps he would not, also. But she refused to think on that. He was still murmuring, more and more faintly; she pressed close to his breast to listen.

"I—I want you to put your head—on my shoulder—Mary. The way you used—used—" His voice trailed into silence.

With hot water and the scraps of rag she bathed him, washing away the yellow pus, elated to find the deadly leaden ball in the sticky stuff. With the last rags she bound the wound, first pressing a pad of cloth over it to protect it. Afterward, exhausted, she slumped in the chair, staring at the stove, hearing it creak and crackle as it settled into cast-iron silence. Rufus came to climb into her lap.

Once, during the night, Rollins stirred in his sleep. "Vapors!" he cried. "All vapors—and smoke! Illusion! Not a damned bit of substance to it, at all!" Then he was silent.

Wearily she went to the bed and drew back the blanket. The wound was still suppurating, but the fluid was now clear and bloodless, without odor. Perhaps that was a good omen. Holding the candle high, she stared at his naked body. Bone Man, the Sans Arcs called him, and with reason. Rollins was very thin, now, with his illness; she had the sudden feeling for him she might have for an unloved child. She felt a rush of compassion; she wanted to help him, to do things for him, to cherish him with kisses and embraces. Almost immediately she was repelled by her thoughts. This was a man; even sorely wounded, and in her care, Jack Rollins was a naked man. Here she was standing shamelessly over him, staring with licentious interest at his unclothed body! Quickly she dropped the blanket, paced to and fro with her arms wrapped about her.

It grew colder. She went to the door and looked out. The night was cold and bright, stars hung like jewels in a sable sky, a dark form foraged around the rusting machinery. The bear! Quickly she closed the door and barred it. Rufus growled; the hair on his neck rose in a spiky ruff.

Already the floor showed a new dusting of frost. She found a few scattered twigs, but they were damp and refused to burn. Wrapping the fur robe around her, she huddled in the chair and tried to sleep. It was no good. The interior of the shack was like an icebox. Shivering, she blew on her hands, holding the dying candle—the last one—near her bosom for its feeble warmth.

Something snuffled near the door. Frightened, she got to her feet, holding the robe about her.

"Jack!" she cried. "There's—there's an animal moving about out there! Wake up!"

He slept, or perhaps he was unconscious—she did not know. Taking the carbine, she pulled back the massive hammer and drew a bead on the door. If the bear broke in—

For a long time she held the gun in quaking hands. Finally it dropped to the dirt floor, and fortunately did not go off. Her fingers had simply been too cold to hold it any longer. She looked again toward the bed. It was unthinkable, of course; why did she let such a sinful thought enter her mind? Still, she was completely clothed. And no one would ever suspect Jack Rollins to molest her, weak and ill as he was. In New England, Abigail had heard, men and women often lay together, fully clothed, in the same bed, as a social habit that conserved fuel in the cruel winters, with the coverlet between them as a safeguard. Bundling, it was called. She thought it a curious aberration, but now she saw its utility.

Teeth chattering, she lay gingerly down, drawing the robe between them. Rufus jumped on the bed, burrowing beside her. They lay thus, the three of them, throughout the night. Abigail drew closer and closer to Rollins, feeling her small warmth begin to reinforce his. After a while, she was fairly comfortable. Rufus, too, seemed satisfied, and went into a deep canine sleep.

During the night she woke. Unaccountably, Jack Rollins had one thin arm around her shoulder. Her head lay comfortably on his upper arm. She started to draw away, feeling embarrassed. But he muttered again in his sleep, calling for Mary, and she was afraid she would wake him.

"I'm here," she whispered. "Jack, I'm here."

That seemed to comfort him; his troubled breathing grew deep and regular. Abigail lay drowsily in the crook of his arm, feeling a contentment she had never known. Slowly she slipped into a deep and dreamless sleep. The distant booming of the cannon had stopped.

CHAPTER NINE

On a cold sunlit morning Jack Rollins woke and stared about. Having strength only to roll his head from side to side, his vision was constricted. There was the familiar log ceiling of the cabin, roots of the grasses on the sod roof reaching brownly down into thin air. Light, a muted sunlight, filtered through the window. From a corner of his eye he could see Rufus lying on the floor, head between his paws. On the other side were the stove, cold and black, his carbine leaning against the wall, a—a— He blinked. A woman's dress, hanging on a nail; in the middle of the rough-sawed table a small Bible lettered in gold.

Rufus saw him stir and lifted his head, whining.

"Come here, boy," Rollins whispered.

His voice surprised him, so reedlike and husky, barely audible. But Rufus rushed to spring atop him, barking and licking his face.

"Stop it!" Rollins protested, trying to turn away from the wet pink tongue. "God damn it, Rufus—stop it!"

The doorway darkened. It was Abigail Brand, out of breath, his old ax in her hands.

"Jack!" Kneeling beside the bed, she put a hand on his brow. "The fever's gone! You're better!"

He had a headache; there was a lancing pain in his thigh when he moved.

"I don't know what better is," he muttered. "What the hell has gone wrong with my leg?" He tried to rise but she pushed him back. Then recollection flooded in. The mounted column, Judge Yount and Major Toomey and Peach, the ball plowing its way through his thigh. "How did we get here? I mean—" The Sans Arc camp, Walking Bull's proud refusal to capitulate; he meant to stand and fight. And his own flight to the New Ophir with Abigail Brand!

"You've been unconscious, off and on, for several days," she said. Her dress was torn and stained; the beautiful hair, lush and thick as a beaver pelt, lay in dank strings around a weary face. But the eyes sparkled. "You're going to be all right now. The Lord has answered our prayers!" She smiled at Rufus, lolling contentedly against his master. "Rufus spoke to the Lord in his own way."

Rollins lay back, scratching Rufus' lop ear. "What happened, really? I remember coming into the cabin, seems to me, and trying to start a fire. After that—" The Adam's apple bobbed in his lean neck. "I don't remember anything."

She told him.

"You—you did all that?"

"With God's help. Anyway, there was nothing else to do. You were—dying."

His eye caught the bucket in the corner. He flushed; the quick tide spread over the wasted countenance.

"That is nothing," Abigail comforted. "In Philadelphia, I volunteered for service at the Lying-In Hospital. I used to spend two days a week there. I am accustomed to sick people." She looked at the butcher knife, stuck in its accustomed place in the post. "The hardest thing"—her voice broke in remembrance—"the hardest thing was to—to cut you, with the knife. But it was necessary. There was this great gout of putrefaction that came out of the wound."

She turned her head away. Awkwardly he reached for her hand, patted it in an unaccustomed gesture.

"I thank you."

For a long time they remained thus, hand in hand, with Rufus dozing between them. After a while Rollins said, "I wonder what has happened at the Sans Arc camp. They had the cannon, and—" He broke off; a muscle flickered in his cheek.

"They fired a long time," Abigail told him. "I sat here, in the cold, and listened. The sounds were faint, but clear. All day the guns went off. Finally, during the night, it stopped."

"We are not too far from the Sioux camp, as the crow flies," Rollins said. "Perhaps ten or twelve miles. We came the long way round to bypass what is called the Slot. That pass was certainly choked by snow."

"When you are well," she said, "perhaps we can go back there, see what has happened. Maybe some of the People are still there. Maybe we can help."

He shook his head. "I have seen enough killing in my time. I can imagine what is there, in that camp, after the shelling." He lifted her hand and looked at it. "Blisters," he remarked.

"The ax was heavy, and I am not used to it. But when it got so cold, we had to have wood to survive. I was afraid, at first, to go outside, because the bear was prowling about."

She rose to put tea on. Rollins watched her move about the cabin. Morning sun streamed through the open door and painted her shadow long and black on the dirt.

"There is practically nothing to eat!" she lamented. "Once I shot a rabbit with your rifle and made some stew." She shook her head. "Poor animal—there was very little meat left when that huge ball struck him! But I made do with it, along with some parched corn and beans I found in the packs. Today, however, there is nothing but flour and a little grease. I shall mix them together with water and make flapjacks, for lack of a better word."

Abigail Brand had saved his life. The thought made him uncomfortable. Yet it was pleasant to lie at ease, watching a woman bustle about the task of preparing his food—their food. He thought of the big kitchen shack at Honey Hill; old Rebecca, black hands pale with flour, making biscuits. Lucas, her boy, stuffed billets of oak into the big stove in preparation for the baking. Biscuits, hot and flaky, nut brown outside, virginal white within. And honey, honey from his father's hives, tended by woolly-headed Julius, whom bees would not sting because he spoke bee-language!

"You don't look like any devil," he said at last. "Anyway, your shadow doesn't!"

She turned, pushing a vagrant strand of hair back from her brow. Her cheeks were flushed from the heat of the stove.

"Whatever do you mean by that?"

He managed a grin, although his thigh seemed filled with a red-hot wire.

"Buffalo Talker never trusted you! He said your shadow did tricks. Sometimes, he said, it would look like a proper woman. Then, other times, the devil would possess you. The shadow would take on the shape of a goat or a bear, or some other animal.

Everyone knows Iktomi, their trickster god, puts on the shape of animals to deceive people, play tricks on them. Buffalo Talker was sure you were Iktomi, sent to plague them, to bring big trouble to the People."

It was the most Rollins had talked for a long time. Exhausted by the effort, he lay quietly while she brought him a cup of tea and a flour cake, tasteless except for the grease she had put into it.

"Perhaps I *have* brought them trouble," she said quietly. "I do not know. Perhaps I *was* sent by some evil influence—my own pride, perhaps, and arrogance. The feeling I could play God, do anything I once set my mind to."

He protested that. "No, you are hardly Iktomi! You are just a woman!" Then, not liking the sound of what he had said, he added gruffly, "A—a—well, a pretty damned fine woman, a woman who saved my life, if that is any consideration." Uneasy, he changed the subject. "Do you know—during the time I was so sick, I remember little snatches of things. Not much; they come and go in my head. The stove was hot, the wind howled outside, an animal prowled around the door."

"The bear," she said. "And he has been back. I saw tracks this morning, in the snow not yet melted." She poured him the last of the tea and sat on the bed beside him. Rufus, satisfied his master was well, was outside chasing rabbits. "You talked a lot about Mary." Her finger traced a complex pattern on the coverlet. "I think she must be very important to you. Who *is* Mary Armistead?"

He lay still, holding the tin cup on his chest with both hands, not tasting it. Finally he asked, "Did I? Did I speak of her?"

"You have done it before, when you were drunk. She seems always in your thoughts, Jack. Do—do you want to talk about her? Perhaps it will relieve your mind."

He shifted uncomfortably, stared at the cup.

"I saw her. When I was in a delirium, I guess—but I saw her, clear as I see you. She was real. In my pain I called out to her. I couldn't sleep, and I wanted Mary. I wanted her to lie beside me, the way she used to do, and put her cheek against mine. I wanted to feel her beside me, warm and—" He broke off.

"There!" Abigail said. She took the cup. "You have talked

quite enough, for now." Gently she drew the coverlet up, but he pushed her hand away.

"No! I want to talk about it. I *need* to!"

"Well, then."

"She came," he went on. "She actually came! It was so real—I don't know how to describe it! I felt her lie down beside me, her weight on the bed, her—her body against mine. I felt it—do you understand?"

"I understand." She fingered the ragged lace at her throat. "It was a dream. When the brain is fevered—"

"It was more than a dream," he insisted. Exhausted again, he sank back. "I have had dreams before. But this—"

"I think you had better sleep now," she said, and covered him. "I will go out and throw pine cones to Rufus. He thinks he is a retriever!"

———◆———

The recovery seemed rapid. There was a life force in the spare body, a vitality she did not suspect in the derelict that had been Jack Rollins—John Fitzhugh Rollins, she remembered from that first day in Wah Chee's laundry in Deadwood. The wound was healing, and was now healthfully closed with a great firm scab. New flesh along its perimeter was wrinkled and gathered like scalloped needlework. But when he tried to stand the injured leg buckled beneath him, causing him to curse, although mildly now. He retreated to the bed, beads of sweat standing on his brow.

"It don't work!" he gasped. "Somehow or other, it just feels dead under me!"

She feared a vital tendon, some sheath of nerves, had been damaged, perhaps severed. But she did not speak of her doubts. Instead, having found her knitting in one of the packs, she sat near the bed and worked at a corner of a projected afghan.

"You always talked about 'causes,' of how you would not under any circumstances commit yourself to a cause. Yet you came back with that dreadful wound to warn the Sans Arcs."

He spoke with some of his old cantankerousness. The limb pained him, she knew.

"I didn't come back to warn *them!*"

"Oh?" The clacking of her needles ceased. "Why did you come back, then?"

He glowered at her, rubbing his leg. "To get *you*, of course."

"To get me?" She decided to poke a little fun at him. "I thought you found me insufferable!"

Rollins rolled carefully across the bed to let a shaft of sunlight bathe his thigh. After the early snow, the weather had perversely turned warm and balmy—what was called in the Carolinas "Injun summer." "I wonder what's going on in Deadwood," he muttered. Propping himself on his elbows, he stared out the door, where Rufus was stalking a jay. "Do you know—the day we left Deadwood I was talking to Lew Searles. He said something that interested me."

"What?"

"Well, Lew never did have any money! He started the *Argus* on a little cash borrowed from his brother-in-law in Omaha. After they burned him out, Wah Chee loaned him that old tent. But when I asked Lew how he intended to eat, buy paper and ink and stuff for the paper, he just grinned; said there was money in Deadwood." Rollins pursed his lips, stared at her. "There's money in Deadwood, of course—lots of it. But Yount and his cronies have got most of it. And they aren't about to give Searles money for a newspaper to attack the powers-that-be in the Territory."

She knitted industriously, frowning at the afghan. Freshly bathed, her hair combed, she had found a ribbon for it, and had sewed back the errant lace at the collar of her dress.

"You know what I think?" he asked.

"What?"

"I think you grubstaked Searles and his paper!"

She knitted again. After a while she said, "Suppose I did?"

He nodded, satisfied. "It fits you, all right. Coming into the Territory like the Society for the Suppression of Vice, all set to shake up things!"

She bit off a strand of yarn. "I will not deny I helped Mr. Searles. Whenever I find injustice or oppression, as are being inflicted on the Sans Arc Sioux, I give my support quickly and wholeheartedly to the foes of injustice and oppression. Mr. Searles and his little *Argus* represented the only obstacle, however insignificant, to the interests represented by Judge Yount and Major Toomey and the Indian Commission in Washington."

"Julian Garner, too?" he demanded.

"And Julian Garner, too, I suppose—though Julian is only a lawyer, doing his job. I do not altogether blame him. I suspect he has a great deal of secret sympathy for Walking Bull and his people."

"Julian Garner is an ass!"

She became nettled at this. "Mr. Garner is a fine man!"

"He is a fop—a dancing master in fine clothes! A tailor's dummy!"

"You are unfair to him!"

"He is too pretty!" Rollins sneered.

"How dare you talk so against him!" She dropped her knitting. "Whatever can you have against him? One would think you—think you—jealous!"

He hooted. "Jealous of that popinjay?" Their brief spell of amity had ended. "Why, I'd—I'd take care of Julian Garner faster 'n an alligator could chew a puppy! Julian Garner is all wind, like a bullfrog!"

"He's a gentleman, something you could never understand!"

He snorted. "I bet you're in love with him!"

"In love with Julian Garner?" She laughed. "Whatever could you know of such delicate matters, Mr. Jack Rollins?"

"I know this," he insisted. "Whenever the talk turns to love you get excited and uncomfortable." He pointed. "Your hand always fidgets up there—"

"Where?"

"To your—your bosom. Look at it!"

She looked. The hand was certainly there, fumbling with the lace.

"It's a kind of—well, a kind of a *protecting* gesture," he said smugly. "Defending yourself against a man that might want to fondle that virginal breast! It's an old habit among females, probably one that Eve used when Adam got too close. Cave women probably did it, too. You're scared of love, Abby Brand! You're scared to death a real man might come along and breach your little fortress! So you prattle about the Bible and Kingdom Come, sashay round more like a man than a genuine woman. But whenever the talk turns to love—real love, not biblical love—that poor little hand flies to your bosom! Ain't I—haven't I seen it enough? Don't I know?"

Crimson flooded her cheeks. Undone, she rushed from the cabin to the sound of mocking laughter. The fool! What business was it of his what she did with her hands? Why had she ever bothered to save his miserable life? Better she had left him to die in that filthy cabin, so full of male trappings, filthy and squalid!

"Here, Rufus!" she called, picking up a pine cone. Her heart pounded; her cheeks were hot. She was still annoyed to find one telltale hand still playing with the ruching at her collar. Resolutely she withdrew it, tossed the pine cone. "Here—catch!"

He bounded away into the rusty machinery, the piles of ore. A moment later she heard him yelp in pained surprise.

"Rufus!" she called. "Where are you? What is the matter?"

It was then she saw the grizzly. Huge, furry, it stood on hind legs and looked at her with piggish eyes. Rufus hobbled on three legs, making small whimpering noises.

The bear continued to watch her. The snout wrinkled as the beast turned this way and that, trying to catch her scent. Bears had poor eyesight, she recalled. Rooted to the spot with terror, she watched the animal drop to huge padded feet and lope toward her, silver-gray pelt rippling loosely over massive shoulders. She wanted to scream but her voice would not come; mouth open, she only gaped soundlessly, veins chilled to ice water. A dreadful lassitude enveloped her. Rufus, valiant in spite of a bloody shoulder, turned and bared his teeth at the behemoth.

"Abby!"

It was Jack Rollins' voice from the doorway of the cabin.

"Stand aside!" he called. "Get out of the way!"

Paralyzed, she was rooted to the spot as certainly as if she had grown there. The grizzly was near, now. It stopped before her, rearing again to its great height, mouth open and slavering, strings of foam dripping from the ivory teeth.

"Abby!"

She flung herself aside just as the shot sounded. Prostrate, fallen almost beneath the rearing bulk, she covered her eyes and screamed.

For a moment there was no sound but the animal's breathing. The foul breath blew in her face. At any moment she expected the grinding impact of teeth in her neck, her breast, her side.

"Abby!" Jack Rollins shouted.

She opened her eyes. The grizzly was lying quite close to her. As she stared, fascinated, the beast gave a shuddering grunt and rolled over, half-smothering her beneath its bulk.

"Are you all right?" He threw down the carbine to pull her from under the furry mountain. "Abby, speak to me—say something!" He held her in his arms, pushed hair away from her face. "Are you all right?"

Dazed, she struggled to sit erect.

"God!" he muttered. "My God!" He looked down at the dead animal, shook his head. "A lucky shot. A damned lucky shot! I—I think it went right between your arm and your body. But it was all I could do. I had to do it that way."

He held out a hand to help her. She was pale and faint; her limbs felt icy cold and drained of strength. A clinging blackness sought to envelop her. With a great effort she finally managed to stand.

"Your leg!" she gasped.

He looked down at the bandaged thigh showing through the cutaway Indian leggings.

"Your leg! Jack, you're walking on it!"

He looked dazed, too, and startled. "By God, that's right!" Earnestly he hobbled about in the snow, the scattered rubble, managing to half-hop, half-stumble, over a timber baulk and a snarl of rusty cable. "Look, Abby, look! The damned thing's well! I can walk!"

Eyes misting with joy and relief, she watched him cavort. Even Rufus, lately mauled by the bear, capered about, barking, until Abigail snatched him up to examine his wound.

"It's not so bad," she told Jack Rollins. "Only a few deep scratches where the claws raked him." She took Rufus into the cabin, and in a few minutes had more water boiling. "For," she said to Rollins, "I am by now quite accustomed to treating male animals!"

Rollins butchered the bear, taking out the steaks and chops and flaying the hide, scraping vestiges of meat from it and rubbing salt well in. Afterward, he hung the hide to dry in the thin sunlight. "Bear meat is right tasty," he said. "Lots of folks don't favor it. But in the autumn like this, when they've had their fill of berries and fish and are ready to go to sleep, grizzly is choice."

They dined on bear filet, along with stewed chokecherries Abby picked from the bushes the bear had not already cleaned. Frying the dark-red steaks, she rummaged on the shelves for a suitable fork, finding a stone bottle she had not noticed before. Dusty, covered with cobwebs, it lay far back in the clutter.

"What is this?" she called, holding it to the light.

Rollins, the action of the carbine on the table before him, put down the bear grease he had been using to lubricate the parts. Limping quickly toward her, he seized the bottle and wrenched out the moldering cork. "Brandy!" he chortled. "I forgot all about that little old bottle!"

She frowned, but he did not appear to notice. Snatching up a tin cup, he tilted the bottle and poured out a measure. The liquid glowed richly in the candlelight.

"We'll have this with our steaks!" he exulted. "Why, we could be dining at Delmonico's in New York, or Willard's Hotel in Washington! All we need is seegars for the gentlemen, and a little Madeira and posies for the ladies!"

She only looked at him.

"What's the matter?" he demanded. "You're awful glum!"

Abigail shrugged, turned the steaks. "I said nothing."

"Is there anything wrong with a little drink to go with the meat? It's been a long time. I deserve a little snort, seems to me!"

She did not speak, only put another stick of wood into the fire. The steaks were almost done.

"Mmmmm!" Rollins said. He sniffed at the cup. "Mighty prime! Well aged."

Still she did not speak. Annoyed, he poured the liquid back into the flask and corked it. For a while he stared at the bottle, cradled it lovingly. Then, with a quick movement that startled her, he flung it at the wall. It shattered into stony fragments; a dark stain ran down the logs.

"You're always spoiling everything!" he declared.

"I did not do anything." Her voice was even. "Whatever happened, it was of your own choice." She bent to give Rufus a choice portion of the bear. "When I say my prayers tonight, I will thank the Lord for His loving guidance of you, Jack."

Glaring at her, he did not speak. His mouth was too full of long-denied meat—rich meat, bear meat, a lot of meat.

One day, the leg hardly bothering him at all, he said, "We'll pack up tomorrow and ride to the Sans Arc camp. Guess I owe them that much." Neither of them had yet spoken of returning to Deadwood. "After that—" he said, and paused.

They were sitting on a long bench in the morning sun. The weather continued unseasonably warm. It was, Rollins told her, the Moon When the Wolves Run Together, according to the Sioux. By rights, there should by now have been heavy snow in the mountains. But only scattered patches remained from the heavy fall the night they came to the New Ophir from the Sioux village.

"After that," he went on, whittling at a pine billet, "I guess we better head for Deadwood."

"But won't they put you in jail? I mean—you rode back to warn the Indians. They—the soldiers—shot at you!"

He stared into the blue haze surrounding the peaks. "Guess they will! If I ride right into town, anyway. But maybe I can just show you the road from the Whitewood Creek bridge. You can find your own way from there. It's not far—maybe a couple of miles."

"What will *you* do then?"

He shrugged. "I'm unpopular around Deadwood, that's for sure! I'll probably head for Cheyenne City or some such place. A man can always find work in a saloon; swamping or room clerk or helping out in the kitchen—pots and pans and stuff. I reckon I've washed a million dishes in my time."

"You'll not take me back to Deadwood!" she insisted. "Not that far anyway, Jack! It's dangerous for you! I don't—I don't want them to get you, after what you did for the Sans Arcs." She put a friendly hand on his knee. "I can give you money, buy you a ticket on the cars from Omaha to the East! At the Iron Works there are a lot of things you could do. Why, you could—"

"I'll not go back east either." He shook his head.

"But why?"

"Too many things back there. Things—to remind me." He stood up, brushing shavings from his lap. "I'll go round up the mules. You get together everything in the cabin you want to take. We won't be coming back here again."

Riding astride, and rather liking it, she urged the bay up the steep back trail after Jack Rollins and the mules, now only lightly burdened. Most of her things had been left in the Sioux camp— the bulk of her dresses, hats, books, paints, brushes. It was unlikely she would find much there after the battle that must have taken place, but she hoped. Warmed by the sun, she began to sing a hymn. Rollins looked quizzically back, but said nothing.

In the afternoon they came to an impasse. Wet snow had softened the ground; a rockslide obliterated the trail. They were forced to ride several miles out of the way, through dense brush and scrub pine. After rolling themselves in blankets under the trees that night, it was again midmorning when they reached the great meadow below Rainy Butte where the Sioux camp had lately stood.

"Look!" she said in a hushed voice.

Most of the lodges had been burned, and were only blackened circles in the scorched grass. Some few still stood, at least the conical structures of lodgepoles, but the skins had been destroyed by fire. Now only mute charred poles pointed skyward. The horse corral was empty, the animals fled or driven away; the meadow was pockmarked with craters where the mountain gun had struck. A smell of rotting flesh tainted the air. A few bodies, some of them women and children, lay about like discarded toys. The trees surrounding the meadow had been splintered, showing stubs of raw new wood. Limbs, sheared by shrapnel, littered the grass. Somewhere, back among the remaining trees, an ax was at work, the sound dull, insistent.

Beside the brook Rollins dismounted. A body lay half in and half out of the water. He got the man under the arms and pulled him onto the bank. Turning him over, he knelt beside the crumpled form, looking into the bloated face. "Walks On The Sky," he murmured.

The eyes had been eaten out by birds, or insects. She shuddered, averting her face.

"I owed him thirty-eight dollars," Rollins mused. He jerked up a clump of frost-browned grass and rose, staring down at the body, letting the wisps of grass sift from his fingers. "Ashes to ashes, dust to dust! Walks On The Sky was a good man. He was good to me, anyway."

Other forms lay about. "There were over a hundred people here," Rollins said. "Where are they all?"

They heard the chopping again.

"Here's where the chief's lodge sat," Rollins said.

He and Abigail Brand stood together in the circle marking the site of the big tipi. It was now only a clutter of burned poles, ashes, a litter of junk. Rollins nudged with his toe at a burned boxlike thing.

"The harmonium," he said. "It was one of his favorite toys. Couldn't play the damned thing—just pumped it and made noise. But it pleased him."

Her portrait of the chief had been destroyed, too; canvas, easel, and all. Walking through the debris, she hoped against hope to find some remnant of it. She had worked so hard, and it had been one of her best, she thought.

"What is that chopping?" she asked Rollins.

A file of figures emerged from the woods. Rollins squinted. "There's old Crow King! And Running Man!" He pointed. "Ugly Woman is still alive! There—do you see her?" He broke off, moved. "They've been cutting poles, for scaffolds."

"Scaffolds?"

"That's the way the Sioux bury their dead." He pointed to a group of spidery structures at the edge of the meadow. "They wrap their dead in their best blankets, and put them up high that way, facing the sun. If the man was a warrior, they drive his lance into the ground, tie his shield and war rattle to it."

"And if it is a child?"

"Playthings." He watched the approaching survivors. "That way, they figure they give the body back to the elements—the four winds, the rain, the birds."

Someone in the band noticed them. Ugly Woman dropped her load of cut poles and lumbered toward them, holding out her hands and weeping. Rollins took the old woman in his arms, speaking softly in the Sioux tongue. Running Man, Crow King, Yellow Bird, the rest—mostly women and children—crowded around them. Running Man's leggings were torn and bloody, a great scabbed gash ran down the side of his face. Crow King hobbled on a stick, a bullet hole in the calf of his leg. Yellow Bird, the younger of Walking Bull's two wives, had a broken arm, splinted with willow twigs and bound with a rag. Abigail gazed with horror at Ugly Woman's maimed hand.

"It's a custom of theirs," Rollins said in a tight voice. "When a loved one dies—her nephew was killed in the fight, she says—the women sometimes cut off a finger in mourning."

They all talked at once, trying to tell Bone Man how it was.

"They had never seen a cannon before," he translated, watching the flying fingers, listening to the shocked voices. "They thought at first that they had done something bad; Rock, the war god, was sending thunderbolts to punish them. Then they saw the white men coming. The Sans Arcs fought, but the lodges were all on fire and the ponies got scared and ran away. The white men took Walking Bull and Badger and—" Briefly he queried Running Man. "Chains, I guess—put them in chains and dragged them away."

"Where are the rest?" she asked.

Rollins spoke to Crow King. The old man still wore the checkered socks his wife had knitted for him according to Abigail Brand's instructions. One was half torn away. It rested on his skinny ankle like a cuff.

"He says they all fought for a long time, fought hard, but finally the white men won. So the younger men left. They went north, to join Crazy Horse and Sitting Bull and the rest of the firebrands." Rollins shook his head. "There's going to be a big gravy-stirring soon, they say. That's what the Sioux call a fight—a gravy-stirring. They say they're not going to put up with the white men any more."

Abigail looked at the weary band.

"They were always singing," she said. "The women were always singing. I went to sleep at nights hearing them sing."

"They're not singing now," Rollins said. "No Sioux is singing, unless it's a war chant!"

There was little they could do for the beaten People. Only one gun had been spared to the Sans Arcs, an ancient muzzle-loading musket with little powder or ball. It was dangerous to shoot, anyway; the barrel had a hairline crack near the muzzle. Rollins left them the carbine, his constant companion, and a sack of cartridges.

In the ruins of Crow King's lodge they found Abigail's charred trunks, and took with them the few things that were undamaged, including the red dress Walking Bull had been so fond of. It was a little scorched around the hem, but otherwise undamaged. There was little else remaining.

As they departed the camp for Deadwood it started to snow again, a gentle drifting down of wide flat flakes. Rollins turned in the saddle to wave good-by. The Sioux stood in the meadow, vague figures half-seen in the falling snow, waving farewell to Bone Man and Abigail Brand.

"When they kill the last Sioux," Rollins said, "it will be like killing the last eagle."

Three days later they sat their mounts at the Whitewood Creek bridge, looking down at the town. Deadwood lay under a mantle of white. Dray wagons struggled through mud streaked with gold where the setting sun shone on water rapidly turning to ice. Lights winked on in windows. Even from that distance they could hear the plink of a piano, a few raucous shouts carried up the hill on the wind. "Hasn't changed much," Rollins said. The sunset cannon boomed.

He blew on his fingers. "Just made it in time. I think a norther's making up." He turned to Abigail Brand, held out a hand. "I thank you for what you did for me, Abby. Not likely I'd be sitting here without your help. I appreciate it."

Quickly she took his hand in hers. "That's not enough, Jack! You don't think I'm going to let you leave like this with just a handshake?"

His face was half-hidden under the brim of the old hat. She saw bewilderment in his eyes, a mixture of regret and sadness, and longing too, she thought.

"Don't!" he muttered. "Don't do this to me, Abby! It's hard enough that I—"

"Put your hands up, Rollins," the Oswego Peach ordered.

Startled, they stared down at Judge Yount's man. Peach stood wide-legged, flat-brimmed hat crowned with snow, pointing a shotgun.

"High above your head!" he warned. He looked at the empty saddle boot. "What in hell did you do with that damned carbine?" He patted Rollins's pockets, legs, pulled off the blanket, ripped open the leggings she had sewed back together and searched inside. "No gun?"

Vainly, Rufus tried to bite Peach, but a blow from the barrel of the shotgun knocked him senseless.

"No gun," Rollins said.

"Wait a minute!" Abigail cried. "Wait a minute, please!" She turned to Jack Rollins. "I'll get you a lawyer. We'll—"

"Talking won't do no good," Peach said.

Tied to the bridge was his horse. Holding the shotgun in the crook of his arm, Peach mounted, jerking his head toward the town.

"Been waiting for you a long time," he said. "Most froze to death out here."

CHAPTER TEN

Back in her suite again at the Grand Central Hotel in Deadwood, Abigail Brand was having coffee with Julian Garner. Sitting at the desk which the management had brought to her rooms, she stirred her coffee pensively. "The Sioux," she told Garner, "call coffee *pazuta sapa*. Did you know that?"

He did not seem interested, only sat on the sofa and turned the brim of his hat in his hands.

"I am so grateful," she said, "that my portrait of the chief was saved. We searched for it in the ruins of his tipi, but could find nothing. I am happy he was allowed to keep it, bring it with him to Deadwood."

Garner shook his head. "You shouldn't be doing all this, you know, Abigail! It's causing a great commotion not only in Deadwood City but all over the Territory. People are stirred up about Walking Bull and the attack on the pack train, and you are attempting to defend him. I hear one of the eastern newspapers is sending out a reporter."

She sipped her coffee. "*Sha* means red, Julian. And *sha sha*—the word repeated twice—means good, excellent. I learned a great deal of the language while I was out there. And a lot about the Sioux, too." Gravely she regarded him over the rim of the flowered cup. "Perhaps—about myself, also."

"You've certainly changed since you left, that's evident."

"A great deal," she agreed. "And yet, in a way, I am much the same." She looked around at the suite. "I am back in the element I know so well, managing things. Temporarily, at least until my own lawyers arrive from the East, I have retained Mr. Lucas Grubb of Deadwood to act as my representative. Even now he is on a visit to Cheyenne City to obtain a writ for the release of Jack Rollins."

Garner shook his head. "That poor fellow! To have meddled so! Now there are federal charges lodged against him, and I dare say—"

"He is *not* a poor fellow!" Abigail objected. "He is actually a fine man, in spite of appearances!"

Garner ran a hand through his hair. "I do not care, really, to hear any more about Rollins!"

She stared at him. "Why, Julian! You seem agitated when I speak of Mr. Rollins!"

He flushed, stammered. "I—I—perhaps I was discourteous! I did not mean to be so. It is only that I am concerned you are putting yourself into the middle of controversy." When she only smiled and began to stack papers neatly on the desk before her, he sighed, balanced the hat carefully on his knee. "In fact, I probably should not be seen here—in your rooms. As representative of the Indian Commission I must appear impartial and objective. But I do not mind telling you that I disapprove of what Judge Yount has done. While the charges against Walking Bull and his Sioux may be true, I think it a poor time to make an issue of it."

"The charges are false," Abigail said.

Garner shrugged. "But with the passions of the town so inflamed—" He broke off, smoothing the nap of the hat. "I have suggested to Major Toomey he detail a detachment of Ninth Infantry soldiers to guard the jail against any attempt to harm the prisoners, but he refused, saying it was a civil matter. As you know, Judge Yount has gotten two of the Indian Police from the new Whitewood Creek Reservation to remain in the cell with Walking Bull and Badger to keep an eye on them. It was a clever move—Yount is a clever man. It makes it appear Walking Bull's own people are against him." He sighed. "Perhaps I am not a very good advocate for the Indian Commission's case! Oh, I make no brief for the Sans Arcs—they have committed their share of misdeeds. But their sins are at retail, ours at wholesale." He rose to take his leave. "You know they say 'Westward the course of empire!—'"

"I am tired of hearing that phrase!" Abigail cried. She came to stand near him, eyes flashing and breast trembling with emotion. "'Westward the course of empire'—that is all very well! But it should constitute no license to imprison and maim and murder simple people whose only offense is to love their country—and to protect it against interlopers!"

In spite of his discomfiture, their eyes met. She continued to stand before him, and the scent of heliotrope came to him; that, and the bouquet of female flesh, warm with passion. Her hair was in slight disarray; she pushed impatiently at it with her hand, forcing it into place.

"Do you not agree?" she demanded.

He could not break the bond her eyes forged on his. He felt completely unlawyerlike.

"Well?"

"I missed you so much! Abigail, I—I—" Stammering inanely, he tried to reach her hand. "When you were gone, for so long, I thought of you all the time—where you were, what you were doing, whether you were in danger. I—I—" Suddenly he turned. Jamming the hat on his head, Julian Garner rushed away, pell-mell, down the steps, into the street. On the way he caromed into a workman negotiating the stairs with a large wooden sign.

"Now what's the matter with *him?*" the workman grumbled. He shrugged, toiled upward again. Seeing Abigail Brand at the top of the stairs, he set his burden down with a sigh of relief. The sign said NATIONAL INDIAN DEFENSE ASSOCIATION, DAKOTA TERRITORY DIVISION, in black letters on a stark white background.

"Mrs. Brand, ma'am," he asked, mopping his forehead, "where did you want this?"

She was gazing abstractedly down the stairwell.

"Ma'am," he repeated, "where—"

"Oh!" She looked at him as if he were a visitor from the moon. "Oh—the sign!" Seeming nervous and distraught, she passed a shaking hand over her brow. "The sign—" she murmured. "The sign I ordered! Yes! Put it—put it just above the door here, will you? And send me the bill promptly."

Everyone in Deadwood, the workman thought, was acting queerly these days.

———◆———

Winter finally set its grip on Deadwood City. The temperature was not severe, only a little below the freezing mark, but heavy snow fell on the town. For pennies, small boys shoveled out entrances to stores and saloons; they were assured of a continuing income. Jamie Burns held the record, having made sixty-five cents in one day.

Jack Rollins languished in the jail, along with Walking Bull and Badger. The Sioux were confined in an adjacent cell, watched constantly by the Indian guards who shared the cell with them. Because of the partition between them, Jack could not see them. But he spoke frequently in Sioux to Walking Bull, which annoyed the Oswego Peach, their jailer and recently appointed deputy federal marshal.

The jail was a stoutly built wooden building at the edge of town. Once it had been a gristmill and the big wheel still turned aimlessly in the waters of Whitewood Creek. Abandoned, the city had taken over the mill for a jail. But with the prospect of gold in Pa Sapa, and the influx of the lawless element, the man hired as constable abandoned his post and fled to Omaha, where law and reason prevailed. Now Judge Yount, under his new cachet as U. S. Marshal, had commandeered the old mill for his three prisoners, awaiting the day when the promised federal judge would arrive to try their cases. Everyone hoped it would be soon; the town was inflamed against the miscreants blocking entry into Pa Sapa.

Peach, new to law-enforcement duties, had not searched Jack Rollins thoroughly. As a consequence, Rollins worked each night with an overlooked jackknife, digging at the oak beams in which the iron bars of his cell were fixed. The oak was tough, the bars set deep; finally, he broke off the blade of the precious knife. Still he persisted, grinding away with the stub of the blade and covering the evidence of the night's work with dust, shavings, and spittle. The back of the old mill bordered the dense forest along the creek. With the snow continuing to fall so heavily, he calculated that if he could only get out through the window his tracks would quickly be obliterated. Of course, he had no clear idea of where he would go, what he would do. But freezing to death in the wilderness was a better fate than being penned up in a cell, awaiting a federal judge and certainly a harsh sentence.

Hearing the approaching strains of the Oswego Peach's mouth harp, he put the broken knife in his pocket and sat down on the cot with its ragged blanket. "Brother!" he called to Walking Bull. "Are you sleeping?"

Walking Bull answered in the sibilant Sioux tongue. "I cannot sleep in this little room. But I rest, and I think, too. I think about—"

Peach rattled the doors of Rollins' cell. "Stop jabbering that way, you bastards! It's against the law for prisoners to communicate! The judge says so."

They knew Peach was powerless to stop them. And the Indian guards only squatted stolidly on the floor and played cooncan.

"I do not like to be caged like this," Walking Bull complained. "But it is a kind of fighting against them, I think. They are trying to scare me into touching the pen. If I do it for them, they say the judge will let me go free. But I will not sign their papers. And so —I fight them, even here in this iron cage."

Rollins lay back on the cot, watching the wink of the lantern on Peach's new badge.

"Go away, Peach," he said. "Your light's in my eyes. I want to sleep."

Peach glowered down at him. He hitched at his coat, showing the revolver in its snug holster. "See that you do, then, and stop that infernal gibbering!"

Walking Bull had been allowed to keep Mrs. Brand's portrait in his cell, an act of compassion for which Judge Yount was praised. After being searched, Wah Chee and Lew Searles were also allowed to visit Jack Rollins daily, bringing him food, and clothing to replace the ragged blanket and Sioux leggings.

"How you feel?" Wah Chee asked. He watched Rollins devour the basket of food the Chinaman had brought to supplement the jail fare of boiled bacon, beans, and hard bread. "You all right, Jack Rollins?" He grinned an Oriental grin. "My goo'ness, you cleaner than I ever see you! You take bath?"

Rollins sampled a mysterious stew, swimming with strands of what appeared to be coarse grass. Seaweed, possibly? But he was hungry. After his long convalescence, all he seemed to want to do was eat and eat, putting badly needed flesh on his bones.

"I feel all right."

"It was a brave thing you did, Jack," the printer said. "Most of the town is against you, that's true. But there are a few that give you credit for standing up to Yount and Toomey and Conway and the miners." He slapped Rollins' thigh. "We're bailing out the ocean with a damned teaspoon, but we don't mean to give up the fight! So long as they've got Walking Bull in their damned jail, we—"

He stopped, seeing the glazed look in Rollins' eyes.

"God damn it, I'm sorry—forgot that was the leg you got nicked in!" Searles was contrite, but went on. "Feelings are running high —they threatened to chase me out of town for a little editorial I printed the other day—but maybe we've got Yount worried some."

Rollins snorted. "What has *he* got to worry about? In this game he holds all the aces! And Toomey's got his successful action against the Sioux—broke their back, he brags! No, it's all over but Judge Yount's coronation, and John Toomey's silver oak leaves—maybe even eagles—and that staff job in the War Department. They've got what they want, and devil take the hindmost!" He took something from his mouth, eyed it suspiciously. "Wah Chee, what in hell are these little bullets?"

"No bullets," the Chinaman assured him. "Water chestnuts! Good for you! Give strength of lion, wisdom of owl, long life like turtle."

"If a turtle ate these," Rollins said, "it would damn sure make it *seem* like a long life!"

"Rollins!" Peach growled. He stood before the cell, unhooking the ring of keys at his belt. "Judge Yount wants to talk to you." He unlocked the door, swinging it open. "You other fellers leave now. And take the rest of that slop with you! You're stinking up the whole jail!"

Roughly Peach pushed Jack Rollins down the corridor. "And don't try anything, Indian lover! By Christ, I plugged you once! I'd have done for you then if my aim hadn't been interfered with!"

It was late afternoon, almost evening. Rollins passed a dirty window, longingly looking out. Perched in a winterkilled bush, a jay sassed him. Whitewood Creek moved black and sluggish along a channel carved from purest white; the mill wheel creaked and groaned. He was not used to captivity. Would he ever smell the airs of freedom again?

"In there," Peach said, gesturing.

Partitions had been thrown up on the main floor of the old mill. Judge Yount sat behind a newly carpentered desk.

"Well, Rollins!" he said cordially. Striking a match, he lit the

lamp at his elbow, and arranged some papers. "Sit down." Peach
withdrew to a corner, arms folded, ready for any insubordination
on the part of the prisoner. "And how have they treated you in
our new federal prison?"

Rollins shrugged. "No outright torture yet, though your bill of
fare could give a maggot indigestion."

The judge chuckled, his deep-pouched eyes amused. Biting the
end from a stogie, he bent over the chimney of the lamp and drew
the tip into a glow. "Got a little proposition to make to you."

Rollins waited. The judge drew deep, exhaled, sat back in his
chair. He watched smoke drift over the lamp chimney, swirl upward.

"As you probably know, your lady friend is causing me—causing
the forces of law and order, that is—a great deal of trouble! I only
wish I knew what she was up to when she first came to Deadwood. Now she's sitting in that suite of hers sending telegraph
messages right and left, hiring lawyers from Philadelphia and
Chicago and Omaha and God knows where else, fighting us tooth
and nail. She's determined to get Walking Bull out of jail, exoner-
ate him. What she's doing, she's getting up steam to wreck the
land deal." He looked keenly at Rollins. "I hear she's even sent to
Cheyenne City to get a habeas corpus or something to get you out
of jail yourself."

Rollins shrugged. "That so?"

The judge sat back in the chair again, examined the ash of the
cigar. "Now no nice lady from the East goes to all that trouble for
a drifter like Jack Rollins unless there's something between them
—isn't that right?"

"What does that mean?"

Yount laughed good-naturedly. "You and Mrs. Brand been
gallivanting around the country for several weeks, all alone, the
two of you. When we had to use force to subdue the Sans Arcs—
reluctantly, I might say—you sneaked her out and holed up with
her for a spell, didn't you? Now Mrs. Brand is a handsome lady, I
never denied that, and I haven't met a female yet who's averse to
a little dallying in the vale when she—"

"That's a damned lie!" Rollins rose and took a step toward
Yount, fists clenched. Peach stepped meaningfully forward, but
Judge Yount waved him back.

"Mrs. Brand," Rollins said, "is a lady! Your comments are coarse."

The judge maintained an air of judicial calm. It was his pride always to remain calm, even under provocation.

"That's as may be," he said. "But let's put it this way. I think the lady cares enough for you, from what I hear, to at least listen to your advice."

"About what?"

Yount leaned confidentially forward.

"The charges against you, as I see them, are circumstantial. We know damned well you went back to warn the Sioux camp, but no one actually witnessed you doing so." He bridged his fingertips together, looked at Jack Rollins through the bridge. "It might be possible to drop the charges against you, with no great harm to the government's case against Walking Bull and his rascals. Drop them that is, if you agree to go to Mrs. Brand and use your blandishments of whatever nature—" He smiled and puffed at the stogie. "Persuade her to get the hell back east and let us alone! I don't mind telling you, Mrs. Henry Brand is not popular with the citizens of Deadwood! I can't speak for her safety if she keeps up her infernal meddling."

Rollins snorted. "Smoke! Vapors and smoke! That's what you're peddling! It's all a sham, and you know it! You and Toomey and Dickybird Conway and the miners—you're greedy land-grabbing scoundrels! I hope Abigail Brand rips the lid off the scandal, shows the whole country how the Sioux are being bamboozled and cheated!"

Yount's composure began to fray. "Now wait a minute, Rollins! You're going too far! Remember, you're a federal prisoner, and there are serious charges against you! I'm only offering you—"

"You know what you can do with your offer! I'm only a cipher in your figuring—just a zero to make things balance—so it doesn't make any difference what happens to me! But I'm an honest man, and you're a damned blackguard, Yount!"

Peach started threateningly forward, but a knock sounded on the barred outer door. The judge stubbed out his cigar. "See who it is, but look through that little peephole first. No unauthorized persons!"

Peach went, looked. "It's Grubb."

Judge Yount was annoyed. "Now what in hell does he want this time of night? Well, let him in, can't you?"

Lawyer Grubb's bearskin coat was powdered with snow, his face chapped, hands chilblained. Spreading a paper before the judge, he said, "Here we are! A writ from District Court in Cheyenne City, all sealed and stamped and proper."

Yount hooked steel-rimmed spectacles over his ears. "Bail," he muttered. "They've granted bail! All right, then. But does any damned fool think Rollins is worth five hundred dollars bail?"

Grubb handed him a slip of paper. "A check for five hundred dollars, drawn on the Merchants and Drovers Bank of Cheyenne City, certified by the Clerk of Court to be acceptable in bail for the person of one John Fitzhugh Rollins, presently in the custody of the U. S. Marshal at Deadwood City, Dakota Territory. And write me a receipt for the check, please, Judge."

Yount sighed, sank back in his chair. "That woman! All right, Peach. I guess we've got to let him go." He turned to his late prisoner. "Only don't try anything funny, Rollins! And don't attempt to leave town. This is only bail until your trial!"

Rollins recovered his scanty belongings from the cell.

"They are letting me out, brother!" he called to Walking Bull.

The chief came to his cell door. He wore the ceremonial coat and leggings Rollins remembered from the night when he had burst in on Walking Bull and Abigail Brand. In the rays of the lantern his face was cut into sharp planes of light and shadow. Behind him was the youth Badger, wrapped in a jail blanket. The two Indian guards squatted on the floor, not looking up from their endless card game. The portrait Abigail Brand had painted stood on its easel in the shadows.

"I am glad, brother," Walking Bull said. He shook hands with Rollins. "If you see any of the People, tell them that Walking Bull does not touch the pen—never."

Peach let Lawyer Grubb and Jack Rollins out into the swirling snow. Together they trudged the rutted road into Deadwood. The town, Rollins thought, was much the same. Men thronged the streets, boots sucking in the mud, cursing and joking. Some staggered drunkenly from hurdy-gurdies, others fell flat in the mire, risking suffocation when they were too drunk to regain their footing. A stage lurched in, wheels sunk to the hubs, horses spattered.

In the window of the *Territorial Argus*, where Lew Searles labored
late over his fonts of type, a light burned. Deadwood Theater and
Academy of Music announced, on a flapping banner strung across
the street, the imminent arrival of Miller's Grand Combination
Troupe, with a Dazzling Array of Stars. Eating houses, saloons,
hotels, and washhouses were packed, and pianos tinkled unceas-
ingly. It wasn't much, perhaps, but it was Jack Rollins' town. He
felt a glow of pleasure.

Dickybird Conway, bearskin coat covering the elegant waistcoat, stepped out from a knot of arguing miners.

"So you're out of jail, eh, Rollins? Now, how did you ever man-
age that?"

Rollins grinned. "Can't keep a good man down!" He was in a
pleasant mood. When he saw Jamie Burns shoveling snow, he
went to rumple Jamie's hair.

"I'm glad you escaped from that dungeon, Mr. Rollins," Jamie
told him.

Watching a lamplit upper window in the Paradise Card
Rooms, Rollins began to think on Zenobia Ferris—Nobie, of the
fox-red hair and silken legs. He had a long-denied craving for a
woman. There was nothing to beat a woman, especially one like
Nobie Ferris.

"Eh?" he asked, startled. He had not been listening to Lawyer
Grubb. Of course, he would never see Honey Hill again, but he
was happy here. His life in Deadwood was probably not much by
eastern standards, but the town had taken him in, brought him
surcease from pain, from regret, from memory.

"What was that?" he asked again. "I'm sorry, Mr. Grubb."

The lawyer took his arm, drawing him into the Grand Central.
"Mrs. Brand told me she wants to see you soon as possible."

He stood on the thick pile of the carpet in her suite, hat in his
hands. Abigail Brand was dressed in black that accentuated the
marble of her skin. A jeweled brooch was at her neck; it caught
the light from the Argand lamp, splintering it into fragments.

"How are you, Jack?"

Lawyer Grubb coughed discreetly. Abigail said, "Thank you,
Mr. Grubb. That will be all for now."

When the door closed she came to him, looking him up and
down appraisingly. "You have not been in that horrid jail long

enough for the experience to have affected you." She laughed. "Do you know—you *have* changed, though!"

"How is that?"

"Always before, you carried that gun, that carbine—wherever you went. It was as if you suspected the whole world, and were ready for a fight. Now, without that weapon, you seem much more agreeable, more at ease, with yourself and with the world."

"A man changes," he murmured. He looked at her. "And a woman, too."

She was suddenly businesslike. Going to the desk, she said, "Here, in this envelope, is the five hundred dollars I promised you to take me to Walking Bull's camp in the mountains. And if you will sit over there and make yourself comfortable, I have so much to talk to you about." She sat at a desk, littered with papers, documents, a few lawbooks, probably borrowed from Mr. Grubb. "Jack, we have just begun to fight!"

"I saw the sign over the door," he said, noncommittally.

"We have the full backing of the National Indian Defense Association! I mean to get the chief out of jail, at least on bond, and take him back to tour the East to speak for his cause. He has agreed, he and Badger both. Then you and I can—"

"Me?" Rollins frowned. "What have I got to do with this?"

"Yes, you, Jack! You can be a great help to our cause."

He shook his head. "I have told you before—I have done with causes!"

"That is what you said, but I do not believe it. You came to the aid of the Sans Arcs, were wounded into the bargain. Is that not a cause?"

"Listen!" he said. "Listen to me! I told you—I came back for *you!* And now, for my pains, I am under federal charges. I have a wound in my thigh that pains me in damp weather, like now." He touched his broken nose. "You wondered about this, where I got it. Let me tell you, Abby Brand—I got it in the late Army of the Confederate States of America, poking it into business that was not my concern. And it hurts me too, in damp weather. So I will have no more of causes—they have cost me enough already!"

She was taken aback by his outburst. Rising from the desk, she came to him. "I had forgotten about your leg! Does it pain you?"

She had forgotten something else too, Rollins thought. She had forgotten how close they had been in the Sioux camp, at his New Ophir mine, on the long journey back to Deadwood. It was insensitive of her; the businesslike manner, the solicitous inquiry as to his wound, like a nurse in a charity ward.

"If it hurts you, Jack," she said, bending over him, "you must tell me! Our discussions can wait until later."

She was very close to him. The jeweled brooch caught the light, lit her face in reflected beauty. He smelled her perfume, or was it simply Abby Brand? When she put a hand on his brow, she said, "Perhaps you have a fever! Is that why you are so flushed, so agitated? I will send to the druggist and get some powders, a draft of some sort."

"No!" he said hoarsely. Beads of sweat pricked his forehead.

"But—"

"Damn it, Abby!" He trembled. "You are either the simplest and purest female yet born, or—or—"

She drew back, startled.

"Or the most guileful!" Blindly he rose, rushing from her unsettling presence. But in his flight he blundered into her. Feeling the soft yielding of her bosom against him, he groped to catch her, prevent her from falling.

"Abby!" he groaned. "Abby!"

She came into his arms; he pressed his cheek against hers.

"Damn you," he muttered. "Damn you! Do you know what you are doing to me?"

She did not speak, only molded her body tighter against his. Locked together, they swayed in the lamplight, her mouth against his lips, soft and ripe. She seemed almost to swoon, hanging heavily on him.

"I—I am not responsible," she murmured into his ear. "Jack, I am not responsible; I cannot control my feelings. But whatever is going to happen, it is in the Lord's hands now."

Together, they went toward the bed with its silken hangings.

———◄◆►———

Afterward, they lay for a long time together. It grew cold in the room. A boy with an armload of wood for the fire was sent away when he knocked; they were warm with their passion. Dark hair cradled in his arm, she looked fondly at Rollins' long white body.

"I have loved you for a long time," she whispered. "It was the—the first time for me, to so love a man." Her finger traced a pattern on his chest, down through the silky yellow hair, so unlike the sunbleached thatch on his head. "When you were deathly ill, there at the mine, I took care of you, Jack. I looked at you then, looked at your body. I felt great love for you. I—I wanted to do things for you, cherish you, nurture you—" She stopped for a moment, looking at the guttering lamp. It was running low on fuel but neither wanted to move, to break the magical spell. "*Sha*," she murmured. "*Sha sha.*"

He frowned. "What do you mean?"

"You told me it meant good, excellent. But it is too frail a word, even in Sioux, to describe what happened to me tonight, with you." Her eyes stared at the lamp but seemed to focus beyond, on something distant, perhaps unseen. "Do you—do you love me?" she asked, drowsily.

He pulled her closer. "There is more to consider than love, now."

She burrowed her cheek deeper into the curve of his arm. "Afterwards, you slept for a while. Do all men do that—after they have loved a woman?"

"I don't know what all men do."

She kissed his ear. "At any rate, I am glad you did not call out for Mary—Mary Armistead."

"Perhaps it is time to tell you about Mary." He rose on an elbow to look down at her. "You are so like Mary. When the war came, I enlisted with the Charleston Horse Guards. Mary and I took our vows just before I left. But"—his sunbleached brows drew together—"during the war she took a lover. She meant all the world to me, Mary did, and she took a lover; I was gone for so long, you see."

She was silent, listening with grave sympathy.

"There was a child. Mary and the little girl both died from the fever. After the war, I went home—to Honey Hill. I called out the man, killed him. It was a duel, all proper; I risked my life, he risked his, and lost. But his family got out a murder warrant. So I—well, I ran away. They sent a detective after me. I ran away again, to Denver. Finally I reached Deadwood. I have been safe here, until now. But I understand there is a reporter in town, from one of the big eastern newspapers. My past will out. And I do not think it will be long before I must run again—perhaps to San Francisco, or the Sandwich Islands. They say a man can live there on fish and coconuts."

With gentle fingers she stroked his cheek.

"You do not need to worry! I will take care of everything. When we go back, I will hire the best lawyer in the East."

He shook his head, rose, put his scarred leg into the jeans Lew Searles had brought him in the jail.

"I'll not go, I tell you! I will not be taken again, put into a jail, locked away from the sun and the wind and the weather! Kept like a shoat behind a fence, the way they are doing with Walking Bull and Badger!"

She caught his arm. "I know what I am doing, believe me! I know the law! We will go back together. We will get the courts to issue a writ, just as I did for you here. Then—you and I and Walking Bull and Badger—we will stump the East, drumming up support for the Sioux. We will cause such a tide to rise that the government will be forced to abandon the scheme to steal the Sans Arc lands! Can you not see it? Walking Bull on the lecture stage, in full Sioux regalia, with you to interpret his remarks! We will win—I tell you, we will win!"

He pulled on his shirt, went to the window, stared out. It was growing late, very late.

"Perhaps Walking Bull and his people are in peril, but then so am I. Can't you understand that?"

"But you love me, don't you?"

"I am—I am very fond of you, Abby."

She threw caution to the winds. "Then—marry me! Together, we can do great things! Marry me, Jack!"

He fumbled with a coat button. "I—I swore, long ago, never to give my heart to another woman."

She sprang to her feet. In her rush she knocked a fluted glass dish from the bureau; it shattered into fragments against the stove.

"You love me! You know you do!"

He turned her aside. "I'm not the man for you, Abby. I never was! Perhaps—once—I might have been. But not now. I'm a wanderer, a drifter; I'm no good for you. What you need is a man that

fits into your world, neatly, like a piece in a puzzle. Someone like
—Julian Garner."

"Julian?" She turned pale. "I don't love Julian Garner!"

He went to the door. "Good-by, Abby." He grinned, the old
wry grin. "Thanks for the bail! But don't be surprised if I run out
on you, forfeit your money. Deadwood isn't a healthy place for
me any more."

"Jack!" she called. "Jack!"

In desperation she ran to the stairwell and called after him.
"You always said money was the thing, didn't you? Well, I've got
a lot of money! A person can do anything with money!"

He was gone. Limping, she went back to the window and stared
into the street. She must have cut her bare foot on the shards of
the broken dish. Watching for him to emerge below, she cradled
the foot in her hand, feeling it slippery with blood. The women—
the Sioux women—gashed themselves when a loved one died.

"Jack!" She opened the window and screamed. "Come back!"

Below, a man was nailing a sign to a post. In the flickering rays
of the lantern propped on a hitching post, she saw it had to do
with a meeting, a big meeting of Territory miners, with free beer
and barrels of oysters.

Conscious of nakedness, she drew the folds of the drapes about
her, still scanning below. But she did not see Jack Rollins. Perhaps
love was *not* the answer, at least not her love for him. Love had
not been the answer for either of them. Bitterly, she wept.

CHAPTER ELEVEN

Late on a snowy afternoon, Jack Rollins and Nobie Ferris sat in her cubicle above the Paradise Card Room. Rufus, head bandaged, lapped bourbon whiskey from a saucer. Nobie Ferris, fondly watching Rufus, was puzzled.

"But why do you have to go away, Jack? Deadwood is your home, like mine!"

Sitting far back in the rocker, boots propped on the bed, he sighed. "It's a long story, Nobie. Besides, I don't want to think. Let's just say the airs of Deadwood are unhealthy for me now." He closed his eyes and linked his hands behind his head. "All I want to do is sit here and rest—be with you for now, feel warm."

Scantily clad, silken legs crossed, she was suspicious.

"You've been with *her!*"

"Who?"

"That woman! That Mrs. Brand! She wants you to go away with her, doesn't she?" Nobie tried to be casual. "I've never seen her, but from a distance. Is—is she pretty, Jack?"

He became sullen. "I told you I don't want to talk about it!"

Knowing his moods, she abandoned the subject. Brightly she said, "You told me once Zenobia was a queen's name." She came to sprawl childlike beside him on the bed. "Jack, don't you think a queen ought to know how to read and write? A queen has got to be smart—someone her subjects look up to."

Before he could answer, a knock sounded at the door. "You in there, ma'am? Nobie? Nobie Ferris!" The voice was male, and expectant.

"Go away!" Nobie cried. "I'm having my monthlies!"

"But Mamzelle Sophie said—"

"Beat it!" Nobie cried. To Jack Rollins she said, "*You* know that ain't so, Jack, but he don't." She giggled. "He's just a rough-neck—one of them miners. And I planned a little celebration to-night, just for you and me!"

Rollins grinned. "Miners aren't refined enough for your tastes any more?"

She poured Rufus another saucer of bourbon; he wagged his tail gratefully. "Major Toomey give me this bottle, just before he left with the soldiers to bring in—what's his name?"

"Walking Bull."

She looked quizzically at the bottle. "A booze bottle this full around here—that's a funny thing. Jack, why don't you drink no more?" When he did not answer, only stared at the ceiling, she asked, "Did you know Toomey's got orders to Washington?"

"I'm not surprised."

"And Mr. Garner—they say he's resigned his job—don't agree with what Judge Yount and the major did to Walking Bull."

Rollins pursed his lips thoughtfully, scratched Rufus' ears. "Well, that's news! Maybe I misjudged Julian Garner."

In the cozy silence the only sound was the crackle and hiss of wood in the stove. That, and an occasional drifting through the frost-etched windows of street sounds; laughter, a fiddle playing, jingle of harness, and a woman's high-pitched laugh. Jack Rollins, hand on Nobie's knee, frowned, listened. "What was that?"

Nobie cocked her head. "What?"

"Sounds like a band."

She went to the window, scratched a clear place with her red fingernails. "Oh, tonight's the big meeting!"

"What meeting?"

She came to sit on his lap, throw her arms about his neck.

"What do we care? Kiss me, Jack!"

Annoyed, he held his head aside. "What meeting?"

"Oh, it's those roughneck miners! Dickybird Conway is having a torchlight rally tonight—parade, free beer and oysters, every-thing."

"What's the occasion?"

Again she attempted to press her lips against his, but he was im-patient. "God damn it, Nobie—answer me!"

"I guess it's about the Sioux business. The miners are mad because nothing's happening. Conway says unless the government takes some sort of action quick, there's bound to be trouble. They want that gold."

He shook his head, sighing. "That's not Conway speaking, that's Judge Yount! Conway has got a big mouth, but not a brain in his head. No, it's Yount's doing, all right. I see his fine Italian hand behind all this."

She stared at him. "Is Judge Yount an Eyetalian?"

He laughed and ran an approving hand along the swell of her thigh. "By God, you're good for me, Nobie! Whenever I get feeling down, you perk me up again!"

Knowing how to take advantage of his humors, she ran to the bureau and brought back a pad of notepaper and a stub of pencil. "Then—will you teach me to read and write, Jack? Right now?"

He groaned, but took the pencil and paper, letting her sit on his lap. What was it Abby Brand insisted? *Love is doing things for people, wanting to help them.* It had been an article of faith with her, unshaken by his jeering. Well, maybe she was right. By that definition, did he love Nobie Ferris?

His brain was tired; he did not want to think. It was enough, now, that Nobie sat on his lap this snowbound night, eager and waiting, loving him. He was, he knew, the center of Nobie's small world. Whether he deserved that eminence he was not sure.

In broad block letters he spelled out her name, ZENOBIA FERRIS. She touched each character with an awed finger.

"That's my name? Nobie? Nobie Ferris?"

"Zenobia," he corrected. "Zenobia Ferris." He took her finger, tracing each letter. "That first letter is a Z." He made an appropriate buzzing sound. "Like a bee, see?" Then he shook his head, dissatisfied. "No, don't think of a bee buzzing! That way you'll get to thinking the damned Z is a B." He bit his lip, trying to think of a way to explain. "Look at it this way, Nobie. If you—"

Another knock sounded at the door. "Damn it!" Nobie complained, "I told him to go away!" Bounding from his knee, she snatched up her wrapper and opened the door. "I told you—"

She fell back, awed. In the doorway stood Mrs. Henry Brand. Abigail's face was pale, but there was determination in her gaze.

"Is Mr. Jack Rollins here? I was told—"

Nobie hesitated. Then she said, "He's here, all right. But what—"

Abigail brushed by her, coming into the room. Outside, through the hall well, they heard the band play louder; a tuba grunted.

"There you are, Jack!" Abigail said.

He sensed tightness in her voice, barely concealed emotion. Brushing snow from the heavy coat, she took off the white-dusted fur cap and let the dark hair cascade about her shoulders. "I—I came to ask your help."

Cautiously he rose, taking care not to stand too near. She was very beautiful; melting snow glistened jewel-like on the long lashes. He felt a familiar stirring within him.

"What kind of help, Abby?"

In the smoky warmth of the room her cheeks became pink, summer flowers in the whiteness of the face.

"There is great mischief planned for tonight. You have heard about the miners' meeting?"

"Yes."

"Since I came to Deadwood, I have managed to establish my own sources of information. What is to happen tonight is more than a meeting. It is a deliberate conspiracy to arouse the passions of the mob. They plan to have the man Conway—what do they call him?"

"Dickybird. Dickybird Conway."

"Yes, he is the one. It is planned to have him get the miners stirred up, attack the jail, drag Mr. Walking Bull and his son Badger out, and hang them up!"

Nobie was looking at him with fear-filled eyes. He reached for her hand. "Perhaps this is all true. I wouldn't put it past them. But—who is planning all this? Maybe it is only rumor."

She looked at him for a moment, appraisingly. "Yount, of course. Judge Yount! Who else? You know that Major Toomey got what he wants, and is to leave for Washington and an important post in the War Department. Now it is time for Judge Yount to get what *he* wants—remove the chief from the land negotiations, open up Pa Sapa to the miners, assure himself of the constituency the judge needs to become governor of the new state certain to be made soon from the Territory."

He knew it was true. But he resisted involvement.

"I can't help you," he said.

"That's right!" Nobie flared. Holding Jack Rollins' hand in hers, she was indignant. "It's nothing to do with Jack! Anyway, why should he help *you?*"

Though she spoke to Nobie Ferris, Abigail's gaze never left Jack Rollins. "He is not helping *me!* He is helping the cause of justice. He knows that."

Rollins sighed. "I think you'd better get someone else to help you, Abby. I don't know what I could do, anyway. What about Julian Garner? I hear he's had a change of heart about the Sioux problem."

"Julian Garner," Abigail said, "did what he could. He went to Judge Yount, accused him of conspiracy, protested the holding of a mass meeting when the matter was soon to be adjudicated in the courts. But a gang of ruffians assaulted him as he left the judge's office, injuring him severely. He is now under a physician's care, in my suite at the hotel."

Garner, Rollins thought. Julian Garner, with his inexhaustible supply of fresh paper collars and lawyer's obfuscations. There had been more to the tailor's dummy than he thought. But still he shook his head.

"I don't know what you expect me to do, Abby! I don't even carry a gun any more!"

If he expected that to close the discussion, to put an end to idle and impractical talk, he was mistaken. Abigail Brand put her hand on his sleeve. She still wore the ruby brooch which caught the glow from the oil lamp on the bureau, sending annoying sparkles of light into his averted gaze.

"You're the only man in town that can help, Jack, and you know that! I have lawyers from the East now—they arrived yesterday—but they speak only of injunctions and indictments and such claptrap! If Walking Bull and Badger are to be saved from the mob down there, it will be you—Jack Rollins—who will save them, and no one else! It is as simple as that!"

Nobie Ferris pushed Abigail aside, jealous of her contact with Jack.

"Stay away from him!" she warned. "It's none of Jack's business, I tell you! You're fixing to get him hurt—maybe killed!"

Abigail disregarded her. "You *must* do something, Jack! Does it mean nothing to you that Walking Bull is your friend? That he sheltered you and me—took us into his camp and gave us hospitality? Does it mean nothing that he is about to be martyred? Is there—is there not *some* bond between you—friendship, compassion, loyalty?"

"I'll scratch your eyes out!" Nobie spat. "All that fine talk don't mean nothing—Jack himself told me it didn't! So you just get out of here, you—you *rich* lady! Don't drag him into more trouble than he's already got!"

Nobie Ferris clung fiercely to his hand; Abigail Brand had a firm grip on his sleeve. Rollins was torn, divided. Swallowing hard, he looked at Abigail, felt Nobie's hand possessive in his own.

"What about Toomey, and the Ninth?"

Abigail shook her head. "In doing what *I* could, I already went to Major Toomey. He was courteous, but evasive; he said it was a civil affair. If the miners wanted to hold a meeting, it was none of his concern."

Against his will, Rollins was being traduced. He began to feel angry, frustrated.

"Wait a minute," he said. He withdrew from Abigail Brand and pulled his hand away from Nobie's grasp. "Now wait a goddamned minute!" He sat down in the rocker, gnawing at his knuckle. What a cockeyed world his own had become! And it was always a female that knocked it awry!

They watched him rock—a frightened Nobie in a gaudy silken wrapper, Abigail Brand elegant and indomitable. Two more different females he could not imagine. And yet—they both had a hold on him. Slowly he rocked, staring at the figures on the carpet. From outside he could hear shouts, cries, the tootle of a fife, the insistent booming of the damned tuba. When the music stopped he heard, through the heavy hangings of the windows, the sonorous voice of Dickybird Conway, an answering roar from the crowd. Rufus was staring at Rollins also, expectantly, a tattered ear lifted. Jack Rollins did not want even to look at Rufus.

"I don't know," he said. "I'm damned if I know what to do. Even if I—"

"Jack," Nobie pleaded, "you don't have to—"

"Be quiet," he said, not unkindly.

The music started again.

"When I was in jail," Rollins said, speaking almost to himself, "there were these bars in the window of the cell. I—I worked on them some, with my penknife, one they didn't know I had. The bars are loosened a little, maybe. And they face on Whitewood Creek, behind the mill."

"No!" Nobie protested. "No, Jack!"

"Beyond the creek, there's only trees. If a man could get in the back way through those bars that I dug at so long—" He got up, paced the floor. Then he shook his head, turned resolutely to Abigail Brand.

"No," he said, "there's no way, Abby! I thought maybe there was a way to get Walking Bull and Badger out of there before they stormed the jail, but there's still Peach and the Indian guards from the reservation, you see. It's impossible."

"Of course it is!" Nobie cried, relieved. "You can't work a miracle, Jack!"

"Listen!" Abigail Brand said. She was the businesswoman, the woman of industry and negotiation, successful negotiation, the manager. "Listen to me, Jack! When I came here, I thought to appeal to you on the basis of my love for you. I know you do not love me—it is humiliating for me to admit it, before this woman— but it is so, and I accept it! So now I am forced to reason on a more logical basis."

He was wary when she was like this, knowing that in business matters her mind worked in the manner of a machine, adding, subtracting, multiplying and dividing, coming out with unassailable reason.

"What do you mean?"

"You took me as agreed into Pa Sapa, the Sioux lands, led me to Rainy Butte, saw I was properly introduced to the chief, bargained to secure his assent to my painting the portrait. You even —through some affection for me which you now deny—returned gravely wounded to rescue me from Major Toomey's attack on the Sans Arc camp. Did you not do all these things?"

Baffled, he admitted, "Yes, I did. But what—"

"And I paid you for your services, did I not? Paid you well?"

He shrugged. "Of course. I have never denied that."

"Now," Abigail Brand cried, "you damned well owe *me* something, John Fitzhugh Rollins! May the Lord forgive me for the profanity, but I am greatly exercised!"

"Owes you what?" Nobie demanded. "Jack, what is she talking about? What do you owe her?"

"I don't owe anybody anything!" he protested. "Look here now, Abby, you can't just—"

"You owe me your *life*, Jack Rollins! Who nursed you, cared for you at the New Ophir, faced bears and other wild things when she was so terrified she could not even find her voice to pray for Heaven's help? Who nurtured you, held your head against her bosom on those frightful snowbound nights when wolves howled about the cabin and water froze in the basin I used to sponge your mangled thigh?"

Her voice broke. Suddenly she became only a woman, grieving. "Who did all these things, hoping against hope that you felt for me a small portion of the love I lavished on you?" Sobbing, she collapsed on the bed, face in her hands, the dark hair in disarray. "I am sorry! I—I did not mean to—to—"

Nobie Ferris stared at her, looked in wonder at Jack Rollins.

"Is she—Jack, is she telling the truth?"

Mutely he nodded, gripping his hands together until they hurt and his knuckles cracked. "It's true, all right, what she says."

Abigail rose from the bed, trying to regain her composure. Her eyes were wet with tears, but she made no effort to touch them with her handkerchief. "I'm sorry," she murmured. "I—I shouldn't have gone on so. I hope you'll both forgive me." She picked up the fur hat, wet with melted flakes. Rufus, remembering, came to her and licked her hand. He whined, looking at Jack Rollins as if to make his master remember also.

"Wait a minute!" Rollins begged. "Abby, please!"

She adjusted the small fur hat, calculating the angle, staring into the cracked mirror of Nobie Ferris' bureau. Almost recovered, she asked, "Wait?"

"Yes! Just a minute."

She shook her head. "I am going to be very busy soon. I don't know what can be done after the fact—probably very little, once Walking Bull is dead. But I mean to labor mightily in the Sioux cause. As you know, I do not give up!"

"I know that," he said, and did.

He stared at the pad where he had lettered ZENOBIA FERRIS. "Nobie," he said, "I've got to go. I've got to try. Maybe it won't turn out to be much, but I—I owe it, I guess you could say."

She clung to him. "Jack, don't go! You can't do anything! They're mean, those men—I know! They won't let anything stand in their way now. You'll get killed!"

Gently he disengaged her grasp, kissed the stricken face. Her tears were salty. "Sooner or later," he said, "a time comes."

"But you always said—"

With a finger he silenced the painted lips.

"Doesn't make any difference, now, Nobie, what I said! Words are just talk—air, like I always told you. It's what a man does that counts." He put on his coat, jammed the felt hat on his head. "All right," he told Abigail Brand. "I owe you something. You're right. I owe Walking Bull something, too, and Badger." He touched Nobie Ferris' fox-red curls. "Maybe I owe myself too. It's a long past-due bill. But we all have to settle up, finally."

Descending the stairs into the cigar smoke, the clink of chips, the whirring of roulette wheels in the Paradise, a man passed him on the stairs, caught at his sleeve.

"Hey! Ain't you the man they call Rollins?"

The man was short and plump and carried a notebook. His hat-band bristled with pencils, and he peered at Jack Rollins through gold pince-nez fastened to his lapel with black ribbon.

Rollins tried to pass by, but the stairs were narrow. The man still detained him.

"Wait a minute, can't you? I'm Frank Chilton, from the Chicago *Tribune*." Reaching in an inner pocket, the reporter took out a sheaf of credentials. "There's a great story here, and I mean to—"

"Let go my sleeve, can't you?" Rollins snarled. "I'm in a hurry!"

"Rollins!" Chilton chortled. "Sure enough! John Fitzhugh Rollins, late of Honey Hill, South Carolina! Once lieutenant in the fashionable Charleston Horse Guards, wasn't it? Wealthy cotton-planting family! Then you killed your wife's lover and disappeared. Now you're Mrs. Henry Brand's paramour, and all mixed up in this business with Walking Bull and the Sioux land grab they're trying to engineer!"

With an oath Rollins flung Chilton away and dashed down the

stairs. He had had the rest of his life planned. There was the Territory, where he was safe from a murder warrant. There were jobs —swamper in a saloon, whatever—to buy the anodyne of liquor. There were friends—Wah Chee, Lew Searles. There had been everything a man needed to live out his life free from care, discharged from obligation. Now the safe haven, the refuge from responsibility, had been snatched away. His past had tracked him down, brought him face to face with responsibilities, attachments long denied. Almost frantically he ran into the snowy night of Deadwood.

CHAPTER TWELVE

That night the area before the Grand Central Hotel was jammed with miners, farmers, woodcutters, gamblers, merchants, a sprinkling of 9th Infantry soldiers—everyone who had an interest in the opening up of Pa Sapa, of freeing it from the grasp of the Sioux who didn't know what to do with it anyway. Gold, minerals in abundance—rich grasslands and forests, all the bounty of a generous Providence for the taking!

Jack Rollins, moving covertly on the fringe of the crowd, stopped in the shadows to listen. The beer was running out and the oysters had long since been eaten; now the spectators listened to Dickybird Conway. The Welsh tenor soared rich and mellifluous. The night was lit by torches affixed to a hastily carpentered platform.

"So how long must we wait?" Conway demanded of the crowd. "Ain't we been patient long enough?"

They roared back their approval. Stamping and moiling in the mud, they called encouragement, nudged neighbors to point out the reasonableness of their claims, drained beer glasses, and wiped beards and mustaches. "You tell 'em, Conway!" roared a behemoth of a man in a red shirt, shaking his fist. "How long does a decent citizen have to take this shilly-shallying?"

In an upper window of the Grand Central, Rollins saw Judge Yount smoking a cigar. He was not sure, but behind Yount in the lamplit room he imagined he saw a moving-about of blue. An army uniform? Major John Toomey? Between them, the powers had the play all laid out.

"Now let's not be hasty," Conway placated, holding out his hands beseechingly. "Let's not have anyone say we're moving too fast!"

Conway knew how to play on a crowd, exhorting them to passion, then calming them down—later to raise them again to another pitch higher than the one before. Almost without knowing it, the crowd would find themselves overwhelmed by passion. That was when they would rush the jail, seize the prisoners from an indifferent jailer, take on the cloak of decent citizens forced to take the law into their own hands.

"Some say," Conway remarked reasonably, "that there's law in this Territory. They say there's a federal judge in Cheyenne City coming to try this case, to pass justice on these Sioux murderers that attacked a peaceful wagon train in the Short Pine Hills"—he smirked—"with the knowledge and approval of their so-called chief, the rascal called Walking Bull." His manner became confidential. "Matter of fact, Walking Bull probably planned the whole thing himself, as an act of defiance!"

I don't have a gun, Rollins was thinking. *No one expects a man to carry out a jail delivery without a gun, surely. But you don't just go up to a man and ask to borrow his gun!*

Conway's harangue went on; he became scornful. "So there's the law, that so-called law that takes a damned long time to operate, seems to me!"

Rollins shook his head, sighed, went to the Star Livery. At least he would have to get his Indian pony, pay the feed bill, ride out to the old mill—the new jail—and see how things looked. He had money now, the money Abigail Brand had paid him for his services.

At the Star Livery he was in luck. Beside a low-burning oil lamp sat Jamie Burns, towheaded and businesslike.

"Jamie!" Rollins said. "What are you doing here?"

"Hello, Mr. Rollins." Jamie stood up respectfully. "I'm watching the animals for Mr. Heck Biddle."

Heck was the night liveryman, a notorious drunk and ne'er-do-well.

"And where's Heck?"

Jamie pointed to a litter of hay, a pile of old clothes, the aroma of cheap whiskey.

"Mr. Heck got to celebrating a little too early tonight, that's what they said. Anyway, I was give fifty cents to keep an eye on the horses."

"Listen, Jamie!" Rollins pulled shut the stable door. "I've got to go on a—well, I guess you could call it a quest, tonight."

Jamie's blue eyes widened. "A quest? Like in times of old, when they went to right a wrong or something?"

Rollins nodded. "There's this prince, you see, that's locked up in a dungeon."

"I didn't know there was kings or princes or anything like that in Deadwood."

"Well, there are," Rollins said. "In fact, Jamie, they may be all round you at times. There *are* some real royalty left in this world, but you've got to look for them." He put a hand on the boy's shoulder. "Now if I'm going to rescue this prince, I have to have a weapon. In the old days, like I told you about, it would probably take a lance, a sword, a shield—things like that. But tonight I need something more modern. Has Heck got a gun?"

Jamie pointed at a nail on the wall. "There hangs that old hogleg. I don't think Heck ever shoots it."

The Dragoon Colt was well-oiled and the cylinder full, though there were no cartridges in the loops of the belt. Rollins cinched the belt loosely about his waist. "Jamie, if you'll just get out my paint, and saddle up a couple of extra horses—"

"For the prince?" Jamie asked eagerly.

"And his assistant prince. Tell Heck I'll settle up with him later."

Quickly the boy ran to the stalls. Over his shoulder he called, "Wisht I could go with you!"

"Someone," Rollins said, "always has to stay to mind the castle. It's not exciting work, but necessary."

The road to the mill was deep-rutted with wagon tracks, now frozen into icy channels. Snow lay heavily on the boughs, and stars glowed fire-bright. Rollins made a wide circle around the jail, where a light burned late in the office window. Near the swift-flowing waters of the creek he tied the horses in a copse at the back of the building. He did not know exactly what he was going to do, or how to do it, but he had to try. A great deal would depend on luck.

Going to the back window, the one where he had ineffectually hacked away at the oak beams in which the bars were set, he pulled himself up and looked within. His old cell was empty, the door swung open. In the corridor was a glow of lamplight; he could hear the soft complaint of a mouth harp. The Oswego Peach was guarding his prisoners. "Weeping Sad and Lonely" was Peach's favorite, the song he had been playing the night he bludgeoned Jack Rollins, put a broken lantern in his hand, and set him up as the miscreant who burned Lew Searles' *Territorial Argus*.

If he could only work the bars loose somehow, climb in, enter the corridor, surprise Peach. But there were Indian guards too. Gripping the bars Rollins listened again, screwing his eyes shut in concentration. The Sioux renegades were there, all right, with Walking Bull and Badger in their narrow cell. He could hear a muffled laugh, the delighted smacking down of a card. The voice belonged to one of the guards, a bandy-legged man named Broken Knife.

His grasp on the bars was wet, clammy. Sinking into the knee-deep snow behind the jail, he wiped his hands on his shirt. First, he had to get into the damned jail. After that was time enough to worry about Broken Knife and Peach.

Moving quietly, Rollins uncoiled the rope from the saddle. It was a good one, braided leather, made for him by Ugly Woman. Knotting one end to the bars, he tied the other to his saddle. Urging the paint with his knees, talking gently to the animal, he took a strain on the rope. But when he drove the animal forward with a slap of his hand the rope stretched, broke, twanged into the snow.

Discouraged, he went back to the bars and tested them. Tight as ever, deep-set in oaken sockets. If he could only get *into* the damned place!

The mill wheel creaked and groaned as it turned in the black waters, buckets rimmed with ice. Holding the broken ends of the lariat in his hands, Rollins stared at the wheel. In sudden activity he lay the two strands together, knotting the ends so he had a rope of half the length but twice the strength. Tying one end around the iron bars of the window, he made a loop at the other and approached the slowly revolving wheel. The buckets were of wood, fastened with rusty iron bolts. One bolt, missing a nut, stood out from the periphery. In the faint light of the stars he watched the wheel turn, waiting for the bolt to appear.

Flicking the noose over the bolt, he stood back. The turning mill wheel stretched the doubled rope, rolled ponderously on. Somewhere in the structure of the barred window a beam cracked, splintered. A portion of the beam and a handful of bars pulled free from the wall, rose majestically over the top of the wheel.

At the open window Rollins paused, listening. Had anyone heard the wrenching, the splintering? The mouth harp stopped. He heard Peach's voice in the corridor.

"What the hell's going on in here? You fellers bust something?"

There was apparently no satisfactory answer.

"I heard *something!*" Peach grumbled.

There was silence again, and the mouth harp resumed its wailing. Rollins climbed through the gaping window and let himself down. Drawing the old Colt from its holster, he set the gun at full cock. The corridor glowed dimly from the lamp in Judge Yount's office. Walking softly, Rollins entered the room.

"Hello, Peach," he said.

The Oswego Peach sat cocked back in a chair, boots on the judge's desk. He stopped blowing into the mouth harp.

"So it's you. Rollins."

"It's me."

"That noise I heard a while back—"

"That was me too." Rollins reached out, took Peach's gun from within his coat. "Don't move! Don't talk! Don't try to give an alarm to those Sans Arc turncoats in there!"

Peach watched him. "You won't get away with it!"

"That's to be seen." Rollins gestured with the Colt. "Hand me your keys."

Sullenly Peach unhooked the ring. "Broken Knife and Red Belt will shoot hell out of you if you try to get into that cell! They got their orders."

"Not," Rollins said, "if you're in front of me, with this old blunderbuss stuck in your backbone. They'll drop their guns when you tell them to."

"What makes you think I'll tell them to?"

"Because if you don't, I'll blow a hole in you a hat could be put through."

Peach paled, but remained defiant.

"Then what'll you do?"

Rollins was becoming uneasy. Peach seemed to be playing for time, debating. "There's a powerful lot of trouble brewing in Sioux country," he said. "You might tell that to Judge Yount and Toomey and the rest, after we've gone. Sitting Bull and Crazy Horse and Gall aren't planning to give up Pa Sapa without the damnedest bloodletting you ever saw!"

"Talk!" Peach sneered. "All talk!"

Rollins gestured with the Colt. "On your feet—get going!"

Peach leaned amicably forward, elbows on desk. "No need to be in such a hurry though, is there, Rollins?" Carefully, his eyes on Rollins, he took one of the judge's stogies from a glass jar, held it out. "Light up, and—"

Rollins felt, rather than saw, the presence behind him. Broken Knife pressed the muzzle of a rifle into his neck, just under the ear. "Do not move, Bone Man," he warned. Carefully he reached around Jack Rollins and took the old Dragoon Colt, tossing it onto the table. Exultantly, Peach rose, took the gun, drew a bead on Rollins' belt buckle. "Get back to the cell, quick!" he ordered Broken Knife. "This tricky bastard might have accomplices out there, behind the jail!"

Rollins spoke to Broken Knife in the Sioux tongue; his remarks were short and obscene in any language.

"Better I kill him right now!" Broken Knife spat. But Peach waved him off. "You don't kill nobody unless I give the word! Now git!" He smiled triumphantly at his captive. "Guess it don't look too good for you, eh, Rollins? You'll get at least twenty years in federal prison for a jailbreak delivery, plus whatever you draw for informing on us to the Sans Arcs at Rainy Butte!"

Rollins never knew where Rufus came from. He remembered the dog in Nobie Ferris' room above the Paradise, but that was before Abigail Brand came and changed everything. Rufus must have gotten out, followed his master's trail in the snow, bounded through the open window. Seeing a remembered enemy, the dog leaped onto the desk and launched himself, snarling, into the face of the Oswego Peach.

Peach dropped the gun and fell back, trying to fend off the dog. Rollins snatched up the pistol but Peach blundered into him, staggering blindly, Rufus still hanging to him with sharp white teeth. They fell together on the floor, men and the dog, wrapped in a maelstrom of biting, kicking, and snarling.

"Help!" Peach found his voice. "Help!"

The gun was between them. Rollins found the trigger, wrenched at the gun, pulled. The sound was muffled. Peach relaxed his hold on Rollins. Rolling over, he wheezed a great sigh, as if tired. Then he closed his eyes and lay still.

Gasping for breath, Rollins struggled to his feet, one hand on the desk to prop himself upright. His side hurt; he wondered if a rib was broken. "Good boy," he said to Rufus, bending to pat the shaggy head. Then he staggered into the corridor. "Friends!" he called out in Sioux. "Where are you? I am coming!"

The cell door was open. For a moment, as in a tableau, he saw Walking Bull and Badger standing in the lamplit cell. Broken Knife and Red Belt, the Sioux guards, stood uncertain, bayoneted rifles at the ready. Walking Bull was straight and tall in the robelike deerskin shirt.

"Bone Man!" he said. He seemed calm, untouched by violence, almost serene. "It is a long time since I have seen you. Friend, what is this all about?"

A sound, a bubbling sound, burst from behind Jack Rollins. Quickly he wheeled. Peach, the Oswego Peach, stood there, one hand clutching a blood-spattered bosom, the other held out in command.

"Get the Indians!" Peach gasped. "Get the Indians!"

Judge Yount had provided for every eventuality. Rooted to the spot in horror, Rollins saw the renegade Sioux stab Walking Bull, plunging in bayonets and withdrawing them with horrible sucking sounds. Badger tried to wrest away Red Belt's rifle but was knocked senseless into a corner.

"Stop!" Rollins cried. "Stop it!"

He shot—once, twice, then the gun jammed on a bad cartridge. Throwing the pistol at the Sioux guards, he ran into the cell and grappled with Red Belt. Broken Knife, shouting a war whoop, slashed the portrait Abigail Brand had painted. Under the fury of his attack the easel splintered, toppling to the floor. Red Belt stamped it flat and capered about, whooping also.

Badger came to Rollins' rescue, throwing himself on Red Belt.

The oil lamp, kicked from its table, fell to the floor and broke; burning oil spread across the floor of the cell.

Suddenly it was silent, the silence of death. The Indians ran from the cell, still whooping defiantly, and disappeared into the night. Rollins stared about him. In the light from the burning oil he saw Peach lying dead in the hallway. Rufus crouched over the body, teeth bared. Walking Bull lay on the floor of the cell in his white deerskin robe, now cruelly torn, and spattered with blood.

"Bone Man," Badger pleaded, "can you do—anything?"

He knelt on the floor, his father's head cradled in his arms. The young face had hardened into sorrow; not the tearful sorrow of a child, a youth, but the grief of a man.

Rollins knelt beside him. "No," he said. "I am sorry, friend. There is nothing that can be done. He is going to the sky."

Rufus shambled up. His job was done.

"We must go," Rollins said.

Walking Bull opened his eyes, filmed and unseeing. He struggled to speak; a whispering rustled from his lips. Rollins wiped the bloody mouth with the tail of his torn shirt.

"Red—"

They bent to listen, straining ears against the crackling of the flames. The wooden walls had caught. The fire was licking upward, eating into dry worm-ridden boards.

"Red Dress Lady—"

"Father," Badger said, "do not worry, up there in the sky. We will never touch the pen, never stop fighting—I promise that."

The eyes stared blindly upward, the whispering ceased. Badger laid his father down. Taking the silver medallion from around Walking Bull's neck, Badger slipped it over his own head. From far away they could hear a muffled roar—the sound of a mob, seeking vengeance.

"It's Conway and his miners," Rollins warned. "They were coming to hang you and your father, to get both of you out of the way so they could go into Pa Sapa and take it for their own!"

Badger stood up. Jack Rollins had not remembered the boy so tall. "I am ready," he said.

"I've got horses outside." Rollins picked up the mutilated canvas, spun it scorched and torn into a neat roll. "*Hopo!*"

Badger did not even look back at his father in the funeral pyre.

"He is not there any more," he said. Together they climbed through the window Rollins had entered, mounted the animals, rode away in the shallow waters of the creek so as not to leave tracks. Upstream, they turned loose the odd horse to leave a false trail. Then they rode up the mountainside, into the dense forest above the creek.

From a rocky promontory they watched the burning jail. A frustrated mob surrounded it; in the flames they could see antlike figures darting about, baffled and confused. Torches lit the night, men shouted hoarsely to each other, there was a scattered volley of gunshots.

Even there, on the mountainside, Badger's face was lit with the flames below. Both of them thought they could feel the warmth of the conflagration.

"A good way to die," the youth said. "My father died a good way, fighting for the People."

CHAPTER THIRTEEN

After a night of violence, fire, and bloodshed, Deadwood awoke to conscience, like a drunk nursing a headache after a binge. Citizens gathered at Van Meulen's harness shop, at the blacksmith's, in the smoky cubicles of the Paradise Card Room. They wrangled, protested, declaimed. The *Argus* fulminated anew. The consensus was that storming a federal jail to lynch prisoners—even Indian prisoners—had been a bad thing. There was even talk that Judge Yount and Dickybird Conway had manipulated people, caused them to do things they never would have thought of on their own, and ought to be chastised. After all, said the more moderate, statehood was coming soon. The Territory would have to give up its frontier image and live within the law.

Abigail Brand sat beside Julian Garner's bed, hastily set up in her suite of rooms at the Grand Central. The lawyer was still sleeping—the aftereffect, the doctor explained, of a concussion. She was to let him sleep unless his breathing became difficult or he showed other signs of distress. In the meantime she kept vigil. From time to time she read in her Bible, but found little to comfort her. The suite was quiet, hushed. In another room her lawyers gathered, discussing what to do next, but she had little hope. Going to the window, she looked out. There was a pall over the city of Deadwood.

Returning, she touched Julian's bandaged head. Dear man—he had done what he could, but he was simply not used to violence! Feeling her fingers, he opened his eyes, looked about.

"It is all right," she comforted. "Julian, you are in my rooms at the hotel."

Wonderingly, his hand touched the bandages. "What—what happened?"

Relieved at seeing him once again rational, she sat beside him and held his hand in hers. "You tried to stop the meeting, but a gang of toughs set on you and beat you."

Remembering, he closed his eyes. "God, my head hurts! Is there—can I have a little water? My tongue—"

"Water, yes—but no food, yet." She went to the washstand and poured him a glass.

He drained it and asked for another, but she was afraid to give him more until the doctor returned.

"I remember trying to argue with them," he said wanly. "I had the legal points, but they owned the clubs, the shillelaghs." He rolled his head restlessly on the pillow, looked at her. "Good lord, is it morning? Have I been—"

"Yes," she told him. "You have been unconscious all night, and on into the afternoon. But the doctor says you will come out all right."

He tried to rise but she pushed him back.

"What happened last night? Did they have their meeting, after all? Is Walking Bull—"

"No one really knows yet what happened." Her face was somber. "My people are trying to find out the details. Mr. Grubb has been about the town, asking questions. But the old mill burned, and there is very little left to show who—who died there."

"Burned?"

She nodded. "Mr. Conway made a long speech to the crowd, pretending to be reasonable, but actually inciting them to violence. I became frightened. When you were hurt and I had no one to turn to, I asked Jack Rollins to help. He went out into the night—he did not even have a gun—and I believe he tried to do what he could. But it was an impossible task. The mob marched on the jail. When they got there, some reported they heard shots inside. Then the jail caught fire. It is an old wooden building, you know, and burned like a torch." She closed her eyes in horror. "Afterwards—this morning, when the ashes had cooled—people went through the ruins, but could identify no one. The bodies were burned beyond recognition. The man Peach had been guarding the prisoners, and certainly the two Indian guards from the Whitewood Creek reservation had been there. Mr. Walking Bull and his son Badger—"

She turned her face away. Awkwardly, he patted her hand.

"Don't talk about it any more, Abigail, please!"

"But I must," she said. "I must talk to someone!" Her face was stricken, but she did not weep. "There are reports, this morning that the two Sioux guards, a man called Red Belt and another named Broken Knife, were seen later at the Whitewood Creek reservation. But they rode away hurriedly, as if afraid of something. Someone said, too, that tracks of three horses were found in the snow behind the jail, but the stories are confused. We—we will have to wait and see this thing resolved."

Still he held her hand in his; she found comfort in it.

"Julian," she said, "there is something more I must speak to you about."

"Not now," he urged. "You are too upset. Wait a while, Abigail, and your thoughts will not torture you so."

"They have tortured me so much already," she said, "that I am in danger of losing my mind."

"Well, then, if it will help you—"

"It will, indeed." She got to her feet, holding the Bible tightly in her hands. "I sat in that chair all night, watching you, listening to the ugly sounds from below. I sought comfort by reading my Bible." Distraught, she tossed it from her. "There was no comfort there, none for a despicable sinner like me!"

He was astonished. "A sinner? You? What nonsense is this?"

Eyes wet with tears, she nodded. "Oh, Julian, I am the greatest of sinners!" She knelt beside his bed. "I must confess to someone! Listen to me, please!"

The room was silent except for the measured ticking of a clock. Afternoon sun streamed through the curtains, lit her form like a figure in a medieval painting.

"Last night," she explained, "I knew what Judge Yount and the rest were up to. They were playing for big stakes, as the saying goes. My people found it out, and brought the information to me. But none was willing to do anything in the face of that mob! I thought of Jack Rollins, the only man who might help me. But what could he do? Nothing, really—he had even abandoned his custom of carrying a gun."

"No one could have done anything," Julian Garner comforted her. "You do not need to reproach yourself, Abigail."

"But that is not the point!" she insisted. "No, you do not understand! I—I saw this tragedy as an opportunity!"

Garner stared at her. "Whatever do you mean?"

"I have long loved Jack Rollins! Perhaps you suspected that, Julian. I even understand there are people in Deadwood City who gossip about the time he came to my rooms, after his release from the jail, and stayed a long time." She looked at him. "Through—through the night, Julian."

His face was pale, confused. "But why—"

"He—he refused me! He said he would not marry me. He went away, and I completely lost my pride. I ran after him, called to him through the open window—early in the morning." She flushed. "So I—" She bit her lip. "I knew he was staying above the Paradise Card Room, at Mlle. Sophie's establishment, with the girl they call Nobie—Nobie Ferris. I wore my best things; the black dress, the ruby brooch Mr. Brand gave me on my birthday, the fur Russian hat from New York City. I put on silk stockings, and Paris perfume. I—may God forgive me—I wanted to show Jack Rollins how common that girl was, how beautiful and desirable I was! Under the pretext of asking for help I confronted him, with that—that girl!"

"Abigail," Julian Garner murmured. "Abigail! Please—don't tell me all these things! I'm sure you meant well. I respect you—yes, love you—and I will not have you demean yourself so!"

Relentlessly, she went on.

"There was nothing he could do, Jack said. I realized that, already, but—" She broke off, staring at the Bible, upturned on the carpet in a ruffle of thin pages. "Seeing him with that girl, I decided if I could not have him, no one should! So I deliberately taunted him. I threw in his face the fact that I had paid him well to go into the Pa Sapa and take me to the Sans Arc camp, but now I felt he owed *me* something; a generous payment for my devotion and care when he was wounded by Major Toomey's column, the time he rode back to the Sioux camp to—to get me. Jack owed me his life, I said, and perhaps he did. But I used that fact, shamefully, to drive him into the street in a desperate effort to help Walking Bull and Badger, save them from that mob." Walking to the window, she clung to the heavy figured drapes as if for support. "So you see, Julian, I sacrificed Jack Rollins to my vanity and now I do not know if he is alive or dead."

For a long time neither spoke. The clock continued its rose-wood ticking. Finally a knock sounded at the door.

"The doctor, I suppose," Abigail sighed. "He promised to look in on you later."

The caller was not the doctor. Instead, it was a towheaded boy, about ten years of age. Under his arm he held a bulky roll.

"I'm Jamie Burns," he introduced himself.

She recognized him. Jamie was the son of the town's best black-smith, and a friend of Jack Rollins.

"Yes," Abigail said. "What is it, Jamie?"

He pulled off the ragged cap. "Can I come in?"

She held the door open and he slipped in, covert in his manner. For a moment he stared at Julian Garner, the bandaged head. Then he said, "I've got something for you, ma'am." He unrolled the bundle and spread it flat. It was the portrait, the one she had done in the Sans Arc camp, the painting of Walking Bull, chief of the Sans Arc Sioux, in all his finery.

"Oh!" She gasped in surprise. "Julian, look at this! It's my portrait!"

The canvas was torn, spattered with red, begrimed by smoke; black holes dotted the fabric.

"Where did you get this?" she demanded. "It was last in the jail, before—it burned!"

"Mr. Jack Rollins sent it to you," Jamie said. "He—"

"He is alive, then?"

"Yes," Jamie said doggedly, "and he—"

She threw her arms about him, danced for joy. "How is he? Is he well? Not hurt, I mean? Is he—"

"I've been trying to tell you, ma'am!" Jamie protested. "There's a note for you. Mr. Rollins writ—wrote it. Said I was to deliver it into your hands, real quick."

She saw the scrap of paper, at first unnoticed. Quickly she un-folded it, cheap colored notepaper, message written in neat block letters. Her eyes swam so with tears she could not make it out. Blindly she handed it to Julian Garner, saying, "Read it to me quickly, Julian!"

He took the paper from her, read in his dry lawyerly tone:

(somewhere in the woods)
"Abby:
This is carried to you by Jamie Burns, a good boy and a friend of mine. As you probably know by now, our good friend Walking Bull was killed by the Sioux guards in his cell. Badger and I got away on horses I rented, and my old paint. I had to kill Peach, though I did not want to hurt anyone. The lamp broke in the scuffle, and the old mill caught fire, which was a good thing to cover our escape."

Garner paused, looked at her, cleared his throat. "This next part—"
"Go on," Abigail said.

"I guess I loved you as much as I loved any woman, but it's too late for all that. I am going to California. Anyway, I must tell you that Badger is safe. Jamie has been running errands for me to friends in Deadwood—Wah Chee and Lew Searles. They arranged to smuggle Badger out of town in a freight wagon bound east. He will be at Lew Searles' brother-in-law's house at 18 Prairie Street in Omaha. Badger is a man now, I think, and wants to go east with you. You are bound to find him a dedicated person, one that could testify before the Indian Commission in Washington, maybe before the Congress itself, and convince a few congressmen that we destroy ourselves when we destroy the Sioux."

Garner folded the paper. "He signs it, 'John Fitzhugh Rollins, late of Honey Hill, South Carolina! I never knew that was his name—his whole name—or where he was from."
"Is that all?" she asked.
"That's all."
She turned to Jamie Burns. "Where is he now? How did you come to find him?"
The boy shook his head. "Ma'am, I'm not allowed to tell you his whereabouts. But I was out hunting with Pa's old shotgun when I saw that little dog, that Rufus. Rufus took me to where

Mr. Jack and the Indian were holed up in a kind of cave. They were cold, and didn't have much to eat. So I brought them grub, and ran errands for them, to the newspaper office and to the Chinaman's. Wah Chee gave me some firecrackers. Then, when everything was fixed up, Mr. Jack said to bring you this—the roll, a picture, I guess it is—and the letter."

She embraced him, which embarrassed him.

"You are a *very* good boy, Jamie," she said, "and have done well." Fumbling in her reticule, she took out a sheaf of bills. "Here —I want you to have some money for your trouble."

"I can't take no money for *that*, ma'am!"

"But why not?"

He drew himself up. "Because he made me his squire, that's why! I always help him when he's on a quest!"

"His squire?"

"That's a kind of an assistant to a knight," Jamie said.

Fresh tears stung her eyes. "I understand," she said.

When Jamie Burns was gone, Abigail turned to Julian Garner.

"It's all so queer," she mused. "My head reels with the unlikeliness of it!" She came again to sit beside his bed. "I traveled out here to the Territory full of righteousness, thinking with the Lord's help I could do *anything!* I was a very moral woman, of high principle, and the Lord was my strength. When I first saw him—Jack Rollins, I mean—I pitied that poor liquor-reeking derelict. But the Lord had put the tool in my hands, and I meant to use him." She smiled, wryly. "Then everything I did seemed to mock my purpose! I caused more harm than good. I got everyone into trouble. Finally, in an excess of frustration, I listened to the devil—Beelzebub himself! A scorned woman, as I thought myself to be, tried to destroy Jack Rollins. And he—" She looked away, through the window, at the distant mountains, where Jack Rollins was—or had been. "The Lord chastened me, properly. He caused Jack Rollins—the derelict, the drifter—to succeed where I failed. Julian, I became the sinner, he apparently the saint. Is it not very queer?"

He kissed her hand, letting his bruised lips linger. She did not respond, only sat motionless in the rocker, staring at the mountains.

"If you are a sinner," he said, "and I do not for a moment stip-

ulate to that, you are now reformed, and have become an angel
that dazzles my poor eyes."

She smiled, distantly.

"I know," he said, "that I am only second best, Abigail. But
will you—will you marry me?"

She laughed, patted his hand.

"We will see," she said. "Some day, Julian, we will see. In the
meantime, there is much to be done." She stroked his cheek. "We
have to pack all my trunks. Then we are going to Omaha."

———◆———

On the patient paint Jack Rollins sat on the heights above
Deadwood. It was dawn—the sky trailed streamers of saffron and
pink, a remembered pink from his mother's rose garden at Honey
Hill. A marauding crow flew low, squawked at him, wheeled into
the rising sun. The weather was cold, very cold. Chill bit into his
body like a driven nail, in spite of the clothing Searles and
Wah Chee had provided him.

Rufus, hunched forlornly on a winterkilled hummock of grass,
whimpered.

"Soon," Rollins comforted. "Soon, little dog, we'll be on our
way to California."

In the growing dawn he watched for the eastbound stage. In
Deadwood there were signs of the new day. Lamps winked off; at
the Paradise a bartender rolled out empty beer kegs. Smoke rose
from chimneys and stovepipes, veiling into the still air to mushroom flat, spread over the town.

Along Whitewood Creek he could see the raw new wood of the
reservation barracks. Listless blanket-wrapped figures shambled
about, waiting for the day's beef issue. Farther up the creek was
the scar burned in the trees by the vanished jail. It was December,
the month the Sans Arcs called "The Moon When Deer Shed
Their Horns."

At Honey Hill, there would be preparations for Christmas;
stringing of colored popcorn, apples glazed with candy, a fat goose
to grace the holiday board. Presents, a lot of presents; Rollins
remembered a small iron locomotive and cars when he was twelve.
But he would never see Honey Hill again. He would not even see
Deadwood City, his friends Lew Searles, Wah Chee. Not even

Zenobia Ferris—Nobie. He hoped Nobie learned to read and
write, someday.

Hunched and chill in the saddle, he thought about California.
It was always warm there, they said; gold in the streams, nuggets
for the picking up, palm trees. He fingered his broken nose,
rubbed his scarred thigh. Both hurt him in cold weather. A
change of climate should help, help a lot of things.

In the street before the Grand Central the eastbound stage
jingled up from the livery stable with fresh horses. A hostler
loaded trunks aboard. A lady came from the hotel, a man accom-
panying her. Even from that distance Rollins could make out a
flash of red. Mrs. Henry Brand was leaving Deadwood City in
style; she must be wearing the scarlet dress Walking Bull had so
admired.

He wondered about the man with her, and did not know who it
was. Julian Garner, perhaps? Searles had told him the representative of the Indian Commission was leaving Deadwood in disgust at the way the Sioux had been treated. Yes, the man might
be Garner. He and Abby were leaving together.

The two got in, the doors closed, the driver whipped up the animals. A moment later the stage disappeared from Jack Rollins'
view, passing into the wilderness of alder and willow bordering
Whitewood Creek.

He sighed. It would take a long time to work his way to California. But a man could always find employment to sustain him
along the way: waiting table, shoveling manure, whatever. He was
not proud.

"*Hopo!*" he said to Rufus. "Dog, let's go!"

Picking his way down the mountainside, skirting the town, he
saw cavalry approaching. The troopers were dirty, unshaven, and
disheveled; probably they had ridden hard all night. A pennon
with a red "7" rippled at the head. In the rear lumbered a blue
Army wagon with a general's stars flying on a staff.

The 7th Cavalry from Fort Abraham Lincoln, Rollins figured,
coming out to reinforce Toomey's 9th Infantry. There was bound
to be trouble soon, a lot of trouble. The Sioux were fighting mad;
the death of Walking Bull was bound to raise their anger to a
new and frightening pitch.

Silently he watched the column jingle by, staring at the heavy wagon rolling on its braces. It was evidently a command vehicle of some sort. In the interior, working at maps under a lamp in a gimbaled bracket, was a blue-uniformed officer. In the rays of the lamp the officer's long hair shone yellow as new-minted gold.

The exhausted column trotted on toward Deadwood, the wagon lumbered after. Finally there was nothing remaining but fresh ruts in the dirt, silence, piles of smoking manure.

"California," Rollins said, half to himself. He was glad to be getting away from the Dakota Territory. He kneed the paint forward, toward the west, and a new hope.

BIBLIOGRAPHY

1. *Red Cloud's Folk*. George E. Hyde, University of Oklahoma Press, Norman, Okla., 1937
2. *The Great Chiefs*. Time-Life Books, New York, N.Y., 1975
3. *Bury My Heart At Wounded Knee*. Dee Brown, Holt, Rinehart, and Winston, New York, N.Y., 1970
4. *Warpath*. Stanley Vestal, Houghton Mifflin Co., New York, N.Y., 1936
5. *On the Border With Crook*. John G. Bourke, Charles Scribner's Sons, New York, N.Y., 1891
6. *The Look of the Old West*. Foster Harris, The Viking Press, New York, N.Y., 1955
7. *Indian Sign Language*. W. P. Clark, Hamersly & Co., Philadelphia, Pa., 1885
8. *Business Atlas of the Great Mississippi Valley and Pacific Slope*. Rand McNally & Co., Chicago, Ill., 1877